The Curvy Side of Life

By Suzie Carr

Also by Suzie Carr:
The Fiche Room
Two Feet off The Ground
Tangerine Twist
Inner Secrets
A New Leash on Life
The Muse
Staying True
Snowflakes
The Journey Somewhere
Sandcastles
The Dance
Beneath Everything

Keep up on Suzie's latest news, projects and podcasts:
www.curveswelcome.com

Follow Suzie on Twitter:
@girl_novelist

For Annie Ocasio, a woman who defines true strength and character.

Acknowledgements

I wish to thank so many people who helped make this story possible. First, to my better half for always being so patient while I disappear for long spans of time into my writer's world. Next, I want to thank Jennifer Morris for providing me with incredible feedback with the story and character development. This book would not be the same without your valuable insights. To Felicia, Deborah, and Dana, I am so grateful for the generosity you showed me with your time and special care to this story. I truly value your opinions and don't know where I'd be without you! To my editor, JoAnne, you helped point me in the right direction by asking important questions and challenging me to dig deeper to discover the answers. Thank you for your honesty and input. To Dorina, for brainstorming names and ideas, and nudging me in the right direction, always. And lastly, I want to say a great big thank you to all who support my writing. Without you, this part of my life would be very static. Thank you for being a part of this journey with me!

Chapter One

Never in Faith Miller's wildest dreams did she ever imagine her life could end up so out of control. That first drop of trouble over a year ago compounded, and then all certainty in life buckled, collapsing faster than she could put it back together.

It all started when her spouse of ten years fell in love with a woman they worked with at the university. Next, came the basement flood. After that, Faith's layoff as a public relations specialist at the university happened. Oh, and then the squirrels.

The fucking squirrels.

On a drizzly morning, Faith sat on a sidewalk curb half a mile away from her home. She waited for a tow truck, which had already surpassed its promise of a thirty-minute arrival. She stared at the smoldering giant nest on her car engine and groaned. Twigs, crunchy leaves, and white puffs of scratchy mattress stuffing smothered her engine. She expected a family of squirrels to pop out of its womb at any moment.

She brushed a piece of lint off the sleeve of her new business suit and laughed at the absurdity of her situation. Her only interview since her layoff, and there she sat in the rain with no choice but to call and cancel.

A few minutes later, the squeaking of the tow truck's brakes brought Faith out of her wallow. She climbed to her feet, pushing aside memories of her former life with its full bank account and ego intact and opened her eyes to the foul diesel truck that would tow her broken car down the interstate. An

1

eagerness rested on the kind face of the man who walked toward her. She latched onto it, grateful to see a friendly, familiar person.

"Third time's a charm, eh?" he said, shaking her hand.

Faith could only shrug.

"Mothballs didn't work this time?"

"They caused my lungs to freak out and I ended up clinging to an oxygen mask in the emergency room. So, no. No to mothballs."

He offered an apologetic nod. "Well, I'll get it hooked up. Then, we can get you off to the mechanic again."

Again. Faith sat back down and watched as he examined the nest. Like the other two times, he pulled the nest apart and placed its contents into a trash bag. "The squirrels worked hard on this one."

Faith understood too well how hard those squirrels worked to keep their home intact, and how easily it could be destroyed.

# #

That afternoon, her sister, Danielle, called for their monthly check-in. "Why don't you and Bristol come spend some time down at the lake house this summer? You've never seen it, and it's been so long since we've gotten together."

Faith guzzled wine and stole a glance of herself in the mirror by the patio door. Despite having smoothed her layers with a large barrel curling iron that morning, her natural waves, too dark and drab from lack of lowlights lately, spiraled more than usual around her shoulders. "I need to find a job."

"I have the internet here. We're not all sand and beach loungers. We even have a stove, refrigerator and, get this, electricity."

"Way to win me over," Faith said, wiping the smeared mascara from under her swollen, dark eyes.

"Seriously, Sis. You've got the summer off and it would do you good to get away from that place for a while."

She hadn't taken an extended vacation in over a decade, well before graduate school. "I don't know."

"I could use the help at the salon."

Faith laughed. "I haven't cut hair since high school. If I visited, and that's a big if, I'm not cutting hair. I'll need to be sending out résumés so I can earn some income."

"Fine. Send out résumés, and in between we'll be silly. We'll drink wine. And, you can watch me cut hair."

Can you put my life back together while you're at it? "I'll think about it."

Faith looked at her watch. Stuart should've returned Bristol half an hour ago. He was probably helping a nice old lady put her groceries into her car. "I have to get going. Bristol will be home any minute and I need to cook her dinner."

"How's my little cutie pie niece doing?"

Confused as ever. "She's doing fine."

"Well, give her a hug from her auntie, and tell her I have a big beautiful lake she can enjoy this summer if her mother decides they should each have some fun."

"Will do."

"And Sis," Danielle said, "Have faith."

She smiled at her sister's favorite closing line. "Love you."

As the next hour passed, and she waited on Stuart to bring Bristol home, she mulled over her sister's invite. Although a trip would do them good, and maybe even Danielle's magical soothing ability could get Bristol to start opening up again to the outside world, she needed to focus. One day, when she put her life back together, they'd take that trip.

An hour later than scheduled, Bristol bolted through the front door with Stuart in her wake. "Mommy, look I'm wearing lipstick!"

Her seven-year-old daughter had painted her tiny lips glossy pink. "You look beautiful, sweetheart." She hugged her daughter and kissed the top of her golden head of hair. She was a mini Stuart with her light hair and blue eyes. "So, Daddy bought you lipstick, huh?"

"He didn't buy me lipstick. Right, Daddy?" She backed out of Faith's embrace.

Stuart's cheek flinched. Then, it turned red.

"No? Then where did you get it?" Faith remained cheerful for Bristol's sake.

"Gilly gave it to me." Her cheeks pinked up in joy, innocent in her admiration for the woman who stole her daddy from her mommy.

Faith glared at Stuart over Bristol's head. He began raking his hand through his thick head of hair. *Screw him.*

"Hey guess what?" Faith smiled down at Bristol, taking her first bold step since the divorce. "We're going to take a trip to Rhode Island to see Auntie Danielle's lake house this summer."

"For the whole summer?" Bristol asked.

"For as long as we like." Faith tugged at Bristol's hand. "Come on. Let's get you some dinner."

"You can't take her away for as long as you like," Stuart said.

Faith stopped and tightened her squeeze around her daughter's hand. "Sure I can."

"But what about my Saturday visitations?"

"Simple. You and your little girlfriend can drive down and see her on Saturdays."

"That's not fair."

"It never is." Faith tugged Bristol along with her down the hallway.

He mumbled something about the contractors needing time anyway to fix the basement flooring and walls from the flood they'd suffered.

# #

Four days later, she and Bristol packed up her rental and headed to Rhode Island.

They both needed the trip. She recited this to herself for the entire two-hour trip south from Boston. Time away from the problems of the failed marriage and her job loss would offer clarity, according to her best friend, Sally.

Faith hoped she was right.

By noon, as she maneuvered the curvy roads of Rhode Island's South County, she relaxed. The air smelled as if it had been kissed by the sea. The plush green grass swayed on the front lawns of quaint lake homes with oversized porches adorned with colorful impatiens. The American flag waved at them from in front of every bay window. Children chased one another and dogs barked. The sun sparkled on the gorgeous leaves of maples and oaks.

Faith forgot how special and welcoming the streets of Rhode Island could be in the summertime. She hadn't visited often since leaving nearly thirteen years before to attend graduate school in Boston. Stuart disliked Danielle's in-laws. Faith liked Danielle's mother-in-law, Lucia. But, Danielle's sister-in-law, Martina, was hard to take with her overbearing personality.

With nothing but time on her hands now, she returned to her home state seeking nourishment, something she knew she'd never find in the cement landscape of downtown Boston.

With each bend in the road, she prayed somewhere on the other side of those curves that her problems would disappear and she'd begin to reclaim a piece of herself.

In the rearview mirror, Bristol looked so small, like a scared pup wanting to remain in the comfort of a crate. Her baby blue eyes scanned the unfamiliar homes and people.

"This is going to be a great summer," she said to Bristol.

"I hope Auntie Danielle lets me play with the turtle."

Ralph the turtle. They had pictures of him all over the side of their fridge. Danielle would send one with each letter she wrote to Bristol. "I'm sure if you ask her, she'll say yes."

Faith caught her daughter's glum stare through the rearview mirror. Her heart sank. Poor kid was afraid to speak to anyone besides her and Stuart. Bristol deserved more than a set of divorced parents and a future filled with uncertainty.

Anything could happen, and that level of surprise freaked Faith out.

# #

When they arrived at Danielle's, Faith flung open her car door and crawled out to stretch her cramped legs.

Her sister ran toward her with open arms, and her happy dimples deepened along her cheeks. Her long thick hair, now colored with a touch of golden brown, camouflaged the gray hair coming into her center part. Danielle's hippy style reminded Faith of better times filled with ice cream cones, roller skates, and hopscotch.

"I've missed you so much," Danielle whispered as they embraced.

Faith gulped back restrained tears. She fell deeper into her sister's hug, comforted by her familiarity and safety.

Danielle pulled away and sought out Bristol. Yanking open the back door, Danielle's smile doubled in size. "Oh my goodness. Look at you!" She extended her hand, and to Faith's surprise, Bristol took it.

When she climbed out of the car, Danielle bent down to her eye level. "You're so grown up." She ran her fingers through Bristol's golden curls. "Your hair. I'm so jealous. You didn't get these curls from me."

Bristol's eyes warmed as she took in the welcome.

Faith's heart ballooned.

Danielle put her arm around Bristol's shoulder and urged her up the driveway. "How old are you again?"

Bristol shrugged.

Faith's heart deflated on a quick puncture. Ever since the marital tension began with Stuart two years ago, Bristol stopped talking to people. Would she ever find her voice again?

"She's seven," Faith answered for her in a singsong voice, even though Danielle already knew.

"That's a great age." Danielle continued leading her up the driveway toward the double garage where her Mercedes shined under the fluorescent lights. "When I was your age, I liked being a great listener, too. I can tell we're going to get along just fine you and me." She squeezed her shoulder, and then set Bristol free. Only, Bristol remained close to her aunt's side as she led them past the Mercedes and up a set of wooden stairs to the door.

Once inside, the scent of maple and sugar greeted them. Aside from the ticking of the second hand on the hallway clock, the house sat silent. They proceeded down a side hallway, passing a bathroom and laundry room. Then, the hallway opened up into her grand kitchen area where beautiful copper pans hung above an island that included five large gas burners and an indoor grill. Tasteful brick dressed the walls and offered a cozy, country charm to what would otherwise be too large of a space to call home.

"This is a far cry from Elm Street." Faith traced her finger along the granite countertop. "When you said you bought a lake house, I thought you meant one of those cottages we stayed in as kids at Spring Lake."

"I do miss the lumpy bunkbeds and even the mildewed windows. The good ol' days." Danielle's voice filled with laughter as she picked up a plate of golden cookies and offered some to Bristol.

Bristol looked to Faith with arched eyebrows.

"Go ahead, sweetie. If you want a cookie, you can have one."

Bristol snatched one up and then smiled at Danielle.

"Enjoy," Danielle whispered.

"It's so quiet," Faith whispered and her voice echoed against the pitched ceiling.

"For now." Danielle smirked and bit into a cookie. She handed one to Faith.

Faith bit into the decadent crunchy sugar cookie and circled her gaze around the open rooms. Peace and tranquility sifted its treasure on them. The trip would be exactly what they needed.

"I should get the bags." Faith turned toward the garage door and noticed the Desiderata poem hanging on the wall. She had sent it after Danielle's husband, Lucas, passed away ten years prior. Faith's note of encouragement hung next to it.

They caught each other's eye, and in that moment, a tinge of sadness curled up around the sharp tick of the clock. Everyone missed Lucas, and no amount of cookies, smiling, or laughter would fill that loss.

"I'll help." Danielle nudged Faith forward. "Bristol, I left you a little surprise in your bedroom. Your room is up the stairs to the second landing. First door on the right. I hope you like pink rooms. It's very pink."

Bristol remained planted in the kitchen, nibbling on her cookie and staring wide-eyed at the vaulted ceilings.

Danielle turned to Faith with a question sitting on her lips.

"She'll be fine." Faith grabbed her sister's arm. "She needs time to warm up."

Danielle's mouth twisted.

"She'll come around, especially if you let her hang with Ralph. She gets a kick out of how he wanders around the house like a dog."

Danielle stopped walking. "There's no more Ralph."

"No more Ralph?"

"He escaped."

"How does a turtle escape?"

"Lucia thought it would be a good idea to create a sanctuary for him on the side of the deck. A place he could sun himself and be in the wild, sort of. I mean, as wild as you can get in Rhode Island. So, she placed huge flat rocks and planted tall marshy grasses. She even dug a shallow hole and placed a plastic pool in it from Walmart. One day out there and he escaped."

Danielle's zany mother-in-law, Lucia, was a hoot.

"Lucia must've freaked."

"She put up signs with a reward. A man called us and told us he found a turtle matching Ralph's description on the side of the street. So, not wanting Ralph to be run over, he brought him to the creek at the end of the cul-de-sac and released him. So, anyway, cheers to Ralph's freedom." She raised her hand up as if offering a cheer.

9

"Freedom?" Faith asked. "He lived his entire life in a bathtub being fed fish food. The poor little fellow isn't going to know what to do out there on his own."

"Well, we looked for him. Lucia dove into the creek, knee-deep in mud, searching for hours."

"Huh." Faith headed out the garage door. "She couldn't wait to see that turtle."

A few moments later, they arrived at the back hatch of her rental SUV.

Danielle hugged Faith again. "I am so happy you came. It's been too long since we've seen each other."

"Well, never again. I missed you too much." They stood at arm's length and grinned. "It's good to be here."

The frantic yelling of a woman chasing a tall and lanky hound dog in the street cut their reunion short. The dog stopped in front of the house next door. It sniffed a flattened plastic bottle. The dark-haired woman, wearing a pair of tight orange shorts and black tank top, fastened a leash to the dog's collar and released an exacerbated sigh. She waved to them, then turned and jogged with the dog back up the street.

"That's Yoga Goddess." Danielle watched them disappear over the hill.

"Yoga Goddess?"

"Yeah, I guess the neighbors must've hired her to walk their dog. No one ever tells each other what's happening. Everyone's so secretive around here. Not at all like where we grew up on Rhodes Avenue where everyone knew everyone's favorite drink or television show."

"Why Yoga Goddess?"

"Lucia, Martina and I see her doing yoga every morning in the grass."

"Martina?"

Danielle nodded. "She lives down here with us for now. After her divorce, it got lonely for her in that big house in Lincoln. With her working at the salon, it's just easier for her to be here rather than dealing with the summer traffic. Besides, my kids love having her around. She and Emmy go shopping a lot. And, Christian adores working with her at the salon now that he's got his cosmetology license."

Faith groaned. "She's so over the top. I don't know how long I'll be able to deal with her."

"She's harmless." Danielle patted her arm. "So anyway, tomorrow morning when we have our coffee on the deck, we'll point Yoga Goddess out to you."

Faith would not need her to be pointed out. She'd spot that long torso and firm butt with no effort. Faith bent over into the SUV and tugged on a suitcase. "I packed for a trip around the world."

"Nice car. I love the color." Danielle helped her guide the heavy suitcase to the ground.

"It's a rental. Which by the way, I need to return to Avis tomorrow."

"Stuart got the car in the divorce?"

"No. The squirrels did."

Danielle grunted and pulled on the suitcase's handle.

"Long story best told over tall glasses of wine." *Very tall*.

"I can't wait to hear this story." Danielle wheeled the suitcase away from the SUV. "We're going to have a blast this summer. Maybe you'll even find someone interesting down here." She winked.

"Why on earth would I want to find someone else?"

Danielle waved her hand up and down the length of Faith's body. "Because you've got the curves going on, and you got robbed on the first go

11

around."

Faith couldn't say the same about the curves for Danielle. With not an ounce of fat on her bones, she could eat anything she wanted. Unlike Faith who only had to look at a sugar cube to gain five pounds. "It's been a year for me. I need to get my life in order before I can even consider treating myself to a manicure, let alone a date. What's your excuse?"

"I already had the best of the best. No one gets that lucky twice in a lifetime. But you. You haven't had the best yet."

Faith stopped Danielle from wheeling her luggage up the driveway. "It's been ten years since Lucas died."

"It could be twenty. Time is irrelevant. I have no desire."

"So, that's it. You're going to dry up and never date again for the next forty or fifty years?"

"I have friends. I have Lucia. I have Emmy and Christian. I have the salon. And now I have you and Bristol. I'm happy." A peaceful glow rested on her golden face. "Oh, and I also have tree removal."

Faith scanned her sister, down to her long polished fake fingernails. "What are you talking about?"

"I cut up dead trees and use the wood in my fireplace. Buying wood is expensive. Not that I'm hard up for money. But, I hate spending money on things that I don't have to."

"Like firewood."

"Yep." Danielle continued to pull the luggage. "My friend Alan and I hunt for fallen trees."

"Alan, huh?"

Danielle laughed. "My *friend*, Alan. We run the bible studies at Saint Joe's on Friday nights. Turns out he loves wood as much as me. It's hard, not to mention unsafe, to cut trees alone in the woods. And, he has a pickup truck. So, it's a thing we do."

"A thing you do." Faith took control of the luggage. She gripped the handle and climbed the steps.

"Is she talking about chopping wood?" Lucia said, coming around the garage entrance carrying a planter box filled with petunias. She lowered it and opened her arms wide, exposing her muddy checkered blouse and freckled chest. Lucia's hair poked out in all directions the way it had last time Faith had seen her. Plump and wrinkled, she wore her happiness like a charm.

"Hey, Lucia!" Faith placed her heavy bag on the steps, and walked down to accept the welcome.

Lucia squeezed her, and then stepped back. "You look like you could use some coffee. A few days in this house and we'll have those bags under your eyes gone like they never existed. Come." Lucia took her hand and led her toward the steps. "And by the way, I think the wood cutting is a cover-up. But, she won't admit it."

"Alan and I are just friends who like to cut wood together. We have a tree to cut up this weekend. It's an old oak that toppled over in someone's front yard a few streets over. Want to help? Hauling wood burns calories. Lots of them." Danielle winked.

Faith sucked in her stomach, self-conscious of her growing curves and now apparently dark circles under her eyes.

# #

Faith found Bristol lying on her back on her pink bed, hugging a teal journal to her chest. "What do you have sweetheart?"

She sat up and placed the journal on her lap. "It's a diary."

Faith glanced at the heart sticker from Danielle. "I used to love my diary." Faith sat down next to her. "I used to write myself a note every night."

Bristol traced her finger on the sparkles. "What did you say in it?"

"I'd write about happy and sad things. Or when your auntie and I would get mad at each other." Faith giggled.

Bristol smiled up at her, revealing her missing front tooth. "I like her."

All tension from the past year released from Faith's shoulders. "She's a good person. She bakes the best cookies."

"She sure does." Bristol lifted a napkin from beside her and revealed a pile of them.

They both laughed and then munched on more cookies.

"Do you think auntie knows I can't talk in front of her?"

Faith weighed her daughter's frustration. "I'll be sure to explain it to her. And to Lucia."

Bristol bit into her cookie. "Yeah, tell her too."

Faith shoved the rest of the cookie in her mouth. "I will." She shifted onto her knees. "No pressure. If you don't want to talk, you don't have to. If you do, then you do."

"Okay."

Faith looked around the pink room. Danielle didn't skimp on the décor. From the lacy curtains, to the miniature table set with teacups, to the adorable stuffed pink teddy bear on the rocking chair next to the canopy bed, the room lifted her spirits. It smelled like fresh rain on a sunny day.

"Where's Emmy?" Bristol asked.

"She's with her Aunt Martina at the mall." Faith tapped Bristol's nose. "I hear she likes to make puzzles, too."

Panic hung in her daughter's eyes. Faith wished she could carry her daughter's fears for once. She wished she could ease the words out of her. She wished she could create that safe place where words flowed and her shyness evaporated under the sun's warmth. In good time, the counselors said. Patience and time.

"Want to race to see who can eat a cookie the fastest?" Faith handed her a fresh one.

Before Faith could grab one for herself, Bristol had already begun shoving hers into her mouth. "I'm winning," Bristol mumbled as cookie crumbs rained down onto her lap.

They busted into giggles, forgetting the uncertainty and emotional baggage for the time being.

# #

After leaving Bristol's room, Faith ventured into hers.

She sat on a white wicker chair in the guest bedroom, admiring the peace for a few more minutes before she headed back down to join her sister and Lucia.

The antique white-framed bed, with its charming louvered accents, boasted sophistication. Everything did, down to the delicate touches of matching washcloths and bath towels her sister put out for her. She picked up a copy of *Rhode Island Monthly* magazine and thumbed through it. Rhode Island had small-town charm with all its local restaurants that hosted happy hours, festive pathways decorated with overflowing flowerbeds and mature thick-branched trees, and concerts on the bustling waterfront in Providence.

Maybe the trip would help her figure out what the hell she should do with the rest of her life.

Chapter Two

"So," Danielle said as she reached for two wine glasses hanging from under the cabinet. "How come you didn't mention Bristol's new shyness to me?"

She wanted to talk with Danielle about it so many times. How do you start that conversation over a phone call? *I messed up my daughter because I can't get my act together?* Something that serious needed to be discussed over a glass of wine and in person so Faith could monitor and smooth over any worry lines. Even though Danielle was only five years older, Faith always viewed her as the matriarch and herself as the clumsy baby sister. "She'll grow out of it."

"Yes she will. I hope you don't blame yourself. As parents, we tend to assume it's all our fault."

Faith brushed off her question with a shrug. Of course she blamed herself. She stopped talking to people right about the same time the marriage began to unravel.

"She's at an awkward age." Danielle wiped the glasses with a white linen napkin.

"She is. That's why I'm confident she'll grow out of it."

Danielle's forehead furrowed. How many times had her forehead furrowed over the past year when Faith whined to her over the phone?

She would not whine during her visit. If she did, she'd have to spend the entire trip convincing Danielle she could stand on her feet and thrive again. That type of a white lie required a lot of energy, energy she didn't have.

17

The openness of the room began to shrink, shriveling and clinging to her. Maybe she shouldn't have come after all. She could always leave after the weekend and blame her sudden departure on a job interview.

"I hope you don't mind boxed wine," Danielle said, pulling it out of the fridge. "It's cheap and tastes okay." She opened its spigot and poured half a glass for Faith, and then handed it to her.

"Half?"

Danielle twisted her mouth in a subtle rejoice. "Oh, there's plenty more."

"Good." Faith opened the spigot and topped off her glass.

Danielle topped off hers as well.

Before they could get a sip in, the front door opened on a whoosh. "I'm starving," Danielle's son, Christian, sang out.

"Christian, we're in here." Danielle turned to Faith. "Wait until you see how much he's grown. And, Emmy too. She and Martina will be back from the mall soon.

A moment later, in walked her nephew, a much taller, more handsome version than Faith remembered. He had his father's full head of dark hair and tanned Colombian skin. His eyes were still large and dark as a forest at dusk. Last time she had seen him, teenage acne dotted his forehead and cheeks, and he sported a colorful blue and pink Mohawk. Now he was a grown man at twenty years old.

"Oh my God," he said to Faith in a soprano voice. "Look at you." He stretched his eyes the full length of her. "And, your hair." He ran his fingers through her tangled mess of mousy brown waves. "I hope you'll let me have some fun with it." He stepped backwards, looking to his mom and back at her. "Did mom tell you I'm working for her now?"

Danielle brushed a piece of her hair behind her ears, deepening the center part and revealing more gray hair. "Christian, let her breathe first. She hasn't even sipped her wine yet."

Faith tapped her nephew's upper arm. "She told me, and I'm happy for you. Hairdressing is a fun way to make a living."

Danielle coughed and rolled her eyes. "This coming from a woman who chose a computer screen over shears."

"You don't know what you missed, then," he said, ducking into the fridge and pulling out a carton of milk. He then searched the cabinet and pulled out a flute glass, filled it, and sipped the milk. "I hear you're going to work with us, though!"

"I never agreed to such a thing."

Danielle lowered her glass. "She'll agree."

Faith opened her mouth to take her stand, when the door opened again. That time, Martina and Danielle's daughter, Emmy, flew through the door, dramatizing their inflections about jewelry. They headed in from the foyer, giggling and screeching.

Martina's voice rang even louder than Faith remembered. No one could get a word in with her around. She trampled every decent thought. She talked without a filter. She criticized every person who disagreed with her.

Emmy mirrored her Auntie Martina's brashness, criticizing the way a top hung like a disaster on the woman who waited on them at the checkout line.

Where had her sweet little niece with the soft brown curls and big infectious smile gone? Who was the diva coming down the hall with a shopping bag dangling from her arm, looking more like a college freshman than a fifth grader?

Bristol would never be comfortable around Emmy. Faith may as well put her flip-flops back on and head out with Bristol before Emmy destroyed what little, if any, confidence the poor kid had.

They stepped into the kitchen and ignored them, still carrying on like a couple of snobs who shopped at places like Nordstrom and sat in the backseat of limousines ordering chauffeurs to drive.

Faith had to protect Bristol. Why did she accept the offer to spend the entire summer in Rhode Island? "I've got to head—"

"Hey, hey, hey," Martina said, opening her arms up wide. She kissed Faith's cheek with her bright red painted lips. "You look gorgeous with that messy hair." She tousled it and examined the curls as if deciding whether to buy them or not. "I love the color. Is that a walnut tone?"

"Nope," Faith tilted her head away. "Just my regular color with a few streaks of gray."

"Ah, yeah, stress. I heard about your little problem. It's tough. I've been divorced twice already, even though my last one turned out to be a good one. Too good. A doctor. A doctor without borders," she sang. "Finally, I found a good one, but then he decided to stay overseas. I would never live in a tent or a dust ball of a city." She opened up her tote bag and out popped a cute little dog with sweet marble-sized eyes and perky ears. "Say hello to our new guest, Henry." She held him up like a glass of wine.

Should Faith fist bump him or shake his little paw?

"No more decent men exist," she continued on the same breath. "My brother closed the chapter on that kind of man when he passed."

Faith gripped the counter to balance herself. The woman's energy ate through the air. She shot words around like a pool ball. From one corner to another. Bing. Bang. Boom.

Faith wanted to curl up and hide under a blanket. She willed for Stuart's impending call to interrupt the nightmare. She could pretend he was a job interview offer. *Come on phone. Ring.*

"Is Bristol here?" Emmy asked.

Faith inched her mouth open.

Lucia walked into the kitchen just then. "Yep. She's up in the pink room. I bet she'll love to see you, cutie pie." She kissed the top of Emmy's head.

Faith feared Emmy's impact on Bristol. "Is it a good idea for her to go into Bristol's room? She's resting."

Danielle refilled her wine glass. "Drink up. She'll be fine."

A few moments later, Faith followed Danielle out to the back deck, and Martina followed closely behind babbling more about the jewelry they saw at the mall.

Faith had landed in hell.

One night. That would be it. Then, back to Boston.

She could last one night. She lasted over a decade in her marriage. She could last a night on her sister's deck listening to Martina ramble.

Faith sank into the warm grey handwoven wicker lounge chair. Its gentle sloping wide arms and plush cushions offered comfort amidst Martina's chatter.

Martina began to sip wine. "I needed this. It's been a doozy of a day." She flipped her long hair over her shoulder.

The three of them glanced out at the grassy field filled with picnic tables and families enjoying the beginnings of the weekend. The lake air quieted Martina like a bottle of milk soothed a baby. A few minutes into their time on the deck and Martina gazed ahead, eyes aglitter to the scene.

Faith took advantage of the moment and eased her head back against the lounger. Something about lake air relaxed her, too. The mist, mixed with the scent of earth and grass, lulled her into a nice peaceful state of mind. Or maybe the wine glossed everything over?

"You're staying through the whole summer, I hope?" Martina asked.

"Not sure yet." Faith swallowed her lie.

Martina stretched into an overzealous grin. "Oh, you'll stay. You'll take one step into the salon and never want to leave. At least I pray that's the way it works." She squeezed Faith's hand. "I'm trying to cut back. Ulnar nerve damage."

"I don't know where everyone got the idea–"

"Oh hey, don't worry. I'm around all the time so I can train you. I hate the forty-five minute drive from Lincoln. Now that Todd and I are divorced, the house is too empty for me. So, I spend my time here. Summer traffic is crazy in South County. This place gets hopping when the heat turns up, especially at George's of Galilee."

Come on Stuart, call me.

"George's of Galilee is the best. I take Emmy there a lot to eat clam cakes. We like to sit on the rocks and feed them to the seagulls. We get quite a crowd if you can imagine."

Gone went any possibility of a relaxing summer. All visions of waking up to a quiet retreat vanished. Those long solo walks around the lake, gone. That woman's need to chat every second destroyed any chance to reflect on life and figure out her next steps.

"So," Martina started again, "Danielle tells us Stuart turned out to be a complete asshole."

Faith shot Danielle an angry look.

Danielle sat taller. "No, no. I never said that." She spoke to Martina in her patient parent tone. The same tone she used on Faith when they worked together at Salon Juliard, back when Faith attended vocational high school. "I never said asshole." She arched her eyebrow at Faith. "I never called him that."

Faith stared out at the community center in the distance. "He's not an asshole."

"Then, why did he cheat on you?" Martina asked.

Faith shot Danielle another look.

"I'm sorry. I shouldn't have said anything." Danielle's face drooped.

"Stuart and I grew apart. It happens."

Martina leaned in. "Oh. Tell me why." Her eyes grew big. "Did you cheat on him first?"

The woman was thirty-two going on twelve. She siphoned drama for fuel.

"Faith would never do that," Danielle chimed in. "Would you?"

"My God, you two are insufferable."

"Okay you're getting punchy," Danielle sat up. "Time to go for a walk or something. What do you say?"

Martina held up her hand. "Hang on. We're just catching up."

Danielle eased back in her chair.

"So, I heard you're looking for a job." Martina stared at her as if trying on a thought.

"I am." Faith sighed.

"I'm resting my ulnar nerve, so you should let Christian do your hair. He's very metro. Danielle does old people, so," she turned to Danielle, "well, no offense of course."

Danielle's eyes sparkled with the love of a parent. "None taken. I love styling my little old ladies."

"What Faith needs is trendy if she wants to work at the salon or a bar, don't you think?"

"A bar?" Faith asked.

"Well, you're not going to find any professional jobs here at the lake. So, it's the salon or the bar."

"What's wrong with my hair?" Faith asked, curious to see how much farther that woman could manage to go.

Martina shook her head. "You need something that'll create impact when you walk into a room. Something that'll get the men swooning." She winked at Faith. "We can go shopping and get you some cute things to wear. A new look. A new life."

Faith gathered her hair and tied it back with the elastic band on her wrist, her one and only accessory. "I like my hair and single life as they are. The last thing I need is more change." Faith smacked her lips together, perhaps a bit too loudly.

"Someone sounds a tad defensive," Lucia said, climbing up the two steps from the patio. Carrying a rusted bucket, she walked with a heaviness across the deck and over to the water spigot near the sliding door. "And you've every right to be. Life has zonked you over the head with trouble. You've come to the right place to escape any more of it."

Faith had some doubts on that.

"Gramma," Emmy walked out of the sliding door and over to Lucia. "How do I get this thing to work?" She balanced a coffee grinder in her small hand.

"Where's Bristol?" Martina asked Emmy.

"She's writing in her diary. So, I left."

Faith sat up, and Danielle nudged her back down with an outstretched arm. "She's fine. She needs space. Let her write."

Faith bounced her legs. Sitting on the deck, surrounded by too many people, she wanted to run. She missed her solitude, and an afternoon hadn't even gone by yet.

"So, how come this isn't working?" Emmy pushed the coffee grinder in front of her grandmother. Lucia, bent over the water spigot, was wrestling to get the hose into the rusted bucket. She craned her neck toward the grinder.

"Well, you have to push the lid down, hard."

"I did that," Emmy whined.

Danielle remained inclined on her lounger with not a care in the world that her eleven-year-old daughter verged on a tantrum over a coffee grinder.

So many bosses. Who was her mother, anyway?

"Why is she drinking coffee?" Faith whispered to Danielle.

"She's brewing it," Danielle said. "She loves to help out in the kitchen. She's eleven going on thirty."

Suddenly, Christian busted onto the scene with gelled hair, and smelling as if he'd taken a bath in cologne. "I'm heading out." He kissed his mother's cheek.

"Hot date?" she asked.

He smirked. "Mike got us tickets to see Julio Iglesias at Foxwoods."

"Please be careful." Danielle cradled his hand, and then let him go. "Tell him I said hello."

He kissed everyone's cheek, including his little sister's and finally Faith's. He turned out to be a good, happy young man.

"Aunt Faith, I'm happy you're both here. We're going to have a good time this summer." He smiled, and then dashed away.

Within a few minutes, calm finally settled in on the sunny deck at Orchard Pond. The group, with all their differing personalities, transported her back in time to a day when she and Danielle would pile into the back of a station wagon with all their cousins and head to the beaches. They'd spend the day holding hands, jumping waves, eating potato chips, and taking naps under the blazing sun on sandy, scratchy blankets.

"I'll be right back," Emmy said, cradling the coffee grinder against her scrawny chest.

Lucia turned on the water, and it sprayed in different directions. She straddled herself over the bucket and fought the power of the hose, slapping it, then yanking it until finally she got the bright sense to turn off the spigot. Soaked, she looked over at them. "Damn thing gets me every time." She bent over and coughed as if she'd run around the block five times. "So, what were we saying earlier?" Lucia dropped the hose and plopped down on the wooden deck.

"We were planning Faith's makeover." Martina flipped her cappuccino-highlighted hair over her toned shoulder again.

"No." Faith shook her head. "I'm not getting a makeover."

"Get the makeover," Lucia said, wrapping her wet arms around her knees. "Otherwise, they're never going to leave you alone. We all go through it. Every new season. Just agree. That's what I do. It shuts them all up. They're like little dogs biting your ankle." She pointed at Martina. "Especially this one."

Well, no shit, Sherlock.

"Mama," Martina pushed a loose wisp of hair behind her delicate ear, "the woman is heartbroken. I'm trying to help. We've all been there."

"I'm not heartbroken."

They all exchanged a look.

"I'm not. Honestly. I'm happy. Everything's good." Faith sat up taller. "I'm on vacation. The sun is shining. It's all good." Faith put on her dark-shaded sunglasses and leaned back.

"What you need is to get into a little bit of trouble." Martina sat forward. "As Katherine Hepburn would say, *if you obey all the rules, you miss all the fun*. I even have someone picked out for you."

"I'm not going out on a date."

"Every woman needs romance," Lucia said, grunting as she rose to her feet. "Even I date Stan on Saturday nights. He takes me out to eat fish and chowder and we dance at The Bluffs. I didn't let my ex ruin my life. I gave him eight years and that was it. You can't let Stuart ruin yours either. You deserve the romance."

"She doesn't need romance," Martina said. "What she needs is to get a little wild." She arched her eyebrow. "If you catch my drift?"

Faith flicked her hand toward Emmy in the house. "There are children here."

"She can't hear me."

"The people five houses down the street playing their music full blast can hear you," Lucia said.

"Great sex can empower a woman. It always works for me." Martina shifted her gaze to the community field's edge. "Like with that guy over there." She pointed her chin over to a greasy, leather-skinned man setting bricks on the boardwalk.

Lucia and Danielle both stretched their necks and grunted in unison.

Faith had no interest.

"He's fixing what a group of hoodlums destroyed this spring. Apparently, they took a sledge hammer to the beautiful bricks and wrote graffiti on it. The cops at least caught the little troublemakers. Thank God for the destruction of bricks in a public park," Martina said on a moan.

Faith stared at her in disbelief. "That's a bit of a stretch to find something good in such a bad thing."

"That's the whole point."

"It's our ritual," Lucia chimed in, taking a seat next to Faith. "There's a good and bad side to everything. We seek the good hiding behind the bad. The search helps us discover the special surprises that often hide around life's curves."

"Cheers to the curvy side of life!" Martina raised her wine glass.

"To the curvy side of life." Lucia clinked glasses with Martina.

"I'm not cheering to that." Faith gripped her glass. "The only thing hiding around those curves are problems."

"Just wait." Lucia patted her hand. "This place will have a different effect on you soon enough."

Faith chuckled and then turned her gaze to the beautiful scene that stretched out before her. A pristine lawn, maple and ash trees, flowering bushes, and a sweeping view of Orchard Pond stretched out behind Danielle's lake house. The lake shimmered in the late afternoon sun and families gathered on picnic tables and blankets. Frisbees flew. Dogs barked and ran in circles. Kids chased balls and giggled.

The community at Orchard Pond offered something for everyone. A nine-hole golf course sat to the far right of the lake. An Olympic-sized swimming pool, complete with a curvy slide and diving board, occupied the area to the left of the brick rec center. A large banquet hall that catered to weddings, proms, and other special occasions took up a large portion of the center. The community offered horse-back riding, rafts, soccer, softball, and even dancing.

Orchard Pond offered the perfect getaway, and one that Faith hoped

Bristol would open up to and enjoy.

Danielle and Martina continued to drool over the bricklayer's muscles. Faith looked toward the brick rec center and noticed a much more interesting site. That same dark-haired woman from earlier. She sat on the lawn, bending at the waist and stretching toward her toes.

Lucia nudged Faith. "She's got quite the flexibility."

"Indeed she does." Faith stretched her neck out a bit more to get a better look for herself.

They all stole glances.

"That's Yoga Goddess," Danielle said. "That dog chase from earlier must've caused her some stress. She's breaking into a double yoga session today."

Faith relaxed her stretched gaze.

Cheers to stress and yoga. Faith eased her glass up to cheer her silent praise.

At that moment, the fine-looking woman glanced up at them.

Martina braved a hearty wave.

Yoga Goddess didn't wave back, which probably meant she had an attitude problem. People graced with long, flowing shiny hair and etched muscles lifted their chins up higher than the rest of them. Women who looked like her broke up marriages with the swing of their hips. They stole furtive glances for the fun of it. They enjoyed playing that game of cat and mouse, leaving people drooling and panting as they masturbated to the image of her curves and flexible muscles.

Just then, Bristol and Emmy came onto the deck. Emmy veered off down to the patio and onto the grass. Bristol walked over to Faith carrying her journal. Happy for the distraction, Faith patted the chair next to her. "Hey sweets. Sit down."

"Oh my God, Bristol!" Martina squealed.

Bristol's face turned flame red.

Faith opened an arm to her daughter to protect her.

"You should put on some sunscreen." Martina straightened up in her chair. "You're going to burn up out here. Before you sit, come here. I'll put some on you." She lifted the bottle to her nose. "It smells like peaches and cream. Want to smell it?"

Bristol took a slow step forward. Then another.

"That a girl. Here. Smell it," she said as if talking to a stray dog. "It's delicious."

Bristol grabbed the bottle. She brought it up to her nose, sniffed, and released a small murmur.

Faith sat up taller.

"Go ahead and dot some on your face."

Bristol did as told, eyeing Martina with great care.

"It's nice and creamy, right?"

Bristol nodded.

"That's what I like to call beauty in a bottle. It's what keeps us girls pretty and wrinkle-free. Now if we can get your mommy to relax a bit, we're going to have a great time this summer."

Bristol glanced at her mother through weary eyes as Martina smeared the cream. Faith wanted to grab her daughter's hand and flee. Run as fast as her little feet could go and not look back. Return to their safe home in Boston where no one questioned sacred things like her sex life or Bristol's love for creamy sunscreen.

At one point, Lucia plopped a blanket over her face to likely drown out

Martina's shrilling voice, and Danielle went inside to use the bathroom. Faith followed her.

"I can't stay here through the summer," Faith whispered to Danielle.

"Martina will calm down once she's used to you. I promise. This is what happens when she's nervous. She becomes chatty."

"Nervous?"

"She might have a gorgeous body and head of hair, but she's scarred. She's been trampled on and hurt all her life by friends and lovers."

"Probably because she has no filter."

"She has no filter because she's tired of being hurt. Her boldness is a defense mechanism that protects her from feeling small."

"So, eventually she'll chill?"

"Eventually, yes." Danielle smiled. "She loves family. She loves being around the kids. She needs them as much as they need her. Being needed is important. It helps us get out of bed in the morning. You know?" Danielle's eyes hinted of a sadness. "Hell, we all need help, don't we?"

Faith released a slight chuckle. "I suppose you're right."

"Please don't leave yet." Danielle gripped her arm. "Give us some time. We'll all grow on you. I promise."

Faith didn't want to promise anything on her end, just yet. "I worry about Bristol. She doesn't do well with attention."

A smile popped up on Danielle's face as she glanced behind Faith's shoulder. Faith followed her gaze.

Martina and Bristol sat close to one another on the lounge chairs. Henry napped on Martina's lap. They glanced down at Martina's cellphone. Bristol giggled, and Martina nudged her with her shoulder. Bristol's face lit up. Even from the distance, the sparkle of Bristol's eyes shone brightly.

# #

Later on, Faith called her friend, Sally. "So, I have something interesting to tell you about Rhode Island."

"You landed a job, already?"

"No, this is a fun kind of interesting."

Sally made a guttural shrill. "Oh? Do I dare guess or let you have your moment of revelation?"

Faith loved her friend's wit and the bond they shared. No one else knew her in quite the same way. "There's an interesting woman who hangs out at the lake. They call her Yoga Goddess."

"Yoga, huh?" Sally asked in a sing-song spirit.

"That and total goddess."

"Give me more details."

"I have none other than she leads a group of people in yoga stretches on the community lawn every morning. That and she has incredible shiny hair. Oh, and totally toned muscles. And legs. Legs that go on forever. She's likely a snob, but nice eye candy. "

Sally giggled. "I already miss you so much."

"I miss you more. But, don't fret. I'll be back in Boston before you know it. That is if I can land a job. Please keep your eyes out for any new opportunities for me, okay?"

"And take away your opportunity to gawk at Yoga Goddess every morning?"

Faith chuckled, and they said their goodbyes.

Chapter Three

The next morning, Faith entered the sunny kitchen on a couple of sneezes.

"You look like you could use some serious caffeine." Lucia put down her steaming mug of coffee and headed to the cabinet. "Large or x-large, dear?"

"If you have jumbo, I'll take that. Otherwise x-large will do." Faith rubbed her eyes, still salty from sleep.

"Jumbo it is." Lucia dragged a hand-painted step stool over to the counter and climbed on it. She stretched up on her tip toes and grabbed a stein. "I hope you've got an appetite."

Faith could barely stop sniffling long enough to consider swallowing food. A surprise visitor approached her last night as she lay her head against her pillow. The smoky cat spread itself across her chest, kneading its paws and purring like a jet engine. "I'm not much of a morning eater." Faith braced for another heart-stopping sneeze.

"Good Lord, woman." Lucia jumped off the step stool.

"Cat allergy." Faith reached for a tissue and sneezed three times in a row.

"Cheers to sneezing," Lucia said, raising her coffee mug.

Faith shook her head. "Not sure I understand your enthusiasm over it." She slid onto a stool. "It's too early for me to figure it out."

"A sneeze is a great way for your body to rid itself of the unnecessary." Lucia beamed as if she'd revealed the great secret to the purpose of life. "Though, be sure to keep your door closed from now on so Felix can't sneak in."

Faith blew her nose. "I'll survive."

"Of course, dear. We all do. Anyway, your sister made her famous flaxseed muffins before she left this morning." Lucia handed her one on a plate. "Be careful on the first bite."

Faith eyed the brown, pokey muffin with caution.

"It's edible," Lucia answered her unstated question. "I assure you. We've all eaten them, and we're all still alive and kicking. Somehow."

Faith fingered it, unable to break it open with her fingernail. She picked it up, examining the seeds and cracks. It resembled a desert rock. "I'd rather starve."

"Wise woman." Lucia opened up the microwave and removed a steaming bowl of oats. "You've got about fifteen minutes before she comes back." She put her hand out for the muffin. "I'll take care of that for you."

Faith handed it to her. "Why don't we tell her the truth?"

"Baking muffins is her way of showing us she loves us."

"With cracked teeth?"

Lucia cocked her head. "We do our part here." She sipped her coffee. "She suffered her first meltdown after Lucas died when I offered to cook breakfast for her and Christian. Emmy was still nursing, of course." A touch of sadness tinted her soft brown eyes. "She liked to be needed, to have purpose. So, we pretended to eat them, and then I began sneaking food to Christian when she went out on her morning runs. Why mess with a good system?"

"It's been ten years, Lucia."

"Now her kids are self-reliant." She shrugged. "They're good kids. Especially, Christian. He gets it. He lets his mom baby him with certain things."

"Where is she?"

"She's at the salon painting the facial room."

The salon. She had seen pictures of it on the company Facebook page. Recently, Danielle had hung up a new True Colors Salon sign on its front lawn. She and Martina stood on either side of it offering a set of thumbs-up signals.

Faith could've ended up standing in place of Martina had she continued as a hairdresser. A pang of jealousy over the salon's success still lodged itself in Faith's heart. That and its accompanying guilt for being jealous of the one great thing that saved her sister after Lucas died of a heart attack. The man jogged five miles a day and ate no sugar, too. Go figure.

When life called you out, it called you out.

"Let's take our coffees to the deck. Shall we?" Lucia led the way. "Martina should be out here any minute."

"This certainly is a full house. How do you all not get in each other's way?"

"I believe we all would rather feel full than empty, dear."

Faith let her statement marinate as they walked onto the deck.

"When Danielle gets back, we'll talk about our dreams and see if we can decipher them."

"Our dreams?"

"Once in a while, we share our dream journals over coffee."

Sharing coffee time was one thing, but dreams? No way. Faith bit her lip and scanned the grassy field. She could leap over the railing and head toward the kayak station. Then, she could squeeze herself into one and paddle out to the middle of the lake where nothing else in the world mattered but the soundness of the plastic, colorful kayak that protected her from the deep, algae infested, murky bottom.

If she accidentally flipped and drowned, that would still be easier than dream sharing.

"Good morning, chickadees!" Martina greeted them with a smile far too wide for eight thirty in the morning.

Faith gulped her coffee, wishing she could inject it straight into her bloodstream.

"Not a morning person, are you?" Martina stretched her neck to see around her mother's sun visor.

"I need a few minutes." Faith put on her sunglasses and stared out over the deck railings. In the distance, people ran. Kids rode bikes on the pathway. Boats floated on the horizon. Blue jays and finches flew overhead chirping. If she could mute Martina for a few minutes, she might enjoy the start to the day.

Martina stretched against the railing. "There's that woman doing yoga again."

Faith opened her eyes wider and stole a glance at the yoga goddess. She bent forward and into a graceful sweep as she worked into a sun salutation.

Several others joined her in greeting the morning sun and arching their backs in celebration of a new day.

"Oh, and looky over there," Martina pointed. "It's the brick man again. I should take up yoga so I can get a closer look at those glistening muscles." She lifted the brim of her sunhat. "Honestly, that is a work of God right there. Ripe for the picking like a crisp apple in the fall."

Faith looked beyond the brick man and out at the yoga goddess. Her sleek arms extended toward the sky, and her long dark hair fell down beyond her shoulder blades flirting with the sexy contour of her back.

Lucia cleared her throat.

Faith caught the playful arch to her eyebrow.

"I have a yoga mat, if you're interested."

Faith's face flushed. "Don't be silly."

Lucia sat on a lounger and rested her head back. "Suit yourself. Best to admire from a distance anyway. God only knows what kind of baggage a person carries."

Faith opened her mouth to try and explain her gawking, but then Lucia closed her eyes.

Martina sat and rested too. Soon after, Danielle joined them, carrying her spiral dream journal under her arm and a red pen in her hand. "For important points," she said. "You'll be amazed at all the things the brain reveals. I've left one for you on your bed."

Faith had given it to Bristol. She had already used up half the diary Danielle had given her on the first day.

They spent the next thirty minutes watching the world come alive. Faith listened as the three of them read from their dream journals and tried to figure out the inner workings of their REM cycles. They spoke about their dreams, revealing silly phobias and pent up anxieties about things like global warming, draining their bank accounts, and saving the world and those they loved.

So began their morning routine, waking up to their entertaining stories of going to sleep ordinary citizens and diving into a world where they morphed into superheroes. Each day, Martina sprang through the slider, back from her morning massage sessions, in time to gaze at the brick man while discussing her wacky, over-stimulated imagination. Lucia pretended she didn't notice Faith checking out the yoga goddess dipping for her downward dogs. Danielle scribbled notes like a shrink. And the kids overslept. All in all, they surfaced from their lazy mornings a little less talkative and a whole lot more relaxed.

At first, Faith dreaded the morning ritual. She wanted to sip her coffee in peace and watch as the yoga goddess bent her long torso forward, and swung her long, dark hair around her toned arms and perky breasts. She wanted silence so she could hear the beat of the sultry music playing in her head.

Then, she noticed that the dream discussions helped keep Martina calm. As soon as her journal opened, her tone changed to that of someone with an important task at hand. Martina, with her ballpoint pen and investigative mind readied herself to jot down the complexities of their warped sleepy minds.

By the end of the first week, Martina grew on Faith. She was a puppy needing constant attention. She circled the room, rolling over and exposing herself with exuberant trust and innocence. She stopped asking so many questions and began to speak at a normal pace, one that didn't suck out the surrounding energy and leave Faith gasping.

When Martina dove into analysis mode, she grew serious and tolerable.

"You need to share, too." Martina pulled off her reading glasses. "You can't expect us to reveal our deepest secrets and you not do the same."

Faith could never remember her dreams. But, she didn't want to lose her morning view of yoga. "I'll bring my journal tomorrow." She had faked her joy in a passionless marriage all those years, surely she could whip up something interesting to toss the women.

So, for the fun of it, Faith began to bake up elaborate details and drizzle some decadence on them. She loved watching Martina and Lucia engage in deep discussion over the fake facts. They created all sorts of reasons why Faith would dream about flying over the lake in a guitar, cooking breakfast in a coffee pot, or, her fondest fake dream, walking on the lake with tennis rackets as floatable shoes.

They tripped over each other's ideas, going back and forth about the true nature of Faith's dreams. They didn't stop until that moment when a united insight clicked, at which point they clasped hands and raised them up in victory. Their debates bought Faith time to enjoy the bold and nutty treat of her freshly-brewed coffee while watching her Yoga Goddess perform on the grass.

One night, she dreamed about the yoga goddess. Faith sat in the middle of an empty room. A lone spotlight shone down on her. Then, a deep and guttural beat rose from beneath her, from the core of mother Earth. Her chair vibrated and began to spin. Then, out of the dark corner of that empty room emerged the yoga goddess dressed in an elegant, white negligee. A sense of longing stood between them, blocking their ability to touch. A steamy haze that smelled of vanilla musk curled up around their waists enveloping them into a secret pocket of space where the outside world could not find them.

Memories of an exchanged past billowed in that haze, memories of when they loved each other and would die for one another. The haze both protected and separated them. Faith longed to touch the woman, to connect to her soul. They could only watch each other and demonstrate their love from the space they occupied, though. So, Faith proceeded to show her love, at first by tracing her finger in those places that she herself enjoyed, on the wetness of her lips, in the hollow of her neck, below her ear, down the edge of her collarbone toward the deep valley leading to her breasts.

The woman responded with gentle murmurs and cries for more. Soon, the woman began a journey down her own skin, teasing Faith with her daring trajectory. As their self-travels took them to that sweet place where pleasure waited, the haze circled and swept them up into a passionate dance that erupted into a series of wild flicks, leaving them hungry for more.

She awoke dizzy and deliriously turned on. She remembered every single detail of that dream, and no way in hell would Martina and Lucia get their curious minds working around it.

That dream etched itself into her memory, and it would remain there. She claimed it for herself. No one would learn of its sexy suggestions. As she ventured out onto the deck that morning, still trembling from the fantasy's power, she pretended she had dreamed of riding on top of the roof of her car while Bristol drove them down the street and onto the narrow path leading to the lakeshore. She had quite the imagination, and it came in handy. She figured, they'd have fun picking that one apart. They'd claw their way through it, dissecting the details like homicide detectives until they lifted their grit-covered hands and shared their findings.

That night, Faith's bath took on a new level of intoxication.

In her fictional rendezvous, she embraced the sexiness of unrestrained possibilities. Fantasy shined brighter than reality. In real life, the yoga goddess would likely snub her on the walking trails or in an empty grocery aisle. But in her fantasies, she imagined the woman to be simple and kindhearted. The kind of person who would open doors for others and never fail to perform random acts of kindness.

#

The next day, after settling back into reality, Faith and Bristol pieced together a puzzle on the floor of the pink bedroom.

Danielle knocked. "Can I ask for your help this morning?"

Faith jumped to her feet. "Of course. Anything."

A blanket of hope sat on Bristol's face, too. A longing to speak, yet she still couldn't. With a little more time, perhaps.

"Both of us can help." She reached down for Bristol and pulled her up.

Twenty minutes later, Faith found herself staring into the big, beautiful display window of Danielle's salon. Two mannequins wearing long flowery sundresses and floppy sunhats posed, pretending to blow into wands to create imaginary bubbles in the form of beach balls. Several of the colorful balls with that month's bonus items hung from transparent strings. Free shampoo with a deep conditioning treatment. Complimentary eyebrow wax with a spa pedicure. A free neck and shoulder massage for recommending someone. "Brilliant."

"That window is Martina's magic." Danielle opened up the door, and they entered.

The salon had a rustic look with brick walls and dangling lights from the open rafter ceilings. Tall mirrors at each station added a sense of depth and richness, offering clients an intimate view of the salon's contemporary touch. Accented in tones of teal and chocolate, Faith could picture herself sitting in one of the massage chairs and enjoying a good book and laughs. Faith headed over to one of the rich, brown cushioned chairs and sat. She twirled, taking in the entire salon. The scent of peppermint essential oils soothed the space.

Danielle brought a sense of hearth and home to anything she touched.

"Let me show you something." Danielle motioned for Faith to follow her behind the circular receptionist desk.

Faith and Bristol followed. She glanced at the computer screen with all of its colorful highlights. Eight columns, sparse time slots, and notes framed the mess of the past week's appointments.

The appointments brought Faith back to her favorite part of life. Back to when she ran the appointment scheduling at Salon Juliard while in college. She loved the hustle of the busy salon and couldn't wait to finish her due diligence to her parents' rule of finishing college before starting her hairdressing career. She couldn't wait to consult with clients looking to her for hair care advice. She couldn't wait to style, cut and color hair as she did when attending the vocational school to get her hair license. Those four years behind the counter of the salon where her sister first started out, crafted some of the best years of her life.

That same excitement of years past trilled on her heart again as she took a closer look at the appointments. Haircut. Forty-five minutes. Highlight. Two hours. Hair color application and cut. One and a half hours. If she were the one making that appointment, she would've buffered an extra fifteen minutes into the schedule and squeezed someone in between while the client's color processed. Faith ran a tight schedule back in the day. The stylists groaned and complained when they'd glance at the book, and then thank her later for padding their wallets with a lot of extra cash from all their Herculean efforts.

But, hey, what did she know? Twelve years had passed since then. Things could be very different in the modern day salon world.

Danielle exited out of the appointment application and opened her browser to a hairstyling site. "I like bangs." She pointed to a picture of a model sporting a side part. "Can you cut my bangs like hers?"

Faith laughed. "You trust me after all these years?"

"If you screw up it grows back."

Bristol giggled on that.

Danielle placed her arm around Bristol's shoulder. "Your mom is very talented when it comes to cutting hair."

Bristol broke out into a huge smile, and looked at Faith with her large expressive eyes.

"We came to decorate for Fourth of July, not cut bangs."

"Did we?" Danielle continued to stare at the screen.

"I know what you're trying to do."

"What? I need bangs!"

They stared at each other. That same excitement from her teen years bubbled up inside her again when she would cut hair in her parent's living room after school. Kids would come by after classes and sit in a chair in the middle of the room while she worked her magic. She'd practice the techniques she learned that day in vocational school. By the end of the week, her mother would have a pile of hair to toss in her composter.

Danielle led her over to her hair station and sat. "I trust you."

"If you say so."

Bristol sat in the chair next to them and watched Faith snip, comb, and re-snip. Thirty minutes later, Faith placed the nozzle of the blow-dryer back in its slot on the counter and spun Danielle around toward the mirror. She clenched her jaw, waiting on her sister's reaction.

Danielle scooted up on the chair. "I love it."

Faith bounced in her sandals. "Sorry it took so long. I'm a little rusty."

"I'll hire you anyway." Danielle stood up and pinched Faith's cheek.

As fun as working at the salon could be, it would mess her up more and take her away from getting her life together. Faith couldn't afford to go backwards. Reality wagged its pointy finger and warned her to stop pretending the world glowed in happy shades of pink.

Danielle turned to Bristol. "Do you want some braids?"

Bristol looked to Faith and stretched her eyes in question.

When would her little girl speak again? If someone as trusting and kind as Danielle couldn't help her find her voice, who could? "If you want braids, tell her you want braids."

Bristol bobbed her head up and down.

A few giggles and braids later, they eventually headed back home.

Chapter Four

The morning after her trip to the salon, Faith ventured out to the deck for another dream analysis session. She carried her stein of coffee and wore some dark sunglasses and a large-brimmed hat.

Danielle and Martina sat next to each other, staring out at the brick man again. Henry sat on Martina's lap and barked at him.

"My mother's out with Stan this morning," Martina said. "They're picking up litter at the far end of the lake. So, looks like it's just a coffee morning for us."

And so, they drank coffee. Martina and Danielle ogled the brick man and Faith eyed the yoga goddess behind her dark sunglasses, recalling the erotic dream from nights prior.

At one point, Martina turned to Faith. "How long as it been for you?"

Danielle choked on her flaxseed muffin. "Martina," she warned.

"What? I'm just asking. It's a legit question, no?"

Faith tapped Martina's hand. "We're not going to go there."

"Ah, so you feel like a virgin. That's all you had to say." Martina adjusted her sunhat. "I'm right there with you."

"I'm fine with my sexless life."

"I'm deprived by it. My ex and I used to have it every other day. Then, he moved to a malaria-infested tent in the middle of some jungle with big ugly bugs. How could I keep our marriage well-oiled when he couldn't even get a decent internet connection?" She plunged forward in a stretch. "I'm frustrated."

Faith would rather eat mud than have to deal with marital sex. "Embrace the break."

"I love sex. Why would I embrace a break from it?"

"You don't ever get tired of it?"

"Never." Martina pointed her eyes at her. "You don't like sex?"

Sex had always been a chore. "I don't miss it."

"Well then you've never been attracted to someone."

Danielle grabbed Martina's wrist. "Enough."

"Of course I have." Faith said. Kind of. If she counted her erotic dreams.

"Trust me. No you haven't. And that is a sin." Martina shook her head. "A serious sin."

"I'm sure once Faith gets resettled into something new, she'll have plenty of time to…" Danielle bit her lip. "Well, to get rid of some of her frustration."

"Frustration is good." Martina winked at Danielle like the two of them were in on a joke. "It causes us to do things we otherwise wouldn't do. It creates new realities." A smile widened on her glossed lips. "It puts us on paths we never would've traveled and introduces us to people we never would've met."

Two sets of intent eyes fixated on Faith as she listened to the oddly poetic insights of Martina.

"Frustration," Martina continued, "gifts us with opportunity for friendship, grace, humility, and let's not forget love!" Her eyes lit up. "I know what you need. You need to reinvent yourself." She slapped her well-nurtured thigh. "Yes, that's it! Let's have a reinvention!"

"Here we go." Faith flung her hands in the air.

"Now wait a minute." Danielle put down her coffee mug and balanced her chin in her hand. "Martina's right. It's good to reinvent yourself. Why do you think I took up tree cutting?"

"I'm not going to start cutting trees."

Danielle laughed. "Fine. Okay, maybe something a little less dangerous."

"Something sexy," Martina said.

Faith didn't do sexy. "No. No way."

"I know!" Martina wiggled in her lounger. "Let's do a Zumba class. It'll get us ready for the patio party."

"Patio party?" Faith asked.

"We have a few each summer. Christian barbeques. Mom cooks for two days straight. Danielle decorates. And, Emmy and I select the music. We're having one very soon. You'll need to know how to dance, so Zumba would be perfect!"

Faith needed to figure out how to put her life back together, not distract herself with looking like an idiot. "Absolutely not. I refuse to do Zumba."

Danielle rose and walked toward the slider. "Even Bristol wants to do Zumba."

Faith tore off her sunglasses. "She told you that?"

"We write notes to each other." Danielle opened up the sliding door. "She also told me you pretend to eat my flaxseed muffins and throw them in the bottom of the trash when I'm not looking." Danielle stepped inside. "She loves them, by the way, because she's open to new things, unlike you." With that, Danielle walked back into the kitchen.

Martina, uncharacteristically, had no words.

Faith chuckled. Shaking her hips and gyrating in Zumba class? She'd look like a baboon screaming for a banana. Stick a pink tutu on her and call it a day. Though, if Bristol wanted to do Zumba, then dance around like a fool it would be.

# #

As the days progressed, Danielle continued dropping hints to Faith about working at the salon while in town. Faith would counter the offer with a maybe.

She needed a real job. Working at the salon would only sidetrack her.

Though, it would be a good opportunity to earn a few extra bucks to help defray the expenses waiting for her back in Boston. The contractor Stuart hired to finally fix the basement flooring from the flood had called the other day with an estimate that caused Faith to nearly faint.

Before long, she made a deal with herself. If no one responded to her latest résumé blast by the end of the week, she'd consider tackling a haircut or two.

She would make the most of her time in Rhode Island. It did begin to grow on her. Her mood brightened every time Bristol giggled and spent time with her cousins and aunts.

Faith also enjoyed when the yoga goddess would find her looking at her. They shared a hesitant glance and timid wave each time.

Faith knew better than to get too familiar with the pleasantries of the easy side of life, though. Whenever too good, fiasco followed. The balance would eventually cock a little off to the side. Ebb and flow. Good and bad. Where good lay, bad waited to pounce.

In fact, she didn't have to wait too long. Midway through her second week at the lake house, Faith glanced at her Facebook feed. She opened up to a new profile picture of Stuart with his young girlfriend, Gilly. She had satin smooth skin, ripened to a healthy glow, and teeth so white they looked fake. Her hair hung in long, shiny golden waves.

Stuart beamed.

He never beamed while married to her. Except for the day Bristol came into their world. Every other day, his forehead always creased in painful folds. That's what a sexless marriage did to a couple. It created crow's feet and deep grooves that swallowed joy.

Now he looked a good ten years younger.

Faith didn't have the magic potion that Gilly had to smooth over the stress and reveal the peaceful glow underneath it.

Faith read through some of the comments, one written by hers truly, Gilly. "This photo sums up my current mood: Overjoyed. I got the promotion! I'm a full-time professor."

Good for you, bitch.

Lucia came out on the deck, and Faith put her cellphone down on the glass table.

"I went out for a nice walk and decided to treat us to lattes."

Faith grabbed the tall cup. "Thank you."

"Next time I go, you should tag along. An adorable barista works behind the counter."

"He's probably a kid in college. Now what would I need with someone like that?"

"Not a kid. Likely about thirty. Artistic with the nozzle of that whipped cream, too. *She* drew us hearts."

Rendered speechless, Faith's skin flushed again. Was Lucia psychic in addition to being a self-proclaimed dream expert? Or had she caught Faith staring at Yoga Goddess too many times? She did create a habit of craning her neck to sneak peeks of her sensual stretching rituals on the plush lawn.

"We can go to get our lattes together tomorrow, if you'd like," Lucia added.

49

Faith stared out at the beauty of nature before them and a giddiness rose. Braving all, she whispered, "I'd rather watch Yoga Goddess."

Lucia sipped her latte, looking straight ahead. "I know, dear."

# #

Later on that afternoon, Faith helped set the deck table for a late lunch. The sun blazed. The air smelled like fresh watermelon. The laughter of families picnicking curled up around the tall maple and pine trees. Summer sprinkled its warmth and brightness on Orchard Pond.

As Faith began to turn the handle to the large table umbrella, she spotted a tall and lean hound with an auburn, shiny coat dart across the grass. It ran toward a tree near the edge of Danielle's property line, and then it leaped against the trunk and howled.

"That squirrel better settle in for the long haul," Lucia said.

"Damn squirrels." Faith neared the deck railing, noticing the hair on the dog's back rise in a Mohawk. "We should get the dog's attention. Howling like that can't be good for its throat or our ears."

"Pretzel isn't going to let up until someone forces her away."

"Pretzel? What an odd name."

"She hasn't gotten loose in a while. I should let her mom and dad know she's on the hunt again." Lucia settled back against the lounger. "But, I'm too comfy."

The hound continued its guttural growl. "Where do they live?"

"Two houses up to the right."

"We should tell them."

"Suit yourself, dear." Lucia lowered the brim of her sun visor. "The howl is like music to my ears. But, if she's bothering you, go right ahead."

Faith climbed down the steps to the brick patio. "I'll be back. I'm going to let them know."

A few minutes later, Faith knocked on the front door of Danielle's neighbor.

When it opened, Faith locked eyes with none other than the yoga goddess. Her stomach flapped, like that moment right before a roller coaster drops from its highest point. Then it dawned on Faith, the hound from the street. Of course. How did she not connect those dots?

The woman's eyes flickered a tease along the charming cinnamon flecks dotting the deep brown of her gaze. She wore her hair in a loose side ponytail. Tiny wisps played with her high cheekbones. The yoga served her right. Her long, sinewy arms and legs looked even more impressive up close.

"Can I help you?"

A hot and delicious surge shot through Faith. She opened her mouth, but nothing came out. Her words hid like bashful children afraid of the first day of school.

"You're the woman from a few houses down, right?"

She knows who I am? The question echoed around her mind. "That's right."

She arched her eyebrow. "Do you need a cup of sugar or something?"

"Um, no. I stay away from the stuff." Like hell she did. She ate it as if it saved her life each day. Her hips and thighs proved that. Her frumpy outfit, an over-sized t-shirt and baggy workout shorts, didn't help her case any.

Yoga Goddess folded her hands over her chest. "So if it's not sugar, what else can it be?"

"I'm sorry." Faith snapped back to the moment. "I've had too much sun. Um, anyway, I came to tell you your dog is in my sister's yard and obsessed

51

with a squirrel in a tree."

"My dog?"

Faith backed up and counted the row of houses from Danielle's. She had counted correctly. "You don't have a dog?"

"I do. Well, the people who live here do. But, she's here." Yoga Goddess looked around confused. "Pretzel." She walked away and down the foyer, leaving the front door open. "Come here girl," she called out.

Faith walked through the door. "Pretzel is over at my sister's house." The dog's erratic howl echoed through the home. "That's her barking."

Yoga Goddess looked out the back window, craning her beautiful neck. "Oh, wow. I guess you're right." She stepped back and scanned the room, pausing when she glanced at a hole in the screen door. "I'll grab her leash."

Faith stood in the center of the room, shifting her weight from one foot to the other. She scoped the view.

A tall bamboo tree with full green leaves added a Zen-like vibe to the peaceful elegance of the open foyer.

A laptop occupied the kitchen counter. A pile of running shoes and sandals sat under the coatrack. Exquisite artwork adorned the walls. Near the entranceway to the kitchen hung a gorgeous oil painting of the beach at Camp Cronin.

"That's a beautiful picture." Faith walked up to it and leaned in closer, admiring the depth of the beach scene. "It looks so real."

"It's remarkable. My ex painted it for the owners a few years back. They took it down after we broke up, but I know how much they loved it. So, I hung it back up for them."

Selfless and beautiful. "Well, your ex is talented."

Yoga Goddess sighed. "Yeah, she's better at some things than others."

52

She.

She strolled toward the leash on the counter. Her hair bounced around the scooped back of her sundress. "So, are you visiting your sister for the summer or do you live there, too?"

"Just visiting. From Boston. With my daughter."

"This is a great place to spend some time in the summer. I love when I get the call from Bob and Mary to ask if I want to house-sit for them."

"They own the house, I take it?"

She nodded.

"So you house-sit often?"

"For the past three summers, I used to teach at a dance school in Providence. But, now I've turned into a pet and house sitter. I travel to different states and take care of everything while the owners are off researching or vacationing. Bob and Mary hate tourist season, so they travel. They prefer Pretzel remain in the house and in her routine. They have a kennel they use in times of emergency, but that's if no one can come. It's a nice getaway for me. I take care of the house. Water the plants. Cut the grass. Things like that."

Faith looked around at the sunny, fun kitchen. The seafoam green countertops and island glistened like sea-glass. The cabinets, with their frosted glass fronts offered a soft backdrop to a set of bright yellow stools. Though, water dripped from the kitchen faucet, which ruined the calming effect. And, sugar ants crawled on the counter and up the sides of the kitchen door.

"By the way, my name is Candace." She extended her free hand.

"Faith."

Candace cocked her head, and her face lit up. "Very pretty."

Faith slipped into a warm buzz. "Thanks."

"Your name is, too." Candace coaxed her with a lingering gaze, then walked past her with the leash. "Now, let's go get the howling beast."

It took Faith a moment to get her feet to move.

#

When they arrived at Danielle's and swept through the kitchen, Bristol followed them onto the deck. They stepped out into the warm afternoon air, and Martina and Lucia's jaws dropped. "Yoga Goddess," they both whispered together.

"Yoga Goddess?" Candace offered a tentative smile, then shifted her gaze to Faith.

"I have no idea," Faith mumbled. In her peripheral view she noticed Lucia's cheek flinched, as if she had gotten caught tossing Danielle's flaxseed muffins in the trash. She angled toward the howling.

"What happened to Mary and Bob?" Lucia asked.

"They're somewhere in the Sahara Desert likely riding on a camel's back, I suspect." Candace twirled the leather leash around her wrist and headed over to the edge of the deck.

"Cheers to a loud Pretzel on the loose," Lucia whispered to Faith.

"Always looking at the bright side."

"No other way, dear. No other way."

Pretzel's bark grew louder and more excited. "I'm sorry about this. I hope Pretzel will listen to me. When she's like this, nothing works. Not even chicken."

Lucia tossed a hand up in the air. "I can solve that." She climbed out of her chair and rushed toward the kitchen. Moments later, she returned wearing her worn, red apron and carrying a container of leftovers. "What'll it be? Sirloin, sweet potatoes, and a little cornbread?"

The dog sniffed the air, and then bolted across the lawn and brick patio. She scaled the two steps up to the deck and headed over to the food medley. She scarfed the medley down in three bites, and then stared up at Candace with expectant eyes.

Candace kneeled and cupped her hands under Pretzel's jaw. "Remarkable. I scratch my head over trying to figure out something to cook that you'll eat. I had to let you run away over here to solve the great mystery."

She lowered her hands, and then Bristol stepped up and petted the dog. When she stopped, Pretzel scooped up her hand with her long nose.

"Oh, yeah, you can't stop petting her once you start." Candace attached the leash.

They spent the next several minutes poring over Pretzel, admiring her shiny coat and affection toward anything that ran, hopped, or crawled in the grass.

"You know," Lucia said. "I've got a bunch of leftovers. Let's head inside and I'll warm them up for her so they taste better."

Candace straightened from her kneeling position. "That's okay. Don't trouble yourself. I doubt she's going to eat more."

Lucia adjusted the straps of her apron over her belly. "It's ok. This isn't the first time Pretzel has visited us." Lucia headed into the kitchen, and like good shepherds, they all followed her lead. "She'll eat more."

Candace's gaze fell to the Zumba brochure Martina had placed on the counter. A sly grin settled over her face.

"Have you ever taken a Zumba class before," Martina asked, lodging herself between Candace and Faith.

"I live for it." Candace looked past Martina and casted Faith a sidelong glance.

Faith stirred at the sudden quiver traveling along her spine.

Martina picked up the brochure and tapped Faith's wrist with it. "See? We need to Zumba."

Lucia spooned more of the leftovers onto a plate and stuck it in the microwave.

"Have a seat." Lucia pulled out a stool for Candace. "Oh, and here's a fresh *arepa*." She placed one of the grilled *arepas* on a plate and pushed it in front of her.

Candace's eyes grew large.

"It's Colombian cornbread. We eat *arepas* every Saturday and Sunday." Lucia sat down and placed her chin in her hand. "Tradition."

Candace picked it up and admired it. "It's so perfect. Mine always come out cracked on the edges. How do you get them so round?"

"You've had them before?" Lucia asked, pushing the container of butter spread toward her.

"Yes, but I haven't had one this authentic in ages. My grandmother used to make them over a fire pit back when I lived with her in Colombia as a little girl."

"You're Colombian?" Lucia asked, excitedly.

"Half." Candace grinned. "My father is Colombian and my mother is Canadian." Candace reached for the butter knife and dipped it into the spread. "Seriously, how do yours come out so round?"

Lucia hopped down from her stool. She went over to the magnetic knife strip on the wall and removed a worn looking plastic wrap. "A Ziploc bag!"

"Brilliant." Candace bit into the *arepa* and sealed her eyes closed. Her eyelids fluttered in delight.

There went that tingle again.

"Where in Colombia do your grandparents live?" Lucia asked, sitting back down again and admiring Candace's ecstasy as much as Faith.

"Armenia."

"Well, hot damn! I love that charming village."

For the next thirty minutes, they chatted about Colombia. Candace smiled a lot. Her smile added a freshness to the air that comforted like the mist on a hot summer day. Faith listened to their conversation like a bystander. They spoke about the miracle that they both had Colombian roots and enjoyed similar dishes like sancocho, sudado, and arroz con pollo. Meanwhile Pretzel kept placing a sock she found on the floor in Faith's hand. They played tug-of-war the entire time. The moment Faith would stop pulling, Pretzel would tap her arm with her paw and yelp.

"We're throwing a big summer party very soon," Lucia said. "You have to come. We're going to have lots of fun. We're going to eat lots of food and dance. There will be lots of dancing. I love to Salsa. Do you?"

"I can't get enough of it." Candace took another sensual bite.

"Faith you love to dance Salsa, too, don't you?" Lucia winked at her, inviting her to join the talk.

Faith didn't have a dance vibe in her body. "I've never tried."

"She's never tried," Lucia said to Candace as if shocked to hear the news. "We need to change this."

Only if Bristol dragged her on the dance floor. Otherwise, she'd never embarrass herself. "I'll be helping with the grill."

"That's Christian's job." Lucia turned to Candace. "Between you and me, we'll get her hips swinging."

Candace's gaze remained on Faith. "It would be my pleasure."

Faith's inner thighs trembled. She turned her attention to Pretzel who had latched onto her fingers and bitten down. Faith placed the sock in between her sharp teeth and swung it side-to-side, trying to ignore the growing palpitations and trickle of blood falling to the floor.

Then, the front door opened, and a moment later, Christian came through the foyer and into the kitchen cradling an arm full of grocery bags. He flinched at Faith's bloodied finger. "What is happening here?"

# #

Soon the whole family gathered around the kitchen island and began digging into the butter spread and crunching down on the crispy *arepas*. Lucia blurted out one crazy comment after another, and Candace laughed with her over each one.

Lucia, with all her flamboyancy, had always annoyed Stuart. They seldom visited because of her. In fact, he'd prefer an injection of poison over a visit. His heart would tighten. His face would break out in a rash. Then, he'd start pacing the room, looking to escape the confines of her chaotic energy. Candace leaned in and took it all in, apparently enjoying the offbeat jokes and crazy rhapsodies about Lucia's day-to-day activities.

"You have beautiful hair," Martina said, admiring Candace's shiny, dark-chestnut ponytail. "I wish mine could be as sleek."

"I wish mine bounced like yours."

How did those two beautiful women not realize their assets?

"So, you're house-sitting for Bob and Mary?" Martina continued to stare at Candace's shiny hair.

"Yes. It's a great gig. I look forward to it each summer."

"How do you get the summers off?" Martina drilled.

"This is my job. I'm a traveling house and pet sitter. At times a dance instructor when the studio in town needs me to fill in for them. It's a great life. I get to take care of these kinds of beasty messes over here who apparently like to chomp on fingers." Candace stretched her eyes down to Faith's freshly-bandaged hand. "I'm sorry."

Faith blushed. "It's okay. She mistook me for a sock."

Emmy bent down to grab the shredded, slobbery tangle of threads. "That was my sock."

Christian sipped lemon water from his fancy flute glass. "I left my socks under the coffee table once, and now I have to do my own laundry."

Danielle lowered her chin and chuckled, and then shuffled through a pile of mail. "Whoever you marry will thank me years from now."

"What about Emmy? It's okay if she turns out to be a slob?"

"Oh, there'll be chores coming her way." Danielle peeked up over the edge of her reading glasses at Emmy.

"It's one sock!"

Danielle clutched the pile of paperwork. "Full of blood stains and drool."

Emmy, Christian, and Danielle wrestled through a few more minutes of sock talk as the rest of them observed with awkward stares.

At one point, Emmy whined about having to wash Christian's stupid skinny glass, and Christian defended his glass choice citing the narrow opening allowed the drinks to breathe.

Candace shifted on her stool.

Martina even began petting the drooling dog with one hand and clutching Henry to her chest with the other. The two sized each other up with steady glances and noses turned up in sniffing positons.

Wanting a better conversation, Faith asked Candace. "So, where do you travel?"

"I have a growing list of clients all over America: California, North Dakota, Florida, Illinois, Georgia, Arizona, and of course here. Rhode Island is sort of my home base. So, I rent a room in Providence. In addition to the summers, I also come back to Little Rhody a few weeks out of the year when I need a vacation from traveling."

Everyone nodded, mesmerized as much as Faith by her charm.

Faith noticed a birthmark the shape of an almond on the side of Candace's slender neck. It sat a mere inch from her soft hairline. Everything about the woman intrigued Faith.

"Who takes care of your place while you're traveling?" Martina asked, letting her hand slip from Pretzel who then headed into the living room.

"My roommate."

"What is your roommate like?" Lucia asked.

"He's a grad student at Brown and reads. All the time." Candace fired back answers with a similar eager cadence to Martina and Lucia.

"Is he cute?" Martina asked, dwarfing back into a thirteen-year-old at a pajama party.

"If you're into long beards and intellectual types, sure."

Faith glanced over at Bristol. She sat on the living room floor now petting Pretzel. Bristol admired Pretzel with a gentle tenderness.

Bristol had begged her for a dog, but Stuart never wanted the fur in the house or to pick up the poo in the yard. Maybe once they returned to Boston, they could adopt one.

"Do you have a boyfriend?" Lucia asked as she poured coffee into a lineup of mugs.

Startled, Faith swung her gaze back to Candace who handled the crazy barrage of questions with a straight face.

"No, I do not have a boyfriend."

"No boyfriend in her life," Lucia spoke to Faith. "You both have so much in common." Lucia winked.

Danielle cleared her throat. "Can I get you something else besides coffee? Water?"

"Coffee is perfect. Thank you." Candace scanned everyone. "My *girlfriend* and I broke up a while ago."

"Oh, really?" Lucia's voice rang high. "Broke up you say?" Lucia nudged Faith's shin.

"Really?" Faith interrupted. "No water?" She rose. "I'm getting myself some. I'll get you a glass too."

Christian, the silent observer, smirked and sipped more from his flute glass.

The conversation continued on with Faith and Danielle doling out vigilant interruptions to protect their guest from Lucia and Martina's questions. Candace praised Lucia's *arepas* a handful of times, and answered her interrogations with polite ease. She answered things such as what color hair dye she used to get the richness and depth. Had she ever pulled a muscle doing yoga? Did she ever get nervous teaching a class full of dance students?

"No," she said. "Well, except for when the mayor of Providence attended and I hyperventilated. But I don't count that. How often does that happen, right?"

"Wow, I'm not the only one who hyperventilates in front of an important crowd?" Danielle asked. "I quit college in freshman year because I feared having to present a paper to the entire Communications faculty."

"Seriously?" Faith had no idea. "I thought you quit because of hairdressing."

"I should've gotten my degree. I would've liked teaching." Danielle struggled to straighten her pile of paperwork. "I ran from my fear. How foolish."

"I get it," Candace said. "I had a meltdown in high school when I had to read a paragraph. I ran out of the room."

The air took on a lighter vibe in the company of Yoga Goddess. She spread her cheer, putting everyone at ease even with the crazy slamming of questions and vulnerabilities shared. Supposedly, Danielle usually remained tight-lipped about personal things even with clients, at least according to Martina. She always stirred the conversation toward them, never to her. Yet she opened up to that complete stranger – someone she'd never met who lived two houses down from her for the past few summers.

Bristol continued to pet Pretzel with one hand and now Henry with the other while leaning against the living room couch. "Is she your daughter?" Candace asked.

They both looked into the living room and watched as Pretzel's eyes remained shut in a content surrender against the lure of chaos. "She sure is. She tends to be a bit shy around new people."

"That's a sign of great listening skills."

Martina raised her cup. "Cheers to great listening skills."

Danielle and Faith shared a private silent chuckle before raising up their mugs and clinking.

# #

After a while, Faith, Emmy and Danielle wandered into the family room.

A large sand-colored sofa balanced the open space with comfort and style. Its skirted base tapered into a plush blue area rug. Accent pillows and window treatments, the color of sea grass and denim, pulled together the entire room.

Though, a colorful ceramic giraffe, with a neck much too short, sat center stage by itself on an end table much too rich in ambiance for such casual playfulness. The black-finished table's lower shelf, supported with charming carved legs, floated above the floor devoid of anything that competed with the giraffe.

Faith would get the story on that piece soon enough.

She sat, and Bristol leaned against her. Then Pretzel snuggled up in a ball on Faith's foot.

Candace and Martina helped Lucia with the dishes, and Faith kept a vigilant ear tuned to their conversation.

"Pretzel doesn't eat well, typically," Candace said. "She surprised me when she gobbled down the food. What special ingredient did you add to it?"

"It's a family secret. I'll send some by to you tomorrow. In fact," Lucia said extra loud and chummy, "I'll have Faith bring it by. Looks like Pretzel would love to see her again."

"I think you're right," Candace said. "We'd both welcome the opportunity."

Faith's ponytail pulled at her temples in a strange and exhilarating way.

Chapter Five

That night, Faith dreamed of a forest. She walked through foggy air, passing by thick trees with double and triple trunks. Their branches swayed. The tree roots sat on top of the soil, creating giant mounds in the middle of the path.

Faith could no longer see what lay before her. Confused, she spun to find a new way, only everyway she turned, the tree roots blocked her. Then, one of the branches plucked her up, lifting her out of the forest and into the canopy. From there, she surveyed the vast lushness of the rolling green hills circling the deep, tangled woods. One giant nest of leaves, branches and knotty roots lay below her – an impassable stretch of land that imprisoned its captives. Free from its grip, she hung in the sky and examined the choices that extended beyond the impossible.

Then, the branch snapped and sent her tumbling back toward the nest. Within inches of hitting it, she awoke.

Despite the dream, when Faith opened her eyes the next morning, the sun took on a brighter shade. It lit up the room in a spectacular tone, highlighting the wicker chair near the window. Faith pictured herself sitting in the chair each morning, sipping delicious coffee as she read a book that took her down a trail of happiness. Under the rays of sunshine, peace would swaddle her. Worries of the mess back in Boston wouldn't unnerve her. The crispness of her mood protected her from the hollowness of the future that only yesterday she had dreaded.

Overnight, the world lightened with a sunny lacquer. Her lungs filled with air that tasted fresh. Reenergized, she stretched and looked out the window at the side yard. From there, she could see the top of Candace's roof. It peaked and sloped toward the green grass her body touched and sank into when practicing yoga.

A few minutes later, Faith joined everyone on the deck and she shared her dream, her real dream.

"Dreams never lie." Lucia passed the sugar across the table to her. "If you would've leaped toward the grass, you wouldn't have fallen back into the woods."

"Oh," Martina bounced in her lounger. "I know what this all means."

"Enlighten us." Faith chugged some coffee.

"Danielle," Martina said. "Now. Ask her now."

"Ask me what?"

Faith studied Danielle's half smile. That look preceded all serious talks. Danielle half-smiled the day she first told her parents she had quit college and would be marrying Lucas. "Well?"

Danielle cocked her head. "I want you to work at the salon. So, I'm asking you again. Please, will you?"

Faith couldn't afford to indulge in things she once played with as an emerging adult with no responsibilities. She needed stability. A career as a hairdresser took time to cultivate. She didn't have that kind of time anymore. She needed to move forward with something that would put food on the table, now, not a year from then. If she spent the day getting lost in hair, she'd get lazy about sending résumés and securing her financial future. What next? Eat ice-cream for breakfast, lunch, and dinner and pretend she'd fit into her jeans forever?

Like any of that could ever happen.

"I need to stay focused."

"Oh, come on," Martina whined. "She needs another stylist. My hand is getting worse by the day. It needs rest."

"I can't." Faith stirred in her seat. What if she left a curling iron on and burned her sister's salon down? How would she live with herself? She couldn't be trusted to select a compatible spouse, get her daughter to talk, or find a job that paid her enough to put a decent roof over her head. How could she be entrusted with something as important as her sister's reputation? Besides, why tangle herself up in anything else that could mess with her already screwed up life? "It doesn't feel right."

"Your dream indicates you need to take a leap to get out of your situation." Martina's words carried a new whine. "What are you so afraid of? Getting a little lost in someone's hair?"

The women stared at her like she'd climbed out of an alien spaceship carrying a two-headed chimp on her back.

"I've only dabbled in it. I can't take on real clients."

Danielle leaned forward. "You're a natural. Even as a student in vocational school, you had a line of clients at home waiting for you."

"Well, only because they received five-dollar haircuts."

"Teens are the vainest. Yet, they trusted you. When are you going to start trusting yourself?"

They were just kids. "Our life is in Boston. Not here. You should find someone else."

Disappointment pooled in Danielle's eyes. "I understand."

She hated to disappoint her sister. "But, I'll think about it."

Danielle reached for her hand and squeezed it. "I hope you do."

The deck door slid open, and Faith looked up from her scribbles. Out of it walked Bristol. "Do you want some breakfast?"

Bristol shook her head and bit her lip.

"What is it sweetheart?"

Bristol lifted her hand and revealed the cell. Her eyes grew large and hopeful.

"For me?"

Bristol nodded and headed back inside without saying a word.

"Excuse me." Faith stood and faced a trio of stares. "What?"

"Nothing," Danielle mumbled. Then, the other two joined in, wagging their heads and looking off into the distance.

"She's shy." Faith defended her daughter.

They continued to look into the distance, nodding in mild agreement.

Faith left the deck on a frustrated sigh. When she met her daughter in the kitchen, Bristol handed her the phone. "It's Daddy."

Bristol headed out of the kitchen on a gallop.

Faith gripped the phone. "Hey."

"So, I've got good news and bad news."

"Go on with the bad."

"The contractor called and said he found more extensive damage under the basement tub. Once he got in there and started looking around, he discovered a bunch of black mold in the wall behind the shower tiles."

"Black mold?"

"I'm afraid so. We're going to need to do an entire shower replacement along with mold removal if we want to sell the house in two years as we planned."

"Stuart, I don't have the money for that."

"Well, that's where the good news comes in."

"Please, let's hear it, then."

"Gilly knows someone at the community college who is hiring a PR rep. She's happy to recommend you. It pays a little less than you earned at the university, but the commute isn't as bad. It's a good opportunity, Faith."

Faith tightened her face. "I don't need Gilly's help."

"Please consider it."

She would not take a handout from him or his girlfriend. She would find her own solution. The time to cut that dependence had longed passed. "I already have some offers on the table I'm considering."

"Well, that's great. Where?"

"I'll let you know when and if I accept an offer."

He sighed. "Fair enough. This weekend, I'd like to spend some time with Bristol if that's okay?"

"We planned to help Lucia plant tomatoes."

"Faith," he whispered. "We have to work together on this."

"You screwed up." Her voice raised too high.

He scoffed.

She clicked her tongue.

She did that too often.

Blaming Stuart became her tool of choice. Not only did blaming him help justify her bad luck, but that blame served as a flotation device. It allowed Faith to float without risk of drowning. But, like any good voyage, one had to eventually let go of such devices and trust in the process of the journey. If life tossed her more than bad luck, maybe she could. For now, she gripped that blame and used it to stay afloat. "Now, if you don't mind, I've some prep work to do for a follow up interview."

She hung up and lowered her head to the counter.

Why couldn't life be simple? Most everyone in her life enjoyed the gift of good luck and simplicity. Why couldn't she find a nice gig like Candace's? Keep someone's house tidy and walk the family dog. Surely, she could do a better job in the tidying department than Candace. Actually, tidy was a stretch. Those ants. That faucet drip. The clutter on the counter. The hole in the screen door.

She stood up and glanced at her puffy eyes in the mirror that hung above the kitchen table.

Mold. New bathroom. No money. Sell the house in two years. Ridiculous job offer coming from Gilly. What next?

Faith stood in the empty kitchen. Thoughts about the future and its potential effect on her and Bristol's life entered and churned up what-if questions. What if she couldn't be hired by another company? What if someone did hire her, but not at the salary she needed? What if she couldn't afford to live in a safe home anymore? Stuart's income ballooned significantly higher than hers. Could she do everything on her own? Stuart would help with Bristol's costs, but not hers. Would she ever be able to afford to buy new clothes again? So long, organic food. So long, comforts like pizza on Fridays and going out for lunch. Oh wait. That no longer mattered. She didn't have a job. Lunches out mattered when she had a circle of colleagues who would invite her to join them. How would she and her bestie, Sally, catch up if she couldn't afford Starbucks coffee anymore?

She watched the three women jot notes in their dream journals on the deck. All they'd been through and they could still smile.

Good for them.

# #

Not soon after, Faith bit into a burnt piece of toast when Lucia and Martina walked into the kitchen wearing colorful getups. A moment later, Danielle entered behind them wearing a much more subdued long t-shirt and yoga stretch pants.

"We're doing Zumba at the rec center." Lucia shook her hips and sashayed over to the cupboard. She mounted the step stool and reached for a water bottle. "And get this, they even have a kids' class mid-week so Emmy and Bristol can try it out. We've all got to get ready for our upcoming patio party."

"Get dressed." Danielle tapped Faith's shoulder. "You're coming too."

Faith bit into her burnt toast again and crumbs fell to the floor. Stress balled up in the back of her throat and threatened her oxygen supply. How could straining her lungs in Zumba class be good for her?

"You go and have fun. I'll clean up this mess instead."

Martina reached for the broom beside the trashcan and swept. "Go," she roared. "Up the stairs." She pointed toward the hallway. "We have exactly five minutes. I don't want to be late and be stuck in the last row."

"I have too much on my mind. My bathroom walls have mold. Stuart wants to sell the house in two years. His girlfriend offered to be a reference for a job opportunity." Faith tossed her toast down on a paper towel. "So, no to Zumba. I have more important things to deal with right now."

Danielle nudged her off the stool. "All the more reason to get your butt up the stairs and get dressed. Let's all go and have some fun. We'll deal with everything later."

Faith climbed back on the stool. "My stomach's in knots. Every time I turn around, something else happens."

"Trust me, sitting around worrying about what's next isn't going to

71

prevent it from coming. It could be something good."

"How do you stay so faithful that everything works out for the best?"

"Because when hasn't it?"

Faith opened her eyes wide. "What about Lucas?"

"I think everything happens the way it's supposed to and if we look close enough, we'll find the beauty even in the darkest places."

Faith crossed her arms over her chest. "How can there be beauty in death?"

"His death brought Lucia and Martina here. They have a sense of purpose and are vital to the people they've touched. Lucia gets to be a doting grandmother and Martina isn't living in a jungle somewhere in the middle of Africa with a man she never loved."

Faith lowered her arms onto the counter. "But what about you? What good did his death do you?"

"This home is full of family and beautiful reminders of how precious life is." Danielle tapped the tip of Faith's nose. "Lil sis, without the bad, we'd have nothing to highlight the good."

Faith had a lot to learn about living. "You're an amazing woman. I hope you know that."

Martina reached over Faith's shoulder to grab an apple. "Totally."

Lucia filled her water bottle. "I agree, she's amazing. When life tosses you a bowl of sugar and some lemons, you mix them together and enjoy the lemonade."

"That's right." Martina clamped Faith's shoulders. "Cheers to Zumba and lemonade." She squeezed Faith's shoulders harder. "Now, go get dressed so we can get wacky. We're not taking no for an answer."

Lucia shimmied her hips. "Zumba! Zumba! Zumba!" she sang.

"You're all wacky," Faith laughed.

Lucia pushed them all toward the foyer. "Come on. Enough with the problems. Time for us to get our hips flicking."

#

They entered the rec center. Latin music blasted from the large meeting room at the backend of the building. Lucia and Martina promenaded forward, sniffing the air like a couple of dogs in search of a treat.

Twenty or so women readied themselves. Faith scoped the crowded area for a good hiding spot. That's when she noticed Candace tinkering with the sound system and an iPad. The music changed to a more upbeat tune and grew even louder. Candace adjusted a headset mic over her sleek ponytail, and then turned to the room full of eager people ready to get their Zumba on.

Faith's heart bucked.

"Oh look," Lucia said. "It's our charming neighbor. I had no idea she'd be here." Lucia winked and whispered. "Lemonade!" Then, she and Martina parted the sea of women and claimed a spot front and center.

"Are you okay?" Danielle asked.

Faith lifted her chin, fighting back the urge to flee and rescue herself from ultimate embarrassment. "Yeah, of course. It's just Zumba."

"You're blotchy."

"Well, it's hot in here." Faith fanned herself and scanned the room for the most inconspicuous spot.

"It's not that hot," Danielle yelled over the music as she followed Faith. They headed toward the back corner near a wall of windows overlooking the kayak station on the east side of the lake.

"Okay, friends. Let's have some fun," Candace said, adjusting her headset mic and teasing the air instantly with her groove. She could move those hips the way professional dancers in music videos did.

They warmed up with some surprisingly easy steps and arm exercises. By the second song, things revved up. With a sensual touch, Candace traveled her hands up and down the length of her taut, tight body. Faith struggled along, hypnotized by Candace's rhythmic undulations, spinning, and gyrating over and over again to the beat of a fast-paced Latin number.

She danced with finesse, a finesse that intrigued, teased, spiraled its way through the room like the tempting scent of decadent chocolate.

Faith attempted to stay on beat, mouthing the one, two, three, four counts. Her feet hit the mark, but the rest of her didn't. If she continued on that tangent, she'd end up on the floor, twisted like a ball of unruly yarn, unable to untangle from the disastrous wreckage of her clumsiness.

She was a hot mess.

If she wanted to survive the next hour, she needed a plan, a map, and a guide to save her from herself. She set her eyes on the woman in front of her. She moved easily. She wouldn't win any dance competition, but she could stand her ground and blend. Faith only needed to blend.

So, like any good student, she studied the woman. And before long, she mimicked her foot movements. One, two, three, four. One, two, three, four. In, out, side, back, side again. Piece of cake.

Then, she added the hip flick and felt a slight pull in her back.

So, feet it would be.

She'd master one body part at a time.

Candace began to circle the group of Zumba enthusiasts, encouraging each with a vibrant whoop. She turned a group of clumsy women into dancers, bringing on the level of confidence needed to step on the stage of *So You*

Think You Can Dance and claim a spot.

As she encouraged, women stepped up their game, shimmying with more confidence, moving with more elegance, and carrying themselves with a sexual prowess. Candace wasn't only an enigmatic force, but also an incredible teacher.

Faith slowed her moves as Candace approached with wide, welcoming eyes. She circled behind Faith, feathering her shoulders with her gentle hands and guiding her in a side-to-side move in sync with the beat. Immersed in Candace's personal bubble, breathing her same air, and warming under her soft and unintimidating touch, Faith eased into the groove. As the sweat poured down her cheeks, Faith's moves lightened. She followed the fun cadence, and continued the gyration on her own count when Candace moved onto Danielle and helped her find her way.

She left everyone in a state of glow. Cheeks flushed. Sweat poured. Voices purred. And if anyone else experienced what Faith did, fantasies ignited.

An hour later, faces aglow and carrying a new swagger to their steps, the four of them approached Candace to thank her for the great workout.

Her eyes, shiny and healthy, sparkled as she listened to Lucia and Martina ramble about the dance parties they hosted back in New Jersey every Saturday night. "We danced all night long under the patio lights in our backyard."

Danielle tossed her arm around Lucia's shoulder. "We should let her go." She motioned to the two women standing behind them. "They have questions."

Lucia cranked her neck toward the women. "We'll just be a minute." Then, she turned back to Candace. "We have to go. These ladies need to get to the salon. We have a salon, you know."

Candace eyed Lucia in amusement. "Oh? I love salons."

"Hmm." Lucia nudged Faith. "She loves salons."

Faith chuckled and pulled at Lucia's hand. "We have to go."

Candace's gaze traveled from Faith's clunky running shoes up to the V-neck of her Nike stretch t-shirt wet from the heat of her instruction. "I'll have to check it out sometime."

Faith couldn't stop the goofy grin that spread across her face. "You should."

Candace studied her closely. "Maybe I will."

Lucia released a foolish chuckle. "Great. It's settled."

Danielle squeezed Faith's arm playfully. "Come on. Let's go so Candace can get back to work."

Before Faith could offer her a farewell wave, Danielle pulled her along toward the door. Lucia and Martina began humming the Ricky Martin song that had closed out the Zumba routine.

A sexy vibe swept in as they walked across the grassy field back to Danielle's.

"You can use the empty hair station near the window," Martina said. "The sun peeks in at just the right angle. You'll see. It's fabulous."

Could life be so simple and joyful? "I didn't agree, yet, by the way."

Danielle's eyes shone with a playful light. "Suit yourself. You never know what could be waiting on the other side of this opportunity."

She regarded the opportunity for the entire walk across the grass, allowing it to marinate with the newfound sexy vibe she'd gathered from the Zumba class. She imagined massaging Candace's scalp and creating a festival of strawberry-scented bubbles. That aroused a spark to ignite between her legs, one that then traveled up and down the length of her spine, pausing to tickle those intimate parts of her that, until then, had never been so excited.

Writing press releases about a faculty member's latest contribution to the academic world never tickled her like that. What harm could cutting hair really cause her? Well, unless she screwed up someone's hair, of course.

It would just be a temporary job until a better one came along. She could continue to send out résumés at night. And if an interview popped up, she could toss on a suit and jump in the car.

All of her arguments from before suddenly shriveled up and blew away.

She was tired of being afraid. If she could dance Zumba and come out intact, she could tackle a temporary job cutting hair.

"How soon can I start at the salon?"

Danielle stopped and dropped her jaw. "Seriously?"

Faith raised her hands. "It would only be temporary, of course."

"Of course."

Martina released a tiny squeal, and Danielle blocked her potential leap at Faith.

"You can start this weekend."

"Fine." Faith walked forward with a confident sexy stride, ready to tackle the new challenge. No reason not to have a little fun while waiting on her next grownup opportunity.

"Fine." Martina mirrored her catwalk across the lawn.

Not until Lucia pulled out her phone, did that sexy vibe vanish. "Look here. I had Christian record us!"

Faith gasped at the video of her ridiculous attempt to dance. "How did I miss Christian?"

Lucia nudged her and whispered. "Well, dear, we both know your attention was pointed elsewhere."

# #

Later that afternoon, Faith sat on the deck and reviewed haircutting techniques on YouTube.

Danielle joined her. "Want a soda?"

Faith removed her earbuds. "No. Not now." Then, she put them back in.

Danielle sat down and took a swig. "Has Bristol seen a counselor?"

Faith stopped the video and removed her earbuds again. "Why?"

She continued sipping and looking ahead at some kids chasing each other near the boat dock. "She needs help, Faith."

Faith studied her sister. "Are you judging me?"

"No. I'm concerned. I mean, why isn't she talking to us yet? She's been here a few weeks and no one's been able to get her to murmur a word. I thought with a little trust, she'd begin to show signs of opening up to us."

Faith fidgeted with the edge of her laptop, swallowing the urge to lash out. "She's shy. Stop making a big deal out of it."

Danielle wrapped her hand around Faith's wrist. "I'm not placing blame or saying there's something incurably wrong with her. I'm concerned because I love her. I want to see her enjoying herself like a kid should on summer vacation."

The counselors had tried many activities to pull the words out of Bristol's mouth. They devised a spreadsheet of activities Bristol liked to do like baking cakes, making jello, playing solitaire on the computer, hiking in the woods, doing arts and crafts. Then, they matched those rewards to activities they'd measure. If she whispered something in school, she'd get to make jello. If the teacher heard her mumbling the Pledge of Allegiance, she could hike. If she said a word aloud, she could bake a cake.

"She speaks perfectly fine with me and Stuart." Faith's defensive walls rose.

"Okay, I'm sorry." Danielle eased up. "I didn't mean to pry."

Suddenly, out of the corner of her eye, Faith spotted an eager Pretzel trotting across the grass. She headed up the deck stairs. Soggy, sandy, and wagging her tail, she placed her head in Faith's lap.

"I'm so sorry," Candace called out from the grass below. "She escaped again. I have to get that hole in the door fixed. One minute she's relaxing and the next she's jumping through the screen."

Well, well. Cheers to the lovely gift of distraction.

Grateful for the shift, Faith sat up taller. "You should probably fix that screen."

"I've never fixed a screen before. I wouldn't even know where to start."

"I can draft a list of things you'll need," Danielle offered.

"And, I'll look into it on YouTube," Faith said.

"Really? I'm not taking you away from anything important?"

"Nothing that can't wait until later," Danielle said. "It's just a list."

Faith tapped the edge of her laptop. "And, just a little research. I also would be happy to attempt fixing it." Faith needed to learn how to be handier anyway.

"This is so nice of you both." Candace hooked Pretzel's leash to her collar. "Would Bristol like to help, too? She can watch Pretzel while we attempt to repair it."

Faith's heart warmed. "I bet she'd love it."

# #

An hour later, Candace called to let her know she bought everything on

79

the list Danielle drafted.

Once she and Bristol headed over, the three of them stood before the broken screen. Bristol tapped Faith's hip and tried to hand her the new screen.

"I'll need that in a second. First I have to remove the old one."

"Bristol, can I get you a juice?" Candace asked. "I have Pomegranate."

Bristol nodded, and then followed Candace to the fridge.

Faith investigated the existing screen and began the initial cut to unhitch it from the fastener, as the YouTube video had instructed. Once she got the advantage, it easily pulled right out of the groove. Faith eventually pulled out the last of the screen.

"Delicious, isn't it?" Candace said from the kitchen.

"Yes," Bristol whispered.

Yes?

Faith froze.

She said yes! Out loud.

She stopped herself from glancing at them. Make too big a deal and the moment might be lost. She resisted, remaining kneeled and gripping the new screen. She swallowed a squeal.

"Oh, wow, so much progress already," Candace said, returning to her side.

Faith looked up at their happy faces.

"We're ready for you to put us to work. Aren't we?" she said to Bristol.

Bristol radiated.

Faith wanted to break out into a series of pirouettes. Instead, she handed Bristol one end of the screen. "Let's measure."

#

Later on, once they returned from their screen repair journey, Faith scaled the steps two at a time up to her room. She closed the door and broke out into a happy dance.

Bristol spoke!

She spoke!

She raised her fists in the air and spun in circles, allowing the joy to sink in and wash away years of anxiety.

# #

Shortly after, Faith and Bristol baked a cake. Bristol dipped her finger into the batter and scooped a glob in between her tiny lips. "Candace invited me to take the kids' Zumba class. I have to ask you, though, she said."

Faith swiped shortening around a Bundt pan with a paper towel. "How do you know what Zumba is?"

"Everyone knows what Zumba is, Mom." Bristol ran her sticky fingers through her strawberry blonde hair, which had grown to three times its volume in the humid air.

"So," Faith treaded carefully. "You like Candace, huh?"

"Yup." Bristol eyed the batter with large eyes. "Can I pour it into the Bundt pan?"

Faith tossed the greasy paper towel in the trash and handed her a spatula. "I'll pour. You spread."

Bristol took the spatula and readied for the batter. Her tongue wagged out the side of her mouth, as it did whenever she concentrated. She guided the batter with the tip of the spatula.

"So, you spoke with Candace, huh?"

"Yup."

"Why her?"

She worked the spatula like a pro, not taking her eye off the batter as it unfurled. "She makes me comfortable."

"How so?"

"She doesn't ask me to speak."

Faith took her time pouring the batter, afraid once it stopped flowing, so too would their words. "Do others force you to speak?"

"Sometimes. But, not you or Daddy."

"Auntie Danielle?"

Bristol shook her head.

"Lucia?"

Bristol shook her head more fervently.

"Martina?" she asked in much too accusing a tone.

Bristol looked up at her, relaxing her tongue back into her mouth. She huffed. "Mom, no. Nobody here."

"Then why don't you speak with them?"

"It's hard."

Faith stopped pouring and sat on the stool, placing her chin in her hand. "I get it. You didn't talk on the first day so now there's too much pressure."

Bristol twisted her mouth.

"Do the counselors force you to speak?"

"Yup. I don't like that." Bristol continued to smooth the batter.

Faith's heart clenched. She needed to be a better parent. What good parent tucked her child into a room filled with bloodsucking shrinks who attacked her and forced her into the corner? She may as well have fed her poor daughter to a pack of hungry wolves while she was at it.

Faith rolled her neck to work out a sudden stabbing kink. "You should've told me."

"I told Daddy."

"What did he say?"

"That he'd talk with you."

Tears stung Faith's eyes.

"Some of the counselors are nice," Bristol said, patting the batter around the edges. "I like Daddy's girlfriend."

Gilly?

Faith stood up. She braced against the granite, rifling through the details in her memory. His girlfriend worked as an instructor in the psychology department. Stuart had said a friend had recommended the counseling center as one of the best in the county. "Daddy's girlfriend is a counselor there?"

"Yep." Bristol climbed off the stool. "Can we put the cake in the oven now? I think it's ready."

# #

The next morning, Faith dropped Bristol off at Candace's house. "I'll have her back in about an hour and a half. The kids always beg me to go an extra few minutes with them. I can't refuse. They're adorable, you know?"

Oh, I know adorable when I see it.

Faith gazed at Candace's pouty lips and expressive eyes, enjoying the tingle that spiraled in her head. "No problem at all."

Faith opened her arms to Bristol for a hug. "Your daddy is coming at three o'clock sharp to pick you up and take you on the ferry to Block Island. So, save a little energy." She hugged her and kissed the top of her head.

Bristol backed away after smiling up at Faith, and then Candace put an arm around her tiny shoulders and led her to the kitchen. "Do you like lemon in your water?"

"I love it." A squeal followed her words.

Overcome with joy, Faith stood in the foyer for a little longer to let the moment seep in. The moment when her daughter bloomed as a kid should, getting excited about something fun instead of worrying about how she'd get a word in.

Candace stretched her gaze back toward Faith and winked.

Faith's heart bucked as she winked back. When she caught her balance, she turned to go.

Chapter Six

Shortly after Bristol returned from her Zumba class, Stuart pulled up in his car. Faith wanted a chance to talk with him about the inept counseling center where his supposedly likeable girlfriend worked.

Stuart climbed out of the front seat and walked around to the passenger side. He opened the door and out climbed the beautiful, golden-haired young woman from his new Facebook profile picture. Her skin glowed even more in person.

He placed his hand on the small of his girlfriend's athletic-built back. "I thought it might be a good time to introduce you to Gilly."

She stepped forward and offered a sugary smile, extending her firm hand. "It's nice to meet you, Faith."

The pleasure is not mine, homewrecker. Faith shook her hand. Not only did her skin feel soft in her hand, but she even smelled like a wholesome spring day, full of the promise of blooming flowers and fresh green sprouts of grass.

After an extended awkward moment, Stuart fidgeted. "Okay, I guess we'll see you soon, then."

Faith needed to be strong. She needed to speak her mind. She needed to stand up for her daughter. "There's something we need to talk about. A family matter." Faith swept her eyes over Gilly and back to Stuart.

"Is it something that can wait until Sunday when we return? Gilly will be heading back to Boston earlier in the day. So, maybe it's better if we talk then?"

Faith liked the idea of having two additional days to compose her argument. She could place all of the ingredients in front of her, let them marinate, and then present them in a palatable fashion. One that didn't sour the point, which was to ensure their daughter received the best care. "Sure."

"Unless it's serious?" Stuart's eyebrows arched. He posed as the concerned dad with one of their daughter's suntanned counselors on his arm.

"It can wait until Sunday."

A moment later, Bristol raced out of the front door looking like a pony escaping through an open gate. It had been two weeks since she last saw her father. She fell into his embrace.

He swung her around, and Gilly radiated with affection. *The bitch.* They looked like they stepped into a toothpaste commercial.

Gilly reached out for Bristol's delicate hand. "Hey cutie."

"Hey," Bristol whispered, allowing Gilly to hold her hand.

Hey? Wait...hey? Hey to Gilly? Not to Lucia? Not to Martina or Emmy or Christian, but to Gilly?

"Okay, well, we should head out if we want to catch the ferry." He cocked his head. "We'll see you Sunday."

Faith stood like an outsider to the new family dynamic and waved, for Bristol's sake, as they drove away.

# #

On Saturday morning, she stole glances of Candace and her yoga class. Candace wore an attractive teal blue fitted shirt with peach-colored yoga pants.

In between gawks, she read from her scribbled dream notes. "At first I drove down the interstate in a convertible, trying to outrun a tornado. Bristol sat in the backseat crying for me to drive faster. Stuart talked on the phone with us asking me if I wouldn't mind if Gilly took over my walk-in closet and summer dresses. She also liked my ankle socks and insisted they'd work well for their morning runs together in the park with her Golden Retriever. I squeezed the steering wheel, and Bristol giggled while pointing at the car beside us. Pretzel drove a Buick. She waved her paw and zoomed ahead, urging us to follow. So, I followed. I drove straight at the tornado without blinking and, at the last second, continued to trail Pretzel as she turned just before the moment of impact with the tornado's winds. Then, I opened my eyes and noticed we landed on a sunny patch of road with nothing but blue skies and fluffy whites clouds as our companion."

"Where did Pretzel go?" Danielle asked.

"I don't know." Faith placed here notepad down and picked up her coffee. "So what does it mean?"

Lucia cleared her throat. "Oh, I'll tell you what it means. It means you need to let go and trust you're exactly where you need to be."

Faith looked around at the trio. "Well, let's hope so. I'm going to start cutting hair today."

# #

Two hours later, standing in the supply room of Danielle's salon, Faith picked up one of the aprons from a wall hook. She looped it around her neck and smoothed it over her torso. Nervous flutters followed. Little prickles traveled under her skin like aliens taking account of a new territory, poking, lifting, prodding, and twisting to get a better look at the fragile ecosystem they now called home.

She peeked out of the door and into the six-chair salon. "I might throw up."

Danielle placed a comforting hand on her shoulder. "It's like riding a bike."

Although a licensed cosmetologist, she had never worked as a stylist in a real salon. The person sitting in her chair would expect a professional, not the nervous woman swimming against a riptide of fear.

Five minutes later, Martina introduced her to Gabe, her first client.

"Please, have a seat." Faith waved at her chair, which offered a beautiful view of the pretty gardens across the street. Her throat tickled and her stomach churned, but she dove into her role as a professional anyway by securing a cape around his neck.

"I just need a clean-up," Gabe said.

"Right." Faith stared at his head afraid to go in and diffuse the unruly hairs. "Martina?" she called out.

Martina rushed toward her. "What is it?'

"You should cut his hair, and I should watch."

Martina tenderized Gabe with a warm glance, and he volleyed a similar warmth back at her. "It would be my pleasure."

Faith sighed relief and handed Martina her shears. "I'll sit here." She plopped down in an empty hair station chair.

"Gabe is a special client." Martina began combing his hair. "He's a scientist."

"Ah, you remember?" His cheeks flushed.

Faith eased back, amused at the flirtatious vibe circling between them.

"Oh, well, how does one forget? You have such an important job."

"It's just biotech stuff."

Red blotches splattered across Martina's chest.

Entertained, Faith settled back further in the chair.

Then, Christian sailed behind them. "Hey, handsome!"

"Hey," Gabe offered Christian a cheery wave.

Christian stopped and ran his fingers through his hair. "I see the sun is working its magic." Then he winked and ran off, saying over his shoulder, "Take care of him, Auntie."

Martina completed her tenth trek over the same patch of hair and dropped her hands. "So, just biotech stuff?" A flirt curled up around her voice. "You need to stop being so modest. What you need is exposure."

Gabe's eyes twinkled. "I'm interested to hear your ideas."

"I take photos. I'm a photographer, you see."

A photographer?!

Gabe's eyes opened wide. "A woman of many talents."

Martina brushed a piece of her hair behind her ear, revealing more of her flushed skin. "Aw, Gabe. Thank you. You're too kind."

"I'm in need of a photographer." Gabe crossed his ankles and leaned back in the chair.

I bet he was.

Martina cradled her hand on his shoulders. "I like the sound of that." She leaned closer and began snipping his hair. "So, you need photos for your website?"

"Yeah. I could always use some. Especially of me in the lab working. I could use them on my brochure, too."

Martina flipped her hair over her shoulders and pointed her smoldering eyes at him. "What kind of stuff do you do in the lab?"

"My lab validates the components found in dietary supplements. We test to ensure the label is accurate. I've devised a software system that investigates the DNA makeup of ingredients. My system is one of the best around for consistency."

"Sounds like you have a story to tell," Martina said.

"No one else has the kind of detailed system I do."

"Have you tried leasing it to others?" Martina asked.

Faith's ears perked. Martina sounded so professional. And serious. Had they stepped onto the set of the *Twilight Zone* without Faith realizing? She expected a director to pop on scene and order Martina to lower her voice more and angle herself toward the camera.

"It's a hard sell."

"Not if you tell your story."

He arched his head up and met her eyes. "I like where you're going with this."

The conversation flowed. Faith passed her eyes back and forth between the two of them as Martina suggested digital storytelling as a means to promote his software to skeptical labs. Gabe fired data, convincing himself he sure did have a story to tell, and he wanted her to tell it.

"If anyone can bring this to life, you can," Gabe said.

"I can't disagree," Martina said. "I am your person."

Martina completed the haircut without talking further. Faith could imagine the ideas speeding through her excited mind. She expected steam to start blowing through her ears at any moment.

Martina picked up her trimmers a few minutes later, then turned to Faith. "I want you to do this part."

Faith shook her head. "It's best if I watch."

Gabe smiled at Faith. "I don't mind."

Martina extended the trimmers toward her.

Faith rose from the chair and tackled his hairline with shaky hands.

The odd meeting at Faith's hairdressing chair ended with firm handshakes and promises to exchange details about his work and Martina's ideas on a storyboard.

Later on, long after Gabe handed Martina a twenty dollar tip and paid for his thirty dollar haircut, Faith met her at the front desk.

"I had no idea you were a photographer," Faith said.

"That's because I'm not." Martina glanced at the computer screen. "I said that because it's always been a dream of mine. So, I saw the opportunity and now I'm going to start studying the art of photography."

"It's not like picking up Zumba, Martina."

"I didn't know how to Zumba either, and I did all right."

"Do you even own a camera?"

"I will later on today after I go to Best Buy."

Faith shook her head. "You are one bold lady."

"I have to be. If I want something, I have to go and get it. I've always wanted to learn photography. Now I have a reason."

"You're not afraid he'll realize you're an amateur?"

"Where's your sense of adventure?" She pulled her long hair into a tight ponytail. "Right now, I see a whole new opportunity shining."

"I've got to hand it to you. You sell yourself well."

"I sure do." Martina slapped the counter and the lipsticks in the tabletop display rolled down to the floor. "Never ceases to amaze me how when things are meant to be, they'll be. If you didn't chicken out on his haircut, I wouldn't have cut his hair, and I wouldn't have a photography gig. There's a bright side to everything. So cheers to your fear."

She raised her fist, and Faith bumped it with hers, taking in the depth of

91

that thought. "By the way, how did his hairline look?"

Martina blinked. "I hadn't even noticed." She walked away, bouncing on air.

As the day progressed, Faith tried her hand at a few more clients. Danielle selected easy ones, like Mrs. Brown who didn't care Faith had styled her part in the wrong direction. "My hair curled! Well, what do you know? Martina can never get the curling iron to work the way you did today."

That little compliment lifted Faith to new territory. So, when she faced her next client, Sue Ellen, Faith commanded the scene by offering her a consultation before tossing her head backwards into the shampoo bowl. To Faith's surprise, Sue Ellen agreed to try a few highlights around her face to brighten her look. She left her a ten dollar tip and asked for a six-week follow-up appointment. "I should still be here, unless a job offer comes through." Faith typed her first rebook into a fresh column and handed the happy customer her appointment card.

Bring on the next client!

Faith dove into the deep end of the ego rush without regard for how she'd pull herself out of it. Like with any distraction from reality, Faith embraced it with the heart of a child, ignoring that dull throb in the back of her head that warned her to turn around before she got in any deeper.

All day, she observed Christian, Martina, Danielle, and their apprentices. She picked up small tips along the way and placed them in her memory for safe keeping.

By the time she sat her last client of the day in her chair, her neurons fired a good healthy dose of creative ingenuity. Faith stared at her client's head full of curls, picked up the clippers and began the tricky trek through it. At first she struggled to get the curls under control. Then, with several deep breaths, she eventually gained her confidence and gave the man a great haircut.

# #

By the time early Sunday afternoon rolled around, Martina completed her work on the storyboard for Gabe's video and shared it with Faith.

As Faith sipped some wine, she read through the convincing plan. "This is incredible. You're good at this storyboarding thing."

"I learned it from an online class I took last night on Udemy."

Martina was totally serious about this video pursuit. She feared nothing and gained everything. She was just like a pup darting through a room full of clutter and discovering the one perfect chew toy.

Martina sat taller. "We must toast this moment."

So, they toasted.

"By the way, did you notice how adorable Gabe is?" Martina wrinkled her nose and her eyes grew large. "Do you think he was flirting?"

"That's a silly question. Of course."

Martina cocked her head. "Do you think he was flirting with Christian?"

"Gabe is not gay if that's what you're asking."

"I think Christian might've been flirting with him, though."

Faith couldn't disagree. "Perhaps."

"Do you think he was just being polite with me?"

Martina dwarfed into an insecure teenager. "Trust me, he was flirting."

"Would you date him if he asked?"

"Me?" Faith laughed. "He's not my type."

"I know. I'm just playing with you." Martina raised her chin. "I know your type."

"Oh really?" Faith chuckled and braved on, "Care to enlighten me?"

93

"You don't need enlightening. It's obvious. To us all, actually."

"I don't know what you're talking about."

Martina sipped her wine. "After a few more of these the truth will follow." Martina winked and gulped. "Drink up."

Martina was growing more on Faith every day.

# #

Two hours later, Faith's head still buzzed from the bottle of wine she and Martina polished off.

"How was your trip?" Faith asked Bristol as she climbed out of the back of Stuart's car.

"We walked around the whole island." Bristol bounced. "I have to pee." She turned to Stuart and hugged him. "Bye, Daddy. So, two weeks, right?"

He patted her back. "Two weeks. You bet."

They both watched her skip up the front walk. When she closed the door, Faith sobered.

"Do you have a few minutes to have that chat?" Stuart asked.

Faith blinked to gather her unmarinated thoughts. "Sure."

"You first. What did you want to discuss the other day?"

Faith poked around her argument points, hoping to bring it to comprehensible life. It lay wilted though, piling up behind her tongue. Her words buckled and landed flimsily in the bland air. "How come you never told me Bristol didn't like her counselor?"

He squinted, glancing toward Candace's house, ignorant to the fantasies that ran around Faith's mind every time she glanced in that direction. "She told you?"

Anger corked its way up Faith's spine. "Of course she told me. She also

94

told me Gilly works there."

He ran his hands through his sun-streaked hair. "It must be worse than I thought."

"If something is wrong with her, you need to tell me. We may be divorced, but I'm still her mother."

"She told me before you left for Rhode Island. We didn't have a chance to talk about it. Gilly recommended that we don't take Bristol there anymore. She noticed Bristol is afraid of the lead counselor. She can see her disposition change the second she enters the room."

A sadness crept in.

Faith had stepped too far off the course of reality with this silly vacation. Playing with hair? Ogling over some hot yoga and dance instructor while her daughter suffered? Who did that in times of trouble? An irresponsible mother, that's who. "Stuart," her voice crawled out a mere whisper. "Did we mess her up by sending her there?"

Stuart wrestled with concern, twisting his mouth. "I hope not."

They stared off toward Candace's house again. Faith dug her fingernails into the sides of her chest. It offered a brief reprieve from the pain swelling in her heart. "So what do we do?"

Stuart cleared his throat. "Gilly is great with her. She offered to help. After the summer, once you return, she can work with her."

"I don't want her going back to that place."

"She won't have to." A hesitancy followed his words. "Gilly is quitting and just focusing on teaching at the university as a full-time professor. The clinic was too much stress. And she can't be under stress."

"Ah, yeah. She does strike me as a bit fragile."

"Gilly is pregnant."

95

# #

Gilly being pregnant meant a few different things to Faith. For starters, Gilly was only twenty-seven. How serious could a twenty-seven-year-old be in life? What if she grew tired of the responsibility of being a stepmom to someone else's daughter? What if Bristol grew attached to her, and then Gilly decided she wanted to backpack through Europe for the kicks of it? What if, like Faith, she grew tired of Stuart?

So many what-ifs.

But more than the what-ifs, why did Stuart get to settle into happiness first? And why did Gilly have to be so nice and likable? Why couldn't she be a back-stabbing monster who swung her ax at marital walls to claim her prize?

Wrestling with that conundrum, Faith sipped iced-tea. She splayed her toes out in the sand and leaned back against her beach chair.

Suddenly, Candace headed over to her. She walked with a seductive swagger, lifting one hip at a time.

Somewhere in the back of Candace's mind, she must have known the power in those hips. That cocky side would emerge soon enough. It always did with good-looking people. They didn't envy others because they had all the goods for themselves. They never concerned themselves with how they measured up against others because others would always measure up against them.

She strutted, flaunting one hip flick at a time, right toward her. To her. Not some other woman wearing an oversized tankini to hide her thick waist, but her. And that excited Faith. Excited her right between the thighs where the unquestionable twitch kicked into full gear, galloping and frolicking.

Candace approached and sat down on the sandy shore. "Perfect lake day."

Faith nodded in agreement, pushing her sunglasses against her face. She couldn't be sidetracked. She couldn't afford to escape her real life to flirt with a yoga and Zumba goddess.

Candace tossed sand on Faith's toes. "You're quiet today."

Faith smiled crookedly. "I have a lot on my mind."

"Like what?"

She wanted to say something, but the lump in her throat created only a mumble. She gripped the arms of her chair and settled on a shrug.

"Hey," Candace said, placing her tender hand on Faith's wrist. "Seriously, what's going on?"

Faith gazed at the dazzling ripples on the lake and swallowed hard. Then, she removed her sunglasses. "I just found out that my ex-husband's girlfriend is pregnant."

With a beautiful sweep of her hand, Candace caressed Faith's wrist. "That's a lot to take in, huh?"

Faith remained silent for a bit longer, craving to unload her distress. The longer Candace's fingers cradled her hand, the more her heart opened. "I'm hurt and a little jealous, if that makes sense?"

Candace swept her eyes out to the kayaks floating at the docks, then released her hand. "All too much sense."

"I'm happy to not be with him anymore. So, why is this bothering me so much?"

"Exes have a way of twisting the knife sometimes."

"Did your ex hurt you, too?"

Candace took a swig of water. "She did. Very much so." Her jaw clenched. "Love can definitely hurt. But, that hurt helps us become a little stronger in the end."

Silence followed.

Finally, Candace stood up and put on her sunglasses. "I should get going. I have a Zumba class to teach tonight." Before she turned to leave, she cradled Faith's shoulder and whispered, "It gets easier with time. You'll see."

# #

The next day, Faith focused on the client in her chair. She combed through his hair and began planning her strategy. First, she'd cut around his hairline and pray she didn't nick his ear in the process. Then, she'd tackle the top and bulkiness. She let go of all tension and indulged in the journey, allowing herself to escape reality for the time being.

Something magical began to happen with each snip. Empowerment surged as she combed and weeded through the hair, shaping and taming his layers. She loved the power of cutting off that which no longer served. Just like an artist, she molded and redirected the hair until it fell into place.

If life could be so simple. Snip, comb, part, repeat until everything fell perfectly into the right spot.

Later on in the afternoon, as she browsed the job listings online, her typical daily activity and requirement to collect her unemployment check, Lucia and Martina entered the kitchen dressed in their Zumba getups. They wore tight workout pants and equally tight shirts that showed off their bosoms.

"You missed a good class this afternoon." Lucia swung her hips in a wide, clumsy loop. "Candace's energy level shot through the roof."

Martina joined Lucia in a series of hip flicks followed by pushing the air above their heads and singing, "The roof. The roof. The roof is on fire!"

Faith placed her hand on her shoulder, to the spot Candace had cradled the day before. The memory comforted her.

"Guess what we're doing tomorrow night?" Martina asked her.

Faith tossed her a questionable look.

"You and I are taking a beginner's class in Latin dance by Candace!"

"I don't dance."

"That's the whole point. Oh, and she said I can bring my little Henry here." Martina scooped Henry out of her bag and kissed his black nose. He grunted and wiggled.

"No. I'll make a fool of myself and knock a few people down in the process."

Martina handed Henry off to her, then whispered. "Candace is excited you agreed."

"I didn't agree."

"Very excited," Martina repeated.

"Very?"

"Yes, very."

So that settled it.

The following night, they arrived at the community center with Henry in tow.

Faith stopped short of the door and peeked in. That's when Candace barged out of the room and smacked right into them both.

Faith straightened up, flushed. "Oh, hey."

Candace wore a flowy black- and red-speckled dress that flared out at the bottom. The neckline plunged, revealing the delicate contour of her breasts. "Ready for your Salsa lesson?" She whipped the right side of her skirt, creating a dramatic effect, and ended on a giggle.

That move managed to stop Faith's breath mid-flow.

99

# #

Something wonderful happened when a person empowered herself with knowledge. The cobwebs that used to scare her off from opening up the doors to certain places and keep her imprisoned by familiarity, cleared. By learning something new, something intriguing, something that revved her engine and left her desiring more, her mind expanded. The more insights she gained, the more her mind ballooned. It wouldn't be able to shrink to its former state prior to her acquiring the knowledge. It craved more nourishment. It wanted to be fed. It wanted to feast upon new things to help satisfy that intense growl from deep within.

Despite her initial insecurities with moving her body to songs filled with twenty different musical instruments, Faith soaked up Candace's tips and tricks. She swiped up every last morsel of drippings and left nothing to rot on the shiny floor. She mirrored her moves, and giggled with pleasure every time Candace cheered her success. The woman, with her über-focused dreamy eyes, had a way of making Faith feel sexy and desirable. When her hips moved in accordance with Candace's, Faith humbled to the magic of creating energy where none existed seconds earlier.

An hour later, Candace had accepted their invitation for drinks. They clinked glasses while cheering their fabulous evening.

Candace looked extraordinarily gorgeous, wearing that black- and red-speckled dress with her hair swept to the side in a soft braid. The braid cradled her long delicate neck.

The server came, and they ordered shrimp rolls, calamari, and bruschetta. Faith ordered a salad as well, attempting health over fat and grease. Her desire to lose the twenty pounds she had gained over the course of the year since her divorce backfired on her. Bristol always wanted ice cream. She couldn't refuse such an innocent and worthy request from someone who had suffered the heartbreak of her parents' breakup. So, Faith did what she could and dug a spoon into scoops of strawberry whenever Bristol asked.

Anyhow, a salad seemed a suitable choice for someone looking after her health, even though she craved something more tasty and sinful.

"Did Faith tell you she's styling hair at the salon?" Martina asked.

"That's a skill that's always intrigued me."

"Well, she's very talented."

A seductive smirk rose on Candace's face. "I couldn't imagine her any other way."

Faith floated in a sea of confidence. She treaded with graceful sweeps, charged with a glow that radiated from her core and extended out in wide ripples. Her newfound buoyancy flirted with the room, creating an energy that beautified the space. The lights cast a warmer tone. The music flirted with the air. The waiters bounced when they walked. Voices rose in a springier melody.

Candace affected everyone and everything in a sparkling way.

"So, tell us about your exciting life as a dancer, Candy." Martina leaned forward and sipped her margarita. "Can I call you Candy? It seems so fitting; you're all sweet and pretty like sugar!"

"Candy and a dancer? I'm not a pole dancer." She laughed. "I prefer Candace."

"Ah yes. Classier." Martina lolled her head around. "I once had someone call me Marty and I wanted to slap his geeky face. We lasted one date." She rolled her eyes dramatically. "Any nicknames for you Faith?"

Yes, but too embarrassing to admit. "Not a one."

Her sorority sisters called her camel toe for her entire freshman year because she didn't know what it meant. She researched it later and learned of its reference to the outline of a woman's vulva when wearing tight clothes. She was the drunk idiot who asked what it meant at a party. In a flash, everyone stared and laughed at her. Sobered, she immediately left the party. Her best friend, Sally, followed behind. "How have you never heard of this before?" She laughed at her expense all the way back to their dormitory and well into the night. The nickname stuck, and by all rights, stuck because of its comedic brilliance.

"So," Faith said to Candace, "What are your plans after summer?"

"I have a few house-sitting offers on the table on the west coast. I've always loved the Pacific." She raised her glass, and then took a long sip, caressing Faith with her piercing gaze.

A goddess sat before her and stole her breath.

"Cheers to the west coast." Martina praised Candace's good fortune.

As the drinks flowed, Faith nursed a fun thought.

She'd be the perfect summer fling. That idea challenged her restraint against guzzling her margarita. Could she have a fling? Was she fling material? Someone like Candace could feed her hunger for a month or two. Then, she'd be satiated for a while. She could get high on the torrid love affair, and then survive for months, even years, off its fumes.

She could do the fling thing. Right?

The more sips she took, the more plausible the idea.

While they waited for their entrees, Martina rambled on about her niece, Emmy, and the trials and tribulations she endured as a young adult, as if none of them had experienced it firsthand. Candace nodded kindly with each of Martina's high-pitched exclamations. "You see, I love that little girl as if she were mine. My ex and I couldn't have kids. He's a doctor. A doctor without

102

borders. Anyway, we tried, but…" She swiped through the air with her hand. "Zilch. Nada. No little babies for me."

"Well, Emmy is lucky to have you."

"I couldn't agree more."

They continued to listen to Martina drone on about her ex and all his fascinating work fixing cleft palates for children in Africa.

At one point, Candace angled herself in such a way that her leg brushed up against Faith's. Her dress tickled Faith's calf.

Faith pulled away. "Oh, sorry. I didn't mean to bump your leg."

Candace offered a sidelong glance and looked back at Martina who waved her hands frenetically while telling them another story about Emmy. One about the beautiful dress she wore at the fall dance. "She had all these delicate sequins that at first she didn't want me to put on the dress, but after that night, let me tell you, she couldn't thank me enough." She slapped the table and sat back. "Let me tell you something about sequins," she whispered across the table.

They both leaned in to hear the secret.

"They make you look like a star."

Candace laughed first, and Faith followed. "You're so dramatic, Martina," Faith said.

A moment later, Candace's dress brushed against her thigh again. Faith flicked her gaze to Candace and met up with her teasing eyes. Candace looked back at Martina and asked, "Tell us the juiciest story ever told by a client." Meanwhile she kept her thigh brushed up against Faith's and listened to Martina go on and on. She didn't reveal a hint of the heat that transferred between her and Faith under the privacy of the white linen tablecloth at a small round table in the corner of Biloxi's Bar and Grille.

Faith sipped her drink and noticed Candace's small birthmark again, the one shaped like an almond on the side of her neck, right below her ear. She wanted to kiss it and taste the saltiness of her skin. A warm pulse passed through her body. If not careful, the series of moans that crawled up her throat would escape.

Yeah, she'd be the perfect summer fling. A temporary reprieve from the endless strife of her life. One little summer fling. What could it hurt? She wouldn't get attached. She had a life back in Boston. Candace wanted to move out west. They were both consenting adults. Both free.

Both obviously attracted to each other.

# #

On Wednesday morning, Faith walked into the salon a new woman. She wore confidence like a dress. It flowed and lengthened her stride. Hints of a hidden talent swarmed and fought to take center stage.

So, when a walk-in client came in looking like she'd lost everything in the world and a haircut might save her from suffocating under the rubble, Faith rose to the occasion.

She took great care with her, consulting and recommending a special conditioning treatment to ease her constant headache. She wanted to be the kind of stylist Candace imagined her to be, a gifted one. As Faith massaged the worries of the world from her, the lady opened up and confessed how sometimes she didn't want to get out of bed, talk to people in her life, or leave the house. "Sometimes these things can be hormonal," Faith said. "Have you talked with your doctor?"

"I'm embarrassed to."

Faith stopped cutting, understanding all too well how anxieties over how others might perceive her could crumble an already fragile foundation. She listened to the woman and after a while, the woman began opening up to her even more. What started out as a haircut, turned into a beautiful conversation between two women who helped each other understand that sometimes life dealt blows, but those blows didn't have to define them.

In the moments that followed their talk, the woman's face turned brighter. And by the time Faith trimmed her hair and styled it, the woman's wrinkles softened and her face lifted in joy. As she left, she handed Faith a tip and whispered, "Thank you for taking me seriously and offering me hope that I'm going to be okay after all."

Faith hugged the new client and wished her well, sending her off with a hearty wave.

Danielle moved in beside her. "That right there is something no office job will ever provide. The power of human touch is amazing. It builds trust between strangers and allows us to help people when they need it most."

Adjusting her apron strings around her neck, Faith turned and walked with a sense of renewed purpose. Even if temporary, Faith owned that sense of purpose. She tucked it inside of her and enjoyed it for as long as it would stay.

A few days later, Faith welcomed another new client to her chair, Roxanne. She learned Roxanne was a two-time breast cancer survivor. Her hair had grown back in and now she wanted to do something fun with it. Faith suggested daring red highlights.

By the time Faith applied shine oil to her styled hair, Roxanne had taught her that despite challenges, the human spirit could thrive in any situation. "I stopped putting myself into other people's drama. I started having fun instead, doing things I desire. It's amazing how fast you learn to appreciate life when you think you're dying."

The unknowns in life had always filled Faith with unease. After a few days of talking to people who thrived on the other side of them, Faith's fear of those unknowns lessened slightly. Perhaps when she landed back in Boston at the end of the summer, she might even be able to face those mysteries without apprehension, too.

Overall, her summer trip had transformed from doubtful to hopeful. She'd certainly walk away from it with fond memories. Hopefully, she could lean on them once she landed back in the reality of wire-eating squirrels and long lines at the unemployment office.

She still had plenty of time before facing that, though. So, in the meantime, Faith would enjoy that summer for everything it offered.

She traveled on the smooth end of the curve for a change, and she wouldn't take that for granted for a moment longer.

Chapter Seven

The next morning, the four women discussed details of their upcoming patio party instead of dissecting their dreams.

"I found plastic silverware that looks metallic," Danielle said. "I bought a few dozen. Will that be enough?"

"I've put the word out at Zumba," Lucia said. "So, we may need more."

"How big are these parties you throw?" Faith asked.

"Between salon clients and Lucia's bingo friends, we typically get around forty people," Danielle said.

"Now that we're making friends with the neighbors at Zumba, I'd say we might get up to sixty!" Lucia said.

"Let's make a list of what we want on the menu." Danielle pointed her pen to her pad. "I say we get premade menu items so you're not in the kitchen all day preparing," she said to Lucia.

"Nonsense." Lucia shot up. "We do this right, or we don't do it at all. Authentic all the way."

# #

That afternoon, Danielle and Faith decided to take a walk along the lakeshore path. Danielle picked up a rock and flung it into the water. "So, it's been a year since your divorce."

Faith looked up from the water. "And?"

"And, Stuart's moved on."

Faith raised an eyebrow in reply.

"When are you going to allow yourself to move on?"

"I am. I have."

Danielle clasped her hands behind her back and strolled. "You need to lose yourself in something greater than what didn't work before. It's the only way you'll find yourself and move on. That's what I had to do."

Faith considered her sister's advice. She had changed things around after Lucas died. She sold their home in North Kingston and bought the lake house, a place Lucas feared would put them underwater in bills. Danielle bought the place because she had already faced her worst fear by losing the one man destined to her soul. Nothing else could hurt her. So, she took the risk and it paid off. The life insurance certainly helped, though.

Then, she took another risk and opened up her new salon location, expanding it to a larger space. She didn't fear anything. She found herself and her purpose and moved forward rather than refusing to stay stuck in a life of sadness and regrets for a planned future that never happened.

Faith continued to walk, but at a slower place. "I'm here for the summer. I'm cutting hair. I'm even dancing. I'd say I've shaken things up enough, no?"

"I mean something bolder."

"Like?"

She paused for a long moment before answering. "Moving here. Permanently."

Faith laughed.

Danielle twirled before her, taking in the full breadth of the lake. "Think about it. You can live with us and work at the salon. Build up the chair and have fun with it. Carve out your own success. Do something more daring for a change."

Faith quickened her pace, attempting to outrun the lure of that idea. Life didn't work so neatly for her. She couldn't package up her life in Boston and roll her luggage down the street of a fantasyland where the sun shone and cast brilliant rainbows in a bright blue sky. Where the air smelled like a garden in fresh bloom. Where she woke up to a family every morning who welcomed her in with their fun-loving yapping. Her life played out in more complicated waves than that.

Besides, she already grew her roots elsewhere, and they tangled up with Stuart's. Like it or not, she choose to dig in and start a life in Boston. She didn't have just herself to consider anymore. Cutting those roots also required she cut Stuart's and Bristol's.

In the distance, Faith noticed Candace jogging.

Tingles sped up her spine and tickled the back of her neck. She had much too much to drink last time she saw her. She probably said a bunch of embarrassing stuff. That's what happened when she drank. Her mouth sputtered stupid things. She vaguely remembered whispering to Martina that she liked the way her stomach trembled around Candace.

"That looks like Candace up ahead." Danielle cupped her hand over her eyes. "Speaking of something more daring."

Faith went to grab her wrist, but Danielle already lifted it to wave at Candace. She waved back, and then ran up to them.

"Wow, it's a hot one out here today," Candace said, placing her hands on her knees. A moment later, she rose and sweat trickled down her face, her neck, past her collarbone and down into the sweet abyss of her cleavage. She tore off her light t-shirt and revealed her bikini top.

Candace gazed past them to Bristol and Emmy who passed a ball back and forth a short distance from them. She ran over to the kids, stealing the ball and rushing away with it. The kids chased her in a fit of giggles.

"She seems good with Bristol." Danielle continued to cup her hand over her eyes.

"Yeah. It would seem so." Faith gazed at the trio galloping past beach blankets. Watching them reminded her of her childhood when her dad used to chase them past blankets and their mother would scream at them to stop kicking up sand at everyone.

Danielle nudged her. "If there's anything you want to tell me, you can. You can talk to me."

Only her best friend, Sally, carried the weight of Faith's secret all those years. Martina and Lucia figured it out on their own. Now her sister opened up the gate and encouraged her to speak her truth, a truth she still hid from Stuart and the rest of humanity.

Faith stumbled back a step before bracing to enter into her sister's invite. "I've never been sexually attracted to Stuart, if that's what you're asking."

Danielle sent her a grateful smile. "Have you ever been attracted to any man?"

Her question squeezed Faith, crushing the air out of her lungs. Did words disappear into the back of Bristol's throat, too, whenever she opened her mouth to talk? Did she ache to speak and want to cry because she had spent too long gripping her silence?

Danielle squeezed her arm. "It's okay. You can tell me anything."

Reassured by her sister's love, Faith whispered, "No, not sexually."

Danielle rested on a smile. "Was that so hard?"

Faith's spirit lifted. A beautiful sense of lightness expanded and allowed her the freedom to open her eyes and see the world in a brighter shade. She laughed and hit her sister's arm. "It's not exactly something that comes out in conversation. Pass the bread; by the way, I'm a lesbian."

"Ah, she says it out loud." Danielle hugged her, then pulled away on a deep breath. "It hurts a little that it took you thirty-five years to talk to me about something so important."

Faith nodded. "Yeah, well, it took me the same amount of years to admit it to myself."

A quiet understanding settled in around them.

"So, have you been intimate with anyone since Stuart?"

"Nah. I'm not exactly sure how to go about it, to be honest. I haven't been in the dating pool in ages." Faith kicked up sand with her toes. "I've never had sex with a woman. So, I'm intimidated. It's easier to be alone and fantasize. You know? I mean that's what you do, right?"

Danielle blushed.

"Have you had sex with someone else?"

Danielle lifted her gaze to the lake. "I did and it was terrible. Very clunky. It left me guilt-ridden, too."

"With Alan? The tree guy?"

"No," Danielle's eyes opened wide. "Not Alan. Some guy from the country bar in Providence. Worst experience ever."

"I'm afraid that's how it's going to be for me, too."

Her sister half-smiled. "You're waiting on the world to open its arms and say it's time. If anyone understands, I do." Danielle walked toward the trio who now frolicked in the water, tossing the ball back and forth.

Faith watched her sister glide toward the lakeshore, always with her chin raised toward the sky and worrying about everyone else's happiness over her own.

She followed Danielle over to the group playing with the ball at the water's edge. She worried with each step forward, remembering bold and erratic statements from a few nights before. She wasn't that person, and hoped Candace didn't judge her by it.

No more drinking for a long time.

Not a drop.

Candace turned toward her and her eyes sparkled along with the sun glittered ripples.

"So," Candace said.

"So," Faith said back, kicking up little splashes of water with her toes. "You enjoy playing with balls?"

Candace tossed the ball at Faith. "Only this kind."

Faith scooped low to get it before it hit the water. She tucked it under her arm and continued kicking the water.

"Throw it," Emmy yelled. "To me, though."

Faith flung it up in the air and let the kids work out who caught it.

Beads of water mixed with the sweat from earlier rolled down Candace's tanned chest.

Faith lost control of her judgments and could easily lose grip on her better sense of self around her if not careful. Having her family right beside her saved her from blurting out more foolish statements. That and the fact she drank orange juice instead of tequila that morning.

"Let's go for a swim." Candace offered her hand.

"Oh, I don't swim. I'm more of a wader," Faith said. "Besides, I'm not wearing a swimsuit."

"It's hot outside. Your t-shirt and shorts will dry in a second out here." Candace turned to Bristol. "Is she chickening out on us?"

Bristol giggled. The two conspired in a shared arching of the eyebrows.

Somewhere between repairing a broken screen and a conspiring set of giggles, trust formed between them. Candace could've asked Faith to shave her head bald in that moment, and Faith would've asked her to hand over the clippers.

A second later, Candace pulled her into the water. Danielle grabbed for Bristol and Emmy's hands and together they all ran toward the horizon, giggling and hooting like fools.

"Swim out to the dock with me," Candace said, back paddling.

"My body doesn't float like that." Faith stretched out onto her back and kicked her feet, but she sank. "See?"

Candace's laughter curled up around them. "We'll work on that this summer."

Faith loved the sound of that statement. She lowered her feet into the squishy lake bottom and gazed up at the expansive sky. "It's such a beautiful day."

Candace floated to her side and pointed up to the clouds. "That one there looks like an ice-cream cone."

"Mmm. Chocolate chip cookie dough."

"With rainbow sprinkles," Candace added.

"Dripping with hot fudge."

"A woman after my own ice-cream heart."

Candace's intense gaze lightened Faith to the point she eventually found herself floating like a pro. Empowered and free, she let go of any worry about what lake fish could be nibbling on her toes and enjoyed the moment for what it presented – a fun trek into life. Something she rarely let herself do with Stuart or anyone else for that matter.

# #

The next day, Faith had three clients booked. A highlight and two haircuts. She enjoyed seeing the appointments in her column.

"Don't forget to write out their prescriptions," Martina said handing her the square pad with the salon's logo. "Pour some product into their hands. A good amount so it works up into a creamy lather they can't resist. They'll be hooked. Then, you come up here, inform them they'll get a discount if they purchase more than two items, and write the recommendations down." She winked. "The more you sell, the more you make."

"Got it."

A few minutes later, as Faith's next client walked through the door, Candace texted her. "When you have a chance, can you give me a call?"

Her heart soared. Her message added the necessary fuel Faith needed to pull off her client's request for pink highlights. Hell, with all the confidence soaring inside now, she could've added purple, orange and blue ones too!

When she finished with her client, she called Candace back.

"I hope it's okay that I texted?" Candace asked. "I could use your help with something if you're not too busy."

# #

Faith keyed in the security code on the lock and opened the front door to Candace's temporary home for the summer. She stepped inside and the foyer smelled breezy and delicate, like Candace. She closed the door and Pretzel bolted down the staircase, howling toward the vaulted ceilings and wiggling toward her. When she landed on the polished wooden floors of the foyer, her toenails tapped out an excited beat.

Faith leaned down to pet her, but she wiggled too much to get a decent hug. So, she settled on the floor and surrendered to Pretzel's intense sniffing.

Once she calmed down, Pretzel sprawled out next to her, exhausted after the greeting. "Candace asked me to check in on you." She bent over and kissed the soft spot between her ears. "She has to work late, I'm assuming."

Pretzel snorted and lay her head down on Faith's outstretched leg. "We can sit here for as long as you like." Faith stretched her gaze around the open foyer. Same setup as her sister's house with its multi-layer staircase. She stopped her gaze on the first level where the master bedroom and two smaller rooms sat. Then, she scanned up to the next landing to the other three bedrooms.

Colorful art filled the house. Unlike Faith's where mismatched décor added to the chaos of life. Stuart collected stuff that looked like it came from yard sales across America. Nothing matched. No rhyme or reason. But in this home, each work of art complimented the other in tone and style. The people who owned it had an eclectic taste for abstract art.

Faith looked down at her dirty shirt, grubby from hair dye. "Thank goodness you don't mind a little staining," she said to Pretzel. "Also a good thing Candace isn't here to see my messiness."

Not that it should've mattered.

She rose and looked around some more, poking into the kitchen. She spotted the ants crawling on the counter again. "Candace can't judge my messiness."

A small creak from the master bedroom startled her. Pretzel's ears perked. "What was that, Pretzel? Huh?"

Pretzel leaped in a circle and lunged toward the stairs, looking back at Faith, urging her to follow. "Well, okay. Only because you asked."

Faith climbed the stairs one slow step at a time. Not to snoop, but to check out the creak. A criminal could be lurking in the whispers of the intimate setting. A creature could be stuck on a dresser, waiting on her to save it. Anything could be happening in that bedroom, and Faith owed it to Candace and the owners to check it out.

Then, of course Pretzel wouldn't take no for an answer. She stood on the top level and yipped until Faith's feet finally landed next to her. Together, they waltzed toward the room. Faith's pulse quickened as they drew closer. Finally, she stepped into Candace's summer territory. The place where she bathed, slept, undressed.

Faith sealed her eyes to enjoy the dizzying effect.

The window was open and the curtain rod clinked melodically against the wall. Mystery solved.

Faith peeked around the soft-palette bedroom with its unmade bed and clothes strewn across the room in small piles.

"I shouldn't snoop," she whispered to an expectant Pretzel, panting and pacing the length of that unmade bed. "I promise, there's nothing to worry about, girl."

She stood in the middle of Candace's bedroom, glancing more closely at the unmade bed. Stately, yet soft, the sleek silhouette of the upholstered sleigh frame with its creamy fabric welcomed Faith into a dreamy state.

Candace's undies lay on top of a pile of cute summer pajamas on the side of the nightstand.

Faith stepped backwards toward the door, and then spotted the bathroom off to the far right of the room. It drew her in. She walked past the ruffled bedsheets and past the window where she could see her bedroom at her sister's house. How many times had Faith pranced around naked? Had Candace seen her? Did the flimsy shades offer some view of Faith's unflattering curves?

Faith stood before a double sink. Cosmetics dotted every square inch of it. Everything from lip liner to skin cream to a half-filled cup of milky coffee took up space. She shouldn't be snooping.

She backed out of the bathroom and looked to Pretzel. She stared at Faith with wide eyes as if saying, *why don't you tell the woman you want to have some fun together while the summer is still hot?*

"You should know that I'm far too busy to consider the thrill of a temporary fling. I need to organize. I need a real job with benefits, you know, go to a place where I sit behind a desk and play solitaire while trying to look busy. That's reality. People don't go to work and play. It's not all fun and games like it is with you. Walk, eat, sleep, and torment a squirrel, then repeat." She knotted her fists into her sides.

Pretzel cocked her head.

"My bestie, Sally, will tell you. I'll get her on the phone and you'll see. She'll state the truth. She'll tell me to get my butt into gear and send out more résumés." Faith pointed at Pretzel's inquisitive face. "You don't believe me."

She yipped.

"Fine." Faith called her friend, Sally, to keep her in the loop of her Yoga Goddess crush. "I'm standing in her bedroom right now and her dog is staring at me. If I'm being honest, I'm feeling a little guilty, and slightly naughty from snooping."

"You don't think she has one of those nanny cams, do you?" Sally asked.

Instinctively, Faith dropped to her knees and crawled out of the bedroom, as if that would clear up any confusion, had Candace been logged into any said nanny cam at the moment. "By the way," Faith whispered, mid-crawl, "I came out to my sister."

"Well, it's about time."

When Faith cleared the bedroom, she climbed to her knees and glanced at the hallway corners for cameras. "She was hurt I didn't tell her sooner."

"Did she expect you to tell her this over coffee and blurt it out somewhere between asking for the creamer and sugar?"

"That's what I said to her! Well, bread in a basket, instead. But, still. We're on the same wavelength, you and I."

"So why are you calling me from her bedroom?"

"I'm in her hallway now. But, anyway, her dog and I just had a conversation and she thinks she'd make a great summer fling. I wasn't sure. So, I do what I always do when I'm uncertain. I call you."

"I'm not making this decision for you."

"You're so good at it, though."

"I told you to buy a CR-V, and the squirrels ate *your* engine, *not* Stuart's."

"Well, in a roundabout way you helped because if I hadn't bought a CR-V, maybe squirrels wouldn't have eaten my engine, and I wouldn't be here."

"Snooping around some yoga goddess's bedroom?"

"Exactly." Faith headed down the stairs. "Well, actually now I'm snooping around her foyer, but only to get the dog's leash. That's why I'm here. She asked me to take the dog on a walk."

"Oh," Sally rolled out her voice in a velvety undertone. "She is totally fling material, then."

"I know, right?!" Faith squealed.

"I was kidding. But, hell, why not? Let loose. Have fun. Take the dog on walks and join her later for yoga stretches in bed. If I weren't married and in love with the best woman under the sun, I'd be all over that opportunity."

"Well, you'd know what to do with her. I have no clue." Faith paused. "You know what? You just made this easier for me. I'm going to walk the dog and get out of here before I do something stupid like knock an expensive vase off a table or slip and break my hip on this shiny granite tile."

"Okay, old lady. Go walk the dog. Call me if things get juicy."

They hung up on a chuckle.

She headed into the kitchen to get Pretzel's leash. She eyed the ants crawling on the counter and in the door and window jams. Then, she spotted an oil burner with a tiny bottle of peppermint oil extract near it. "Ah ha!" She looked down at Pretzel. "After our walk, I'm going to solve this little ant problem."

When they returned thirty minutes later, Pretzel lay over an air conditioning vent while Faith busied herself spreading cotton balls of peppermint oil extract around the edges of the counters, windows and doors. "That ought to keep them out."

Satisfied, Faith turned the knob to the front door and exited.

# #

Later that evening, Lucia, Martina, and Emmy went to the grocery store to get all the supplies they'd need for an outdoor party the next night. Danielle and Bristol went to the bookstore to get some books on gardening. Christian disappeared, leaving a wake of cologne behind.

So, Faith relaxed with a cup of tea and her laptop. She watched her last of the hair-cutting techniques she'd found. She learned of a new way of coloring the ends of the hair while keeping the roots a stable color. She couldn't wait to get her hands onto a willing client.

After that, she reviewed a set of discovery questions Martina drafted for her interview with Gabe. She wanted everything to be perfect, and so asked Faith for her help.

Martina's bland questions excited no part of Faith's brain. She needed ones that would create the important element of surprise in order to get the raw, genuine emotion and story. Otherwise, what Martina would get would be a boring interview of someone who memorized his answers and spoke to the camera like a scared robot. Everything should sound like a natural conversation.

Faith wished she had practiced that more while writing press releases at the university. Maybe then she'd still have a job. Then again, if she still had a job, she wouldn't be sipping tea in her sister's lake house planning how to turn ordinary heads of hair into works of art. Nor would she be wrestling with fantasies of Candace's sweet-smelling shampoos and creams because she never would've met Candace.

Cheers to my job loss, I suppose!

The house simmered in silence for the first time ever. Faith leaned back and enjoyed it for a moment longer before she jumped into the shower to wash the grime off from hours earlier. But, before she could, someone knocked on the deck door.

Pretzel's perky ears rotated at her like little radio antennae. She pressed her snout against the window, creating a wide circle of steam. Then, Candace knocked again and waved. She balanced a plate wrapped in foil in her free hand.

Faith waved her in as she tried her best to get up from the couch without looking like a total clumsy goofball wearing a shirt speckled with color stains.

"I wanted to bring over a plate of Colombian sweets to thank you for stopping by earlier today."

Faith accepted the plate. "You didn't have to." She smelled the sugary heaven. "But, I'm glad you did."

"I appreciate it. I got called into an important meeting that lasted too long."

120

Faith's curiosity piqued. "I hope it was a productive meeting, at least?"

"Yeah, Candace bobbed her head. "It was." Her eyes lit up. "I met with some friends about a potential studio they're thinking of purchasing in California. They asked if I wanted to teach for them."

"Oh wow." California loomed so far away across vast mountain ranges, rolling green fields, deep valleys and deserts. "Are you considering it?"

She held Faith's gaze. "Nothing's ever off the table when it comes to dance."

Faith swallowed the bad taste of disappointment. "Speaking of dance, Lucia is depending on you tomorrow night to lead her party guests in whatever kind of dancing you do." Faith pointed to Candace's hips and wagged her finger. "Whatever you do there."

Candace laughed. "It's called Cuban Motion." She flicked her hips. "Everyone assumes it comes from the hips, but it's all in the footwork and knees." She moved slower, exaggerating the flow.

Heat surged from somewhere deep within Faith. To release it, she giggled. "My hips and my knees don't work that way."

"Tomorrow night." Candace turned toward the door and looked back over her shoulder. "We'll see about that."

"Is that a threat?" A hint of tease trailed Faith's words.

"Maybe." Candace tugged on Pretzel's leash. "Enjoy your treats. See you tomorrow night."

Chapter Eight

The patio party began at dusk. Despite having snacked on chips and salsa with the kids earlier, Faith's stomach growled as Lucia passed through the sliding doors carrying a tray of pork chops seasoned with herbs and lots of oil. "We're going to party all night long," she said, shaking her hips and twirling.

Faith caught the tray of meat. "I'll take this over to the grill."

"Tell Christian he has to heat up the grill before placing them on or else they'll stick and half the delicious skin will be burnt off."

"Yeah. Yeah." Faith walked down the deck stairs and toward Christian on the patio. Tiki torches illuminated the early evening. The back patio and grassy yard turned into an island getaway.

She passed Bristol and Emmy who kicked a soccer ball back and forth. Bristol wore a plain pair of jeans and a cute halter-top while Emmy dressed for a night out in New York City. She wore looped earrings and a beaded necklace to adorn her silky dress that flared out in beautiful ruffles at the edge. She should've brought Bristol something more party worthy.

"Did you call Daddy?"

Bristol nodded, still not able to speak in front of Emmy.

Small steps, Faith reminded herself as she neared Christian with the plate of meat.

As the sun began its slow descent toward the horizon, Candace finally arrived. Bristol approached her first and led her to the edge of the patio where no one else stood. She whispered in Candace's ear. Candace smiled widely.

123

Faith fingered the rim of her glass, mesmerized by how easily Bristol trusted Candace. That trust could hurt her, though. What would happen at the end of the summer when free-flowing Candace, with her flippy dress and pretty sandals, traveled to her next stop in life and they traveled back to Boston, away from their crazy, fun-loving group of relatives?

Faith could possibly protect herself against the heartbreak of someone like Candace, but she couldn't protect Bristol.

# #

Faith helped Lucia feed the guests. Lucia had spent the entire day stirring, chopping, sautéing, and marinating. The resulting feast filled the evening air with a festive, summery scent. The thirty guests piled rice, fried plantains, lentil salad, stuffed avocados, adobo chicken, blackened ribeye steak and savory pork chops browned to perfection onto their plates.

Once everyone settled in, Faith shooed Lucia toward the plates. "You've earned some for yourself."

Lucia's face hung in exhaustion. "I'll grab a plate in a few minutes. I'm not hungry."

Faith handed her a plate. "Eat. Or I'll force you."

"You're no different from your sister. Both pushy as hell when you think you're right." Lucia grabbed the plate. "Fine. Just a little for now. I don't want food jostling around my tummy when I'm dancing."

Lucia dug into the sautéed drumsticks, piling three on her plate. Then, she scooped two helpings of rice with scallions on top. She shoved a drumstick into her mouth and mumbled something about the Tiki torches being too close together. She looked back over her shoulder at Faith. "You better be ready to Salsa dance in a few minutes." She shimmied her wide hips, while gnawing on the stubby end of the drumstick. "Lots and lots of salsa dancing."

She walked up to a group of four and began laughing, placing herself into their lively banter.

Like most people, Lucia loved a good party. Often, the moments in between parties paled in comparison. The fun times sat ahead on the mundane path of life, a constant mirage to keep them moving forward. The anticipated buildup kept people in a state of joy. It created a nice distraction to the everyday grind, allowing people, for even the briefest moment, to indulge in a fantasy of what might be.

Life became one giant pathway filled with rest stops like that party. It's what kept people taking those curves along the path with reckless abandon, to capture the thrill that might lay on the other side of the bend.

Candace, seemed to love the curvy path. People hadn't even eaten through half their plates before that woman grabbed Lucia's hand and led her to the center of the dance floor. *La Camisa Negra*, an upbeat song created with lots of instruments, bellowed out from each of the four speakers. Candace raised her arm and led Lucia into a series of turns. Lucia's skirt twirled along with her. They flowed from one intricate move into another. Their bodies swayed in harmony as if engaged in an intimate conversation.

The partygoers grew enthusiastic as the dance ensued. Before long, the dance floor filled, brought to life through the energetic swaying of hips. Their movements matched the sound of the music, strung together beautifully by the cooperation of the partnerships gathered.

At one point, Martina walked around with a tray of Jell-O shots. She stopped in front of Faith. "I'll pass."

Martina took one of the shots, placed it to her red-painted lips and swallowed. She exaggerated a sigh. "Life is short. The summer is even shorter. Now, have one Jell-O shot with me." Martina lifted one and stared at her like a sad puppy waiting for someone to stop walking by her crate and pay her some attention.

"Oh, fine." Faith swallowed the cherry-flavored Jell-O in one easy roll. "But, that's it. Don't be coming around here in five minutes with that pathetic begging face."

Martina swallowed another one.

The delicious cherry-flavored taste lingered on Faith's tongue. She stole another one and swallowed it.

Martina swaggered away on a chuckle.

Not more than a minute later, Faith stood up to clear some of the dishes. She brushed some crumbs from the white table linen and found herself clumsily swaying to a sexy Kenny G song.

Summer always projected good times in the glow of great music and good food. Why couldn't life be one big party after another? Why did people have to worry about paying bills and finding their next job? Why couldn't they all live as their ancestors did, tucked together in the safety of numbers, cooking and eating as a family, not distracted by television or cellphones. Just one delicious spoonful of lentil salad after another.

She hummed along with the romantic song that teased the night air as she cleared plates and glasses from the tables. Martina walked past her carrying that same tray almost empty of shots. She leaned in and whispered, "I see Zumba wasn't a total waste of your time."

Faith stopped swinging her clumsy hips. "I like the song."

"Well," Martina nudged her with a hip bump. "Enjoy the song then."

If Faith wanted to survive the night with a yard full of dance-loving partiers, she'd need to stop obsessing about her lack of rhythm. She eyed the lonely Jell-O shots on the tray. "Those are sinful. Good thing we're almost out."

"Oh, no honey. We don't host a summer party and run out of Jell-O shots. We've got another two trays ready to go." Martina headed toward the sliding door, but before she got too far away, Faith grabbed the last two remaining shots and swallowed them.

"By the way," Martina said. "Your girl knows how to dance."

"She's not my girl." Faith followed her into the house. Though she did like the sound of that.

Danielle washed some dishes and gazed out the window to the backyard. "Who's not your girl?"

Faith's head began to take on that delightful swirl effect of a gentle buzz. "Martina thinks Candace is my girl, I suppose."

"Who said anything about Candace?" Martina opened the fridge.

"You did, silly." Faith braced herself against the counter to keep the room still.

Martina shared a chuckle with Danielle. "Someone's drunk already."

Faith backed away from the counter, but then the room spun a bit too much. "You might be right. I should've eaten more than lentils."

Martina placed the new tray on the counter, and hung her arm around Faith's shoulder. "We'll let Danielle pass these out. Let's you and I go greet some guests instead."

Faith looked back over at Danielle who wiped her hands on a towel and shooed her away. "Go have fun. I'll take care of these."

"I don't need to have fun," Faith said. "I'll hang in here with you."

Martina snorted. "Let's go see your girl dance."

"She's not my girl," Faith said. "But, do you think she'd want to be?"

127

"Trust me," Martina laughed and urged her through the slider. "She's your girl, and no one else will do."

Faith stepped out into the night. The fresh summer air swaddled her in a sense of carefree whim.

"See? Look." Martina pointed to Bristol and Candace. Bristol followed Candace's lead, giggling and talking with her. "Your girl loves to dance."

Faith rejoiced at the sight of her girl. "You meant Bristol."

"It's amazing what Jell-O will reveal." Martina winked, swaying to the addictive, chaotic beat of a song new to Faith. From somewhere, Martina revealed two more Jell-O shots. "Here you go, and you're welcome."

Faith eyed the shot. "Where did that come from?"

Martina swallowed one. "You're not the only one here who needs a little liquid bravery to get started."

Faith refused and stared at Martina in disbelief. "You?" Her word came out strong and too loud, as if someone else said it.

"I invited Gabe." Martina stretched her neck toward the grill where Christian and his new boyfriend were grilling more pork chops. Gabe stood with his hands in his pockets chatting with them. "I made sure Christian wasn't crushing on him before I invited him. And you know what he said?"

Faith cocked her head waiting on her reply.

"He said not a chance. He's in love with his new boyfriend. And besides, he said Gabe is straight, so he'd never have a shot even if he *was* crushing on him."

"Well, that's good news on all fronts."

"Yes." Martina lifted her chin as she stared ahead at them. "Yes, it is, isn't it?"

Faith latched onto her turn to offer Martina a hip bump. A giddiness rose in her. "Why are you standing here with me? Go." She pushed Martina.

Martina pulled back. "Why did I invite him? Look at him. He's too handsome. Why isn't he wearing a geeky pair of glasses and mismatched clothes like scientists do? Why does he look like he dates random women every night of the week? Why does he look so natural and comfortable?"

Faith began to giggle from somewhere deep inside. She derived cynical pleasure in observing the brave Martina collapse under a little social pressure. It leveled the playing field and lifted Faith out of the negative and into a world where her presence mattered.

Martina needed her. So, Faith tugged at her, leading her over to the grill. "Get it over with. It's always the first step that's the hardest."

Martina trailed behind, fighting Faith every step closer. When they finally arrived at the grill, Gabe's face opened up into a genuine smile. "There you are."

Martina's shyness fell to the ground. There one minute keeping her safe, gone the next like training wheels shed at the foot of a bicycle. "Shall we dance?" She extended her hand to him.

He took her hand, and whisked her toward the bricked patio.

Faith landed her eyes on Bristol and Candace again. Bristol came to life around her. She could dance. "Where does she get that from?" she asked aloud.

"Not from my mom's side of the family," Christian said.

"No doubt." Faith watched as her daughter transformed before her eyes into someone with confidence.

Then, she spotted Martina flirting with Gabe as they moved around the dance floor. She stroked his cheek with the tip of her fancy nail.

Time blurred in the minutes she stood watching the dance numbers unfold. The Jell-O shots flowed through her in warm, intoxicating ripples. And, before long, she was spun, coming face-to-face with Candace, the leader of that spin. She followed her lead. Her body flowed with Candace's moves, going in and out of turns with uncanny ease. At one point, Candace drew her in close and stared deeply into her eyes. A heat intensified as their bellies touched and Candace pressed her closer with a gentle nudge on her lower back. Her head buzzed, as she danced in the arms of a woman who smelled as if she had emerged from a field of wildflowers.

At one point she looked out over the dance floor and giggled into Candace's bare shoulder. Christian dipped his grandmother into a pose that caused her to become even more dramatic than usual. Candace joined her in that giggle, and then led her into a series of intimate steps that eventually resulted in a dip of Faith's own.

# #

The next morning, Faith sat on a beach chair inhaling the refreshing air. She clung to a water bottle, recalling the night before. She downed so many Jell-O shots that she lost count.

Small pieces of the night patched themselves together like random curls pinned to form a fancy updo. She vaguely remembered Lucia dancing on a chair at one point. She did remember Martina and Gabe enjoying a lustful kiss. And Candace. She remembered something about a question Candace asked her. What was it? She mentioned Salsa. Then she brought up lessons. Candace said Bristol's name. Bristol. Dance. Salsa. Bristol wanted to take Salsa lessons?

Faith tossed her hands up in the air. "Yes! That's it." Faith's sudden outburst caused her head to pound.

The last time Faith suffered a hangover, her life turned inside out. Stuart confessed his love for Gilly and she drank herself to oblivion. Not out of sadness. In pure celebration for her freedom. She thought she should've marked that crucial point by downing a quarter of a bottle of coconut rum. She and Sally sat in the middle of her living room cutting up her wedding pictures with dull kitchen knives, the ones that squashed tomatoes instead of sliced them. Before they stabbed the pictures and tore through them, she painted Stuart's face with a pen, drawing funny moustaches and unflattering dark circles under his eyes.

That's when she began her blame game against Stuart.

She spent the night hovering over a pile of pictures, reflecting about how she never wanted to end up again. She'd never put on another wedding dress and walk down an aisle. She'd never order another crummy wedding cake from Pastry Farmers because to that day she couldn't eat vanilla cake. The fly she almost bit into ruined any chance she'd trust another bakery cake again. Don't even get her started on the crazy flower prices. For what she spent on her bouquet and some table settings, she could've paid off a good chunk of her mortgage.

A full year being hangover-free impressed her, considering she spent a good portion of her married years hiding liquor in her steel coffee mug. How else could she get through hours of listening to Stuart yell at the television because his Patriots didn't toss a football at the right time? Of course Sally argued Faith could've solved that by telling Stuart she didn't want to watch football.

That would've been antagonistic and led to a fight.

Faith hated fighting. So, she'd sip her wine and brainstorm on how she'd decorate the house differently if Stuart left one day. She'd remove all the

131

stupid old, black and white pictures of cars manufactured back when seatbelts didn't exist. She'd also throw away all the excessive blankets, especially the scratchy ones. He stored them in a closet in the spare room, and every time Faith opened one of the louvre doors, one would inevitably come crashing down on top of her head.

She would never buy milk again. She hated it. Stuart drank it from the bottle. He'd always leave a little on the bottom and start a fresh bottle. On recycle week, Faith had to open the lid to rinse it and smell its foulness.

She'd get rid of the television and replace it with a fireplace instead. A real one, not the fake electric one Stuart installed after he found it on the side of the road one day.

A lot of furnishings came to them as toss-aways from neighbors. They'd go for walks with Bristol and he'd pick at the garbage, finding lamps, stools, once even a desk with broken drawers. He insisted he'd fix them.

Well, that never happened.

That night overflowed in satisfied gulps and hiccups. In between swigging rum and Sprite, coloring in Stuart's face with a pen, and then slicing through it, they piled all that junk he had collected over the years onto the curbside. Trash night wasn't until three nights later, and Faith didn't even care. She couldn't wait to get rid of it. If a neighbor did that, Faith would've never stop cussing him out every time she glanced out the window. But, that night, payback arrived. Screw the neighbors. Screw the desk. Screw the stupid pictures of old hunks of rusted metal. Screw Stuart. Most importantly, screw married life.

Faith was single.

Faith was free.

That night, after taking her last sip, she mounted her roof from Bristol's window and screamed out to world, "I'm drunk and damn well happy about it!"

Had it not been for the video Sally had taken of her waving her hands around like a lunatic out there in the shadows of a full moon, Faith would've protested the outrageous insinuation. She didn't even know someone had called the police on her. Sally fended them off.

Thankfully, Bristol had been sleeping over her friend's house that night.

Back then, Bristol used to talk to people besides her parents.

As Faith sobered to her new reality of unknowns, Bristol's voice had vanished. God, how she missed the excited tempo of her giggles and outbursts with the outside world.

That seemed so long ago.

Now in the present day, Faith's head pounded. She opened her water bottle and chugged, willing the sharp headache to go away.

Then she spotted Candace strolling up to her.

Candace arrived along with a dusting of sand, and plopped down. She looked equally hungover. Even her oversized sunglasses couldn't hide her swollen eyes. "Morning," Candace whispered.

Faith smiled.

Candace wore her hair down and it cascaded onto her tanned shoulders.

Those shoulders.

That's when Faith remembered their dance and her giggling into those shoulders, right at the part where her skin met her collarbone. Then, she recalled the brush of Candace's hand down her arm as she said goodbye.

Faith's heart quivered.

"How are you feeling this morning?" Faith asked.

Candace lifted her sunglasses and revealed two swollen eyes.

133

Faith gasped. "What happened?"

"I touched the switch to the garbage disposal. Then, unfortunately, I rubbed my eyes."

"I don't understand." She looked like she had taken a bath in pollen.

"Well, from the look of all the cotton balls along the kitchen counter, I think someone had doused that switch with peppermint oil."

Faith's hand flew up to her mouth. "Oh my God. I'm so sorry. When I let Pretzel out the day you called, I tried to stop the ants. They crawled everywhere. I spotted the oil and remembered hearing ants didn't like it."

"Neither do my eyes." Candace replaced her sunglasses. "Of course, you can always make it up to me."

"Sure. Anything. Tell me what you need."

"Have dinner with me. I know the perfect place that has pretty tables, wine, and quiet music playing in the background."

Faith swallowed a tickle that threatened her throat. "You mean like a date?"

Candace lowered her sunglasses and peeked up at her. "If that's all right with you?"

A date. That escalated her fantasy to a state of realism. As a fantasy, it tucked safely into the way-back crevices of her overloaded mind. It placed her in a fanciful scene where she could twirl and be the star of a light-hearted show that highlighted her good points. The realities of her failure as a wife, mother, and employee faded in the limelight of her fantasy. On that stage, she didn't concern herself with finding a job or running out of money to keep her house and car. She didn't focus on how she'd pay for black mold removal or have her car engine repaired if the squirrel didn't stop fucking with her. Nope. Everything shined in her favor in her fantasy world.

She drew a line in the sand with her pinky, bringing herself back to reality and to the fact that, aside from protecting herself, she needed to safeguard Bristol's heart, too. "You do know I live in Boston, right?"

"Do people from Boston not eat food?"

They both laughed, relieving some of the pressure. Could she trust Candace with their hearts? How else would she know unless she allowed Candace the opportunity to prove she could?

"So, a date?"

Candace leaned back on her elbows and arched her back. "If you're into labels, then a date it is."

Faith looked out to the calm lake and enjoyed the pull on her heart. The last time someone pulled on her heart, she was twelve and a girl named Emily kissed her cheek to thank her for signing her birthday card.

Candace's hand brushed her arm. "It's just dinner. It'll do us both good."

With that, Faith offered Candace her first wink. Then, she wished she could take it back because it came out all wrong. It fell heavy and her eyelashes stuck together. She blinked a few too many times to release the pressure, and that's when her eye began to tear up. "Sorry, I have an eyelash in my eye."

Candace sat up and pulled a tissue out of her pocket. "Let me help. Scoot closer."

Cheers to eyelashes in the eye!

Chapter Nine

After returning to Danielle's, Faith stumbled over a chewed up flip-flop. "Who does this belong to?" She examined it at arm's length.

"That's Henry's," Bristol said aloud.

Everyone shot up from their reclined positions.

Bristol's eyes grew large and her face reddened, realizing she had spoken aloud. She gazed around the room; at Martina's widening grin, Lucia's bright eyes and Emmy's curled up lip. Christian still slept, blowing snores into the silence that pervaded.

Faith wanted to cheer, but settled on delivering a distraction instead to take the pressure off her daughter and place it on her. "Martina?"

Martina sprang up from her chair. "Yes, darling."

"Can you look after Bristol tonight?"

"Of course! Why?" Her voice curled up in a shrill.

She glanced at Bristol and noticed her skin color returned back to her normal ivory. She braved forward. "I'm going out to dinner tonight."

"You have a date!" Martina squealed.

Lucia jumped up from the couch. "Wait. What did I miss? You have a date? With Candace, right? Tell me it's Candace."

Faith's face flushed.

A small sprig of joy crept onto Bristol's face.

"Who has a date?" Christian yawned.

The unfolding scene caused Faith's nerves to gallop.

"Of course, I'll watch her." Martina leaped forward and swung an arm around Bristol. "We'll be fine while you go on your date. Right, Bristol?"

"Yes," Bristol whispered, looking right into her mother's eyes.

Faith's eyes teared. An entire lifetime of worry evaporated in that moment. She and her daughter floated, suspended by a loving energy that whispered of a bright future, regardless of anything else.

Martina lay her hand over her heart. "Well, all right then. That settles it. Bristol and Emmy go get your shoes. We're going shopping."

"I'm not leaving until six o'clock tonight." Faith laughed.

"You, get dressed, too. We're going shopping for you, silly. You're not going on a date with what I've seen you wearing. We've got to get you into something sexier."

"No." Faith crossed her arms over her chest. "We are two friends going to dinner. Casual will do just fine."

"Oh, whatever!" Martina waved her off. "Go get your shoes girls."

Faith admired the chaos. Everyone, even sleepy Christian, engaged with life and found joy in the simplest of pleasures, a nap, a romp to the mall, and the combined joy over a lonely woman landing a date.

Later, as she sat in the passenger seat of Martina's car, she reflected on how much things had changed. Stuart would've hated the chaos and the excitement over a shopping spree to find a fun outfit for a dinner date. Faith loved it. For the first time since before she met Stuart, she embraced the giddiness of good old-fashioned girl time.

# #

Martina ordered the girls to fetch as many red dresses in size fourteen that they could find. Meanwhile, she stuffed Faith into a few black cocktail dresses.

"I can hardly breathe." Faith sucked in her tummy. She turned and glanced at her backend in a tight black dress that plunged low toward the middle of her back. "No way." She pointed to her waist. "I've got back fat. I need to go up a size."

Martina stared at her backend in the mirror. "Those are curves, not back fat." She placed her hands on her skinny waist. "You're not going up a size. You'll look frumpy."

"How will I enjoy myself if I can't even talk because I'm too busy holding my gut in? I'll have gas pains within an hour. No way." She slipped out of the dress. "This was a stupid idea."

"Shopping?" Martina looked about ready to cry.

"The date." Faith slipped back into her oversized Rhode Island t-shirt. "I need to be looking for a real job, not an opportunity to eat expensive food at a romantic restaurant."

The girls knocked on the dressing room door. Martina opened it up and Emmy revealed a navy blue dress that looked more casual than sexy. Faith grabbed it out of her hands. "That's more like it."

Martina glared at it. "You're going to shove yourself right back into a potato sack." She folded her arms over her chest. "I guess I'll stand back while you figure it all out for yourself."

Faith rested it up against herself. "This is more my style. It says pretty, but not fancy. I can eat and breathe at the same time. Imagine that!"

Martina rolled her eyes. "Fine, put on the comfortable dress."

She said comfortable as if it reeked of garbage.

"We get to choose the accessories." Martina tilted her chin up. "Girls, can you grab a few chunky beaded necklaces and colorful scarves?"

They trotted away with an air of purpose to their steps.

Faith slipped into the navy dress. Before turning to face her reflection, Martina squealed. "Oh, I like what I see!"

Faith whipped around to catch a glimpse. It fit without clinging. "So do I."

"That dress is going to put a sparkle in her eyes."

"And not make me look like a slut," Faith added.

"You look sexy in a casual way." Martina narrowed her eyes, examining every inch. "Don't be surprised if she's going to want to get you out of that at the end of the night."

Sex with Candace.

Faith's stomach rolled.

She could look at it as a hijacking to her plan to get more focused on her future or a great opportunity to challenge herself and move forward.

Faith let the seasonings from her fantasies blend as she stared at the scooped neckline. She floated so far out of her fantasy comfort zone. Performance in a fantasy didn't matter because she'd never meet any of the women in her dreams. In her years of fantasizing over women, Faith grew her skills. At least in theory. She always brought the women of her fantasies to that point of ecstasy.

But, Candace was more than a fantasy. She was real. What if she disappointed her? What if she discovered she didn't have the sophisticated touch to bring a woman pleasure? What if Candace didn't like the way she kissed?

"Accessories will be too much." Faith began to gather her clothes into a neat pile. "I've got a simple necklace at home that will do fine."

"Are you talking about that cheap, faded piece of fake metal with the itty bitty turquoise blunder hanging from it?"

Faith rubbed her fingers around her neckline. "Well, yeah. I bought that when I went on a cruise with Sally."

"Fifteen years ago?"

Faith sucked in her tummy. "Yup."

"Chunky beaded necklace it is, then."

# #

Faith stared at herself in the mirror as she waited on Candace to ring the bell. Her stomach waved. She smoothed her hands down the length of her sides, ensuring her curves hadn't grown since indulging in the triple scoop sundae at Dairy Queen after their exhaustive search around Providence Place Mall for the Aquamarine beaded necklace. She leaned in closer to the mirror to examine it better.

Aye. Too much?

What if Candace wore jeans and a t-shirt? What if it was just dinner with a friend? After all, Candace didn't plop the date label on it. Faith did. Or what if Candace expected the night would end up with them rolling around under the sheets of her bed?

She needed to change. She went over to the closet and pulled her pair of Levi's from a hanger. She could hide her muffin top with a blazer.

Before she could pull her dress over her head, the doorbell rang.

Her heart bucked.

A moment later, Danielle knocked on her door.

Faith opened it and pulled her inside. "Help me get out of this."

Danielle scanned her face. "You look stunning."

"Stunning? Stunning is too much pressure." Faith began to hyperventilate. "I don't want to go. I want to get out of this dress, scrub the

141

makeup off my face, and put on a pair of flannels. Then, I want to slip under my covers and read a book. Why would I want to date? Why would I want to put myself through this torture?"

"Get ahold of yourself." Danielle grabbed her shoulders. "It's dinner with someone you already know. That's it. Dinner."

"Tell her I'm not feeling well."

"I will pinch your forearm if you don't get down the stairs."

Danielle's pinch could topple a three-hundred pound man. She witnessed it one day when one of Lucas's college friends accidentally stepped on her toes. She pinched him so hard he cried.

"What are you afraid of? You've spent time with her, and you both get along fine. Why is having dinner different?"

"Because it's a date. I declared that to her. I've been out of the loop for so long. Who pays? Do I grab the check first? Does she? Do we both? Do I kiss her goodnight? Does she expect sex? Maybe so. Do you see why I'm panicking?"

"Go with the flow. Stop planning the details."

"That's dangerous."

"Dangerous? You're not driving ninety around a bend in the road. You're picking up a fork, and possibly a spoon, and digging into some chow. Get a grip." Danielle scoffed. "Dangerous. Give me a break."

"Well, it's dangerous because what happens if I end up liking her past this friendship we've started?"

"Then you do."

"I've got a life to get back to living after this summer break. I can't spend my mornings lounging in the sun with my toes in the sand and my afternoons and evenings playing with hair. I can't drink margaritas every night while I watch the sunset. I can't continue to entertain Lucia and Martina's crazy antics."

"You're going to dinner, not getting married." Danielle patted Faith's arm. "I'll let her know you're coming down. I'll tell her you had an eyelash stuck in your eye or something."

"You can't," Faith blurted out. "I've already had that happen."

Danielle shot her a confused look. "Just get downstairs. Don't take too long. I promised Bristol we'd bake a cake tonight."

"She told you about baking cakes?"

"Told me what?"

Faith decided to keep that secret tucked away. No one needed the inside scoop to the stupid therapist's reward system. Bristol spoke that day not because she had a sudden appetite for cake and frosting. She spoke because of the love in that home. It wrapped her in its comfortable embrace with all its cushy pillows, frilly curtains, and delicious home-cooking smells. It would be a great place to settle with Bristol if it wasn't for the horrific, traffic-jammed drive separating her from her father.

"Only that she's not a fan of chocolate."

Danielle opened the door. "That's not going to be an issue. I bought confetti cake."

Her sister closed the door, and Faith took one last look at herself. *I can do this.*

#

When Faith reached the bottom step, she glimpsed into the kitchen. Candace laughed with the girls over the sizes of the bowls Danielle had taken out for the cake batter. They were big bowls. They could bake a wedding cake if they wanted.

Candace wore another one of those beautiful dresses Faith liked. She wore a teal-green and cream one and it hung in pretty layers down to her knees. The tank style top accentuated her toned arms.

When Faith entered the kitchen, Candace turned to greet her. She wore makeup. Light, but still there. A giddiness surged in Faith. She took the time to get ready for their date. That had to mean something, surely.

Candace traveled her eyes up the length of Faith's new outfit, stopping for an extra moment along the cleavage, and then finally landing on her eyes. Her stealthy smile didn't communicate friendship. It smoldered.

Faith tucked a loose strand of hair behind her ear, and then swung the rest of her loose waves over her shoulder so they rested along her breasts.

Candace cleared her throat before opening her rosy lips to say, "You look beautiful."

Faith steadied her breaths so her voice wouldn't come out all shaky. "As do you."

Lucia, Martina, Danielle, Christian, Bristol and Emmy all stood as silent sentinels.

Faith's frazzled breath crawled up the back of her throat. Then, Henry scratched his ears, filling the room with something worthy of attention.

"Oh, Henry." Faith crouched down and picked him up, thankful for the distraction. She kissed his wet nose.

"You two go on now." Martina pulled Henry from Faith's arms. "We're going to eat popcorn and bake cakes full of confetti. It's going to be grand." She spun Henry. "Isn't that right, my baby?"

Henry wiggled and barked.

"Girls, get your mixers ready," she said, and then turned to Faith and

Candace, shooing them away. "Go on now. Skedaddle."

# #

Candace drove under the speed limit. Not by a little, but by five whole miles per hour. Faith had spent nearly ten years clawing the leather on the passenger door and stomping an imaginary brake pedal when Stuart drove. Now, she could actually keep her eyes open and hands folded in her lap, admiring the subtle beauty of wild grasses swaying and the fluffy clouds drifting.

Not only could Faith relax in the good hands of Candace, but she also didn't have to grit her teeth when the wind blew her hair all over her face. Instead of riding along as if on the set of an eighties music video, like when Stuart drove, Faith enjoyed the cool, refreshing air conditioner and windless drive.

They arrived at the parking lot to the quaint seaside town with not a hair out of place.

Faith hated to jinx herself, but things shined brightly for the first time in many years. Something was bound to go wrong. She'd probably twist an ankle on the cobblestone or end up spilling red wine down her new dress. As long as she didn't hiccup or catch her hair on fire by candlelight, everything would work out.

Charm filled the short walk from the parking lot to the restaurant. They passed adorable shops filled with tourists buying t-shirts, cotton candy, salt-water taffy and postcards. They passed an ice-cream parlor where families sat at picnic tables and lapped at their maple walnut and peanut brittle ice creams to catch the drips. At one point, they passed a dance school. Candace stopped in front of it. Inside, couples danced what looked like a Waltz. "My friends

145

own this place. They have dance parties and they allow me to invite students from the community center to join in so one day they might consider studying dance under them year-round."

Faith gazed at Candace's easy smile as she watched the couples. "Are these your friends who are considering opening up the dance studio in California?"

"Yes. They like the idea of having multiple locations. They're considering turning their business into a franchise."

"Ever think of opening up your own dance studio?"

Candace turned away from the window and continued their stroll toward the restaurant. "It's a huge commitment, one that would take a lot of careful consideration."

Not into commitments. Got it.

As they walked, Candace's arm brushed up against Faith's. A tangible electric jolt transferred between them that caused Faith to wobble slightly.

"So how's the hairdressing going?" Candace asked.

"I'm enjoying it. It's fun being creative." Faith liked the sound of that rolling off her tongue. The creative type. The type who didn't let a little layoff destroy her. The type who persevered amidst uncertainty. Give her a little more time in that happy bubble and she might even be able to pull those things off.

"Maybe I can sweet-talk you into styling my hair."

"I'd love that." Her answer came out too quickly.

Candace's arm brushed past again, that time remaining. "The sweet-talking?"

Faith's insides fluttered as they rounded the street corner. "Yeah. Something like that."

They stopped in front of a colorful golden stucco building. "So, here we are. Are you okay with Peruvian food?" Candace asked. "If not, we have plenty of other choices."

"Sure. Peruvian is great," Faith said as if she'd eaten Peruvian food all her life.

As they entered the restaurant, Candace placed her hand at the small of her back and guided her. Faith prayed the food didn't have too much hot spice to it. Even Italian dressing made her choke.

# #

An attractive woman with hair the color of beach sand showed them to their table in an intimate corner. A votive candle created a soft glow. Cream-colored napkins, folded like tuxedos, sat between the silverware. She handed each of them a wine list and two hardcover menus. "I would suggest the sangria if you like fruity wine," she said, smiling and exposing her high cheeks. "Antoine will be your server tonight."

They both thanked her and watched her stroll away.

"The sangria is delicious. Though, I'll warn you to sip it slowly. It has a kick to it that doesn't hit until well after you've polished off a glass."

Water it should probably be, then.

Candace tilted her head and pinned Faith against the back of her chair with her playful gaze. Her eyes were still swollen from the peppermint oil.

"I shouldn't have put the oil on the switch. But, the ants were crawling, and I got all OCD."

She continued to gaze at Faith. "We've got the rest of the summer for you to make it up to me."

Faith ventured a daring step forward. "Oh, so dinner isn't going to be enough?"

"I don't know. We haven't even raised our forks, yet."

"Or sipped sangria."

"A woman taking a risk. I like it." Candace clicked her tongue. "Seriously, I'd order a water with it."

Faith understood wine. She drank the strong red kind. Really, what harm could a little sangria cause? Faith opened up her menu. "So, what would you recommend eating?"

"Uh-uh." She shook her head. "If we're going to be risky, let's go all in. You order for us."

She scanned the menu. Everything was written in Spanish. What if she ordered them a plate of crackers and cheese for dinner? She never took the lead on such things. She stayed in her comfort zone eating at the same restaurants, ordering the same old menu items, and shopping for the same produce and snacks. The craziest she got that summer was when she and Bristol went to Dell's lemonade and she ordered a cherry flavor instead of lemon. She tossed out the entire jumbo cup.

Risks never panned out, as they did for Stuart. He could order a random meat on a stick from a street vendor and not question it. Faith once ate a mango from a fruit truck in New York and ended up in the hospital for two days with severe food poisoning.

"There are so many choices," Faith whispered, leaning back against the seat to stop the beads of sweat rolling down her back.

Antoine arrived at their table with folded hands. "Ah, I see you've jumped right into the menu. No famous sangria first? Whet the appetite, no? How about a nice spread of various breads and cheeses?"

"We'll have two sangrias," Candace said.

"And two waters," Faith added, sensibly.

"And appetizers?"

"Um, the tray of bread and cheese sounds amazing," Faith said.

Candace sat back. "You have no idea what that menu says, do you?"

"I took Spanish class in high school. Give me a little time and I'll have it deciphered."

Antoine arrived in a flash with a beautiful pitcher of sangria adorned with strawberries, pineapples, and mangoes. He placed tall flute glasses down and poured each one half-full, and then he lowered the pitcher onto the table.

"Enjoy." He left on a whisper.

Faith picked up her glass and sipped from it. It tasted fruity and innocent enough. Then, she noticed Candace steadying hers in front of her.

"Oh, sorry about that." Faith clinked her glass.

"In paraphrasing a little *Casablanca*, here's to the beginning of what is turning into a beautiful friendship," Candace said.

Friendship?

Faith's heart dropped in disappointment. "Yes, here's to our new friendship." She took a sip, embracing the sweet aftertaste of the fruit. "Tastes like summertime."

Candace examined the glass, sweating with water. "Reminds me of hot summer days spent jumping in and out of the community pool. My mother would always have a cooler filled with Kool-Aid." She took another thoughtful sip. "It's scary how easily this goes down."

"Right?" Faith took her third short sip. Light and airy music, coupled with the golden candlelit space, tickled Faith's core.

Danielle was right. She needed to go with the flow. Relax and let the night unfold.

Antoine returned with the tray of breads and cheeses. He poured more sangria into their glasses before waltzing away.

They chatted while they munched on the warm bread and creamy cheeses. Faith learned Candace started dancing when still in diapers. That she arrived to the United States from Colombia when she was Bristol's age, seven. And that she didn't speak a lick of English upon arrival. Neither did her father. Her mother, being from Canada spoke perfect English. Her father never quite adjusted, and needed both Candace and her mother to translate for him.

"So where are your parents now?"

"In Colombia. They left when I got into college. They assumed I'd be okay. My father prefers working and living on the farm. My mother also adores the countryside."

Faith refilled their glasses. "You must miss having family around, huh?"

"So much." She sipped. "It's hard. You have no idea how lucky you are to have yours only a couple of hours away."

Faith should've appreciated them more.

"One day I'll go to Colombia and make up for it. I'll take a month-long trip and visit everyone. It'll be one huge party."

"Sounds like a future adventure awaits."

Candace lifted her freshly filled glass and lobbed a playful gaze. "In more ways than one."

Faith let that comment travel all the way through her. It spilled its warmth on her tongue, down her throat and into her belly where it swam in a dance with the sangria.

Faith's eyes landed on Candace's delicate hands. She could imagine their softness. She wished she could summon the courage to bring them up to her lips and kiss them, and to have the power to tease her into wanting more.

Candace was so much more than some beautiful woman to have sex with, though. She was real and kind. She cared about kids and dogs. She laughed at Martina and Lucia's half-baked comments as if she found them hysterical. And Bristol trusted her.

She wasn't just any beautiful woman.

She was Candace.

And she already had Faith smitten beyond repair.

Faith continued to sip her sangria. It didn't taste potent like Candace had warned. It was probably watered down and no more potent than the Kool-Aid from Candace's childhood.

At one point, when they talked about some of Candace's travel adventures to the Midwest, a woman approached. Not any woman. A gorgeous, sophisticated blonde who towered over Candace by at least eight inches. Candace stood and opened her arms up wide to the woman wearing a soft pastel sundress and heels much too high to be legal.

"What are you doing here gorgeous?" The woman kissed her cheek.

Gorgeous?

Candace's cheeks flushed red, as they regarded each other at arm's length. "I'm here with my new friend enjoying the sangria. Definitely order it. It's better than the last time we had it."

New friend? Last time they had it? Faith sank in her chair.

"Latin dance party tomorrow night, right?" The woman shook her hips. "It's been quite a week, so I'll fill you in then. I don't want to hold you and your friend up now." The woman crawled her eyes down to Faith and offered her a smirk.

Faith matched her smirk with an accidental eye roll.

Candace, in her typical charming self, cradled the woman's arm. "I'm looking forward to it."

Faith sat like a third wheel, drinking her watered-down sangria. It rolled down her throat with delicious ease, at least.

As the two of them exchanged flirty innuendos about their dance party for the next night, Faith reprimanded herself. Why was she so gaga over a woman who didn't even know her middle name yet, let alone her birthday or favorite song?

The blondie droned on and on about dance contracts and shows, captivating Candace and causing an odd jealousy to take hold of Faith.

Ugh. She wasn't cut out for the fling thing and all the weird insecurities it stirred in her. Give her a cozy blanket, dramatic television show, and a bowl of popcorn drizzled with maple syrup and butter any day.

The woman may as well have pulled up a seat with the amount of time she stole from them. Candace offered her an apologetic smile in between laughing at the woman's remarks.

Faith drank another glass of sangria to pass the time. She stared at the fruit in the bottom of her glass and thought maybe that was where all the alcohol had gone. She certainly didn't feel any affect. The stuff was delicious. So, she poured herself some more.

The longer she sat, the punchier her thoughts. How could someone be so rude? Couldn't the woman see how uncomfortable Faith grew?

Finally, the woman hugged Candace goodbye.

Candace sat back down. "I'm sorry that went on for so long. She's the friend who owns the dance studio we passed by earlier."

Friend? The blonde had outright flirted. A friend doesn't flirt like that!

A satisfied smile had stretched across Candace's face, the kind Stuart used to come home wearing after flirting all day with his mistress.

Well, Faith was just a friend, too, after all. Friend. The word rolled off Candace's tongue easily when introducing Faith to the blondie. Should they start roasting marshmallows over their romantic candle and sing camp songs while they were at it?

"I'm sorry. I have to run to the bathroom," Candace rose, placing her hand on Faith's. "I'll be back in a snap."

Faith watched Candace walk away, flicking those hips and showering everyone with an eyeful of her sexiness, including the blonde bimbo as she passed her table.

Faith sighed and helped herself to the fruit at the bottom of her glass. It tasted sweet on her tongue and bitter as it descended. She devoured it all anyway.

Friends. At least she knew where she stood with Candace. Oh well. Too bad the sexual part didn't work out. She would've liked adding fling to her list of adventures around life's curves. What would she dream about now, if they were only friends? Friends didn't dream up torrid love affairs about each other.

Stupid beautiful blonde woman.

Screw every beautiful woman who ever passed her by with an indifferent shrug. She had things to offer, too. So what if she couldn't dance great? Okay and big deal she was semi-jobless and likely homeless soon, too. Stuart would end up getting the house and moving in his beautiful Gilly who would pretend to like his idea of home décor. She was young and dumb, like Faith used to be, too naïve to stand up for herself. Well, thirty-five years on the planet taught Faith that if she didn't latch onto what she wanted, others would file in and stake their claim to it instead.

Candace returned in what seemed like a blink, carrying that same satisfied smile.

The jealousy waved through her again. Faith entered into a far different world as a single person now than she had as an early twenty-year old. Now she had to deal with smartphone apps that helped her decide if someone hated or liked the same things as she did. She dipped into the far end of a pool, the side she had no right occupying. When had she ever swum so deep before?

The dating world freaked her out.

In fact, her mind went back to an earlier thought of a cozy blanket, good television show and maybe some plain crackers instead of sweet and salty popcorn. She'd even take Felix the cat over sitting in the hard chair in that restaurant – which by the way, could've used some cushioning – across from a woman who stared at her with concern. Enough with the concern. Stuart had doled out enough of those concerned stares the entire ten years of their marriage.

Antoine, at one point, had snuck up on them and was waiting patiently on Faith to decide their meal plan for the night. The sangria caused everything to blur. She could barely read the bold subheadings on the menu, let alone the items. So, she let fate take over. She twirled her finger, adorned with a new red apple nail polish, in the air. Finally, when Candace and Antoine had suffered through enough anticipation, she dropped her finger to the menu. "She will have the," Faith looked down at the choice. "The Tall..arin Sal..ta.."

"Ah, the shrimp, calamari, and octopus," Antoine said. "Great choice."

Faith cocked her head playfully. "Didn't think I could handle ordering in Spanish, eh? Antoine understood me." She gazed up at his half smile. "Didn't you?"

"Yes, ma'am."

Ma'am?

Oh no he didn't.

"Faith. Not ma'am." The sangria kicked her bold attitude into high gear.

"Right." He swallowed a giggle.

Faith opened her mouth to put him in his place. Then, Candace stopped her when she cupped her hand over hers. "She'll have the Pesaro a Lo Macho."

"Yes. I'll have the Pesaro thingy."

Antoine twisted his mouth into a weird curved line, as if restricting a fart. He bowed his head, and then glided toward the kitchen.

Faith glanced back at Candace who had at some point switched from Sangria to water. They both had water. Where did the sangria go? When did Antoine steal it from their table? Where had all the bread and cheese gone? Had she eaten it and forgotten? Had she missed the part when they fed each other the creamy cheese with the tips of their sultry fingers, gazing into each other's eyes? Candace sat before her a creamy goddess she wanted to lick.

Oh my God.

Get a grip.

You're zonked.

Drink water.

Screw shrimp.

Get more bread.

She began to hyperventilate.

She could sneak off to the bathroom and steal a loaf from the kitchen. No one would see her. Or she could, at the very least, dig into the large bowl of mints at the host station. Anything to soak up the alcohol and stop her mad dash down the road of foolish regret.

She opened her mouth to tell Candace she'd be right back. But she couldn't. The room spun, and she couldn't find the seat of the chair to lift herself. At least not without falling. Could she even walk across the room? She sat still, and looked at Candace who smiled back, having no clue of the war that brewed within Faith's drunken mind.

"Do you want some coffee?" Candace asked. She blurred before her. "You look like you could use some."

A tide of emotions rolled in, bringing in its wake an enormous amount of jibber-jabber, nausea, and spinning. Lots of spinning. The alcohol rocked against her stomach, threatening something terrible. A huge doomsday to her first date as a single woman. "I'm not feeling well." Faith attempted to steady her rise from the chair, but fell back into it.

Candace rushed to her side and helped her up. "Let's get you home." She pulled Faith up by her underarms.

Candace carried her through the restaurant like a puppet. Faith's legs wouldn't work on their own. What did they put into that sangria? It should be outlawed. It should come with a warning label. Nothing that delicious should ever be placed in front of unsuspecting guests on first dates. It ruined the chance for second dates. It destroyed any chance they'd share a first kiss. A bed. An anniversary where they'd exchange chocolates and cute cards with puppy dogs on them. It tossed Faith over the side of a mountain too steep and slippery to fasten a grip and pull herself back up to where classy people hung out.

Candace whispered something to Antoine.

"Of course. Call us once you're safe. We'll settle then," he said in his fake Peruvian accent. He was probably not even from Peru. He was probably from South Providence and learned to talk with an accent from Nova television.

They exited the restaurant and headed up the sidewalk toward the parking lot. The cool breeze sobered her enough so she could see the shapes of cars and streetlights. Even people. A sense of partial control returned to her legs. Maybe the night could be redeemed. Then again, Candace still carried her by the armpits.

Oh my God. Someone shoot me. Right now. Aim and shoot. I don't want to remember any of this. Put me out of my agony.

She recited that all the way back to Candace's car. "You don't mean that," Candace whispered.

"I said it aloud?"

Candace protected her head while she stuffed her into the passenger side. "We'll just get you home," she said again before shutting the door.

On the drive, Candace spoke with someone over Bluetooth. To whom did that voice belong? The blonde bimbo? No, wait, her voice had dripped with too much sex appeal at the restaurant. Concern, not sex appeal, trailed the voice that floated through the car.

"Can you unlock the front door? We'll get there in about ten minutes."

"I'm sorry about this," the concerned voice mellowed. "I'm sure she's going to be too." The voice softened even more. "She's been through a lot."

Candace placed her hand over Faith's hand. "Apparently so."

Faith closed her eyes and finally recognized the voice to be her sister's loving, safe voice.

She was so tired. So very tired.

Chapter Ten

Sitting in a room teeming with black mold would've been a gift compared to opening her eyes to the brightness of the new day. Faith's head pounded, as if someone had taken a nutcracker to it, not once, but repeatedly. If she turned to the right or left, the pain worsened. So, she lay, still in her dress and sandals, on top of the unmade bed and tried not to move. The sound of clanking pots and pans from the kitchen below sounded like a firing squad had moved in and practiced hitting their metallic targets.

Each clank caused her to stiffen.

She peeled her eyes open and squinted at the sun. Her stomach rolled along with her head. Then, memories of her disastrous night emerged like a devil, pointing its ugly fingers at her and laughing. Not a pleasant cajoling. No, a deep, guttural laugh. The kind that lifted the little hairs. She remembered the tears rolling down her cheeks. Then, she recalled begging Candace to pull off to the side of the street so she could throw up.

Faith rolled over and waited for the nausea to catch up.

Who accepts a playful offer on a date and ends up needing to be carried back to the car? By her armpits, no less.

Mortified, Faith buried her head under a pillow.

She had done some pretty stupid things in life, but nothing left her with that kind of dread. How would she face Candace?

Eventually, Faith managed to climb out of bed and go to the bathroom. When she returned, she glanced out the window at her daughter walking her bike up and down the driveway. Bristol feared not being able to stop the bike, so she walked it instead. She was such a delightful and peculiar child. Afraid of so much, but willing to at least face it with some action, be it body language for speaking or walking her bike for thrills.

As long as she had Bristol everything would be okay in the world. Bristol was her life. Faith needed no one else. Eventually, with enough time to buffer the bad luck in her life, she could get through anything.

She had great purpose with Bristol. She would dote on her the way she deserved, always being there when it mattered most. Like when she would finally, one day, mount that bike seat and pedal her feet far away from whatever turmoil led her to walk it in the first place. She would help her daughter be brave and strong.

She would focus on Bristol and erase the grime left behind from all the years she wasted trying to fit the mold of a happy wife. That would help reengage her in a search for a stable profession instead of the unpredictable world of hairdressing so late in the game. She would stop the nonsense of pursuing dates with women like Candace, too. From then on, she'd live a balanced, healthy life complete with a healthy glow and firm butt cheeks.

Yeah, right. Maybe when she won the lottery or ended up on Ellen's Twelve Days of Christmas.

A woman could dream.

She leaned her forehead against the window and sighed. Distress collected in between her groans. Would she ever get the "happily ever after" everyone else did? Even Martina struck gold with the lab scientist guy. They looked like they'd been happily married for twenty-something years the other night. They beamed like a couple on a postcard advertising a romantic cruise or trip to Paris.

What about ten years in the future? Bristol would pack up her clothes and diaries and head off to college. Would she go to a local college and still be a part of Faith's life? My God, what if she decided to go to college in California? Would Faith become some lonely mother who began wearing curlers to bed and grocery shopping in her housedress? Would she become that old woman on the hill yelling at little kids who played too loudly and straddled the line between her property and town property?

Bristol would never let that happen. She would ask her mother to join her in California. They'd get a nice apartment, one with a study for Bristol. She'd never have to eat cafeteria food or worry about sharing a room with a bunch of party girls who didn't include her in their plans. Her devoted mother would take care of all of that because it would be her primary focus.

By then, her fantasy of a love with some random woman she met one summer at her sister's lake house would be long faded away, like the blue of a good-fitting pair of jeans. The image of Candace in her red flared dress and shiny bouncy hair that flirted with her breasts would be replaced by years of being a good mother and writing press releases for another company.

Oh, God. No. She didn't want to write press releases ever again. She didn't want to pitch ideas to the media or pretend she cared about shares of a corporation.

Candace would long have forgotten her by then, too. She'd no doubt, be engaged or married to a hot dancer with moves and grooves that turned her on and stirred her libido like a well-supplied cocktail. They'd start their journey together as wives who ruled the Latin dance world with their charm and ability to get parties started. By day she'd impress dance students with her wisdom of rhythm, and by night, she'd tear up the dance floor, leaving all with a sense of wonder. And faintness. Let's not forget faintness. The woman had that kind of power.

161

Faith couldn't get in the way of that.

She lay back down again and rested her eyes, wishing the headache would melt away.

Some time had passed, and the sun filtered through the windows and under the pillow to torment her again. It poked its sunny little rays in her face and mocked her. Why couldn't it be a rainy dreary day? Why did the sun have to shine? Why did her stomach have to hurt like a dull knife twisted in it?

"Faith," Danielle's cheerful voice stabbed her in the head as she entered.

"Stop knocking."

"I'm not knocking." Danielle sat on the side of her bed. "You look like you've spent the night in a dumpster." She picked at something in Faith's hair. "How did you get cheese in your hair?"

Faith groaned. "I made a huge fool of myself."

"I know. I helped put you into bed, remember? Or do you not remember that part?" She twisted her face in a question.

Faith tossed a pillow at her. "Tell me the truth. How bad did I leave things?"

Danielle studied her. She opened her mouth, and then Emmy and Bristol barged through the door.

"Before you say no," Emmy said much too loudly. "You have to hear us out."

Bristol pressed her lips together waiting on Emmy to sell her mother on something.

"Use your indoor voice." Faith's voice came out raspy as if she'd spent the last month in a smoke-filled nightclub.

"Girls, not now." Danielle shooed them out the door.

"Candace is waiting for us. It has to be now."

Faith shot up, and her head exploded into a series of electric shocks. She feared opening her eyes too wide and discovering those electrical impulses had short-circuited something vital in her optic nerve and left her blind, mute, and well, if possible, more irresponsible. "Candace is here?"

"No," Bristol whispered.

Faith eased open her eyelids a little more, careful not to tear a cornea or worse, bring on a migraine. "I don't understand."

"Phone," Bristol handed her cellphone over.

Faith looked at her cellphone through suspicious eyes. Bits of the night before broke through. Faith had dropped her cell and Candace had picked it up and told her she'd leave it on the counter by the breadbox. Then, Danielle had giggled and said something about the headache she would have the next morning and possibly for days.

Faith groaned again and passed the phone to Danielle. "I can't. Please take it," she whispered.

Danielle answered and bobbed her head up and down in between yeses. "I'm sure that'll be fine. The girls would love that." Then she creased her forehead and looked at Faith. "She'll be all right in a few hours once she's had some coffee and a muffin." She giggled into the phone and exchanged pleasantries before hanging up.

Faith waited on Danielle to share. When Danielle walked over to the nightstand and placed the phone down, she turned to the girls. "She's waiting for you."

"Well hang on." Faith sat up. "Where is she taking you?"

"She's taking us to a dance studio in Providence!" Emmy's body bobbed up and down.

"On a bus," Bristol whispered.

"A bus?"

"A Greyhound bus." Danielle said, impatiently.

Had Faith missed that part of the conversation last night, too?

They screamed as if someone had handed them free passes to Disney World. Bristol leaped to the bedside and kissed Faith's forehead.

"Thank you, Mommy."

Faith hugged her daughter in exchange for a thank you she hadn't earned. "I'm not the one to thank."

"Ms. Candace said you talked about it last night," Emmy said. "And you told her to call you in the morning to arrange the details."

Danielle nodded. "It's true. Right before she placed a pillow on your side so you wouldn't get sick in the middle of the night."

Faith's stomach lurched again.

Emmy grabbed Bristol's hand and tugged her out of the room. "Come on, she's waiting." More squeals faded along with them down the stairs.

Danielle folded Faith's wet towel from the floor. "I've got coffee brewing, and Lucia swears she has the cure of all cures for a hangover." Danielle rolled her eyes. "Tread lightly." She walked out the door and said over her shoulder. "You've been warned."

# #

A hangover cure never should've included lemons.

Lucia swore by it, though.

She brewed freshly-grated ginger tea and squeezed a whole lemon into it. "Cheers to the gift of lemon trees." Then, she placed it under Faith's nose and ordered her to sip it. "It works like a charm. You'll be eating hotdogs by noon."

Faith pushed it away, in no mood for Lucia's sunshine and her little *cheers to* philosophy. And certainly not hotdogs, either.

Martina grabbed her shoulders from behind and Lucia forced the tea cup under her nose. "Drink."

Faith gasped and bucked under the restraint, and when she lost the battle, she finally caved and sipped it. It swam right to her brain. Faith worried those synapses she destroyed the night before would revolt and take out the rest of her brain cells. She coughed and bent forward.

Martina rubbed her back, while Lucia rubbed her temples. "That a girl. Give it a second." She continued to rub her temples, lulling sense back into Faith's brain.

Three cups of ginger tea later, Faith could walk around the kitchen without fear of throwing up. She couldn't eat hotdogs, but possibly a piece of toast.

As if reading her mind, Danielle plopped a piece of multigrain bread into the toaster oven.

Lucia plucked an avocado out of a hanging basket. "So, we heard you had quite the night."

Martina stopped flipping through the Vogue magazine she had been studying. "A perfectly good waste of a great outfit, that's what happened last night."

"It's fine." Faith said, opening up the fridge to fetch some butter for her toast.

Lucia grabbed it from her. "I butter it. You sit and talk to us. Tell us what happened. We're all ears."

No doubt about that. "I'm not ready to date. I'll never be. It was a stupid idea."

165

The three women shared equally amused grins.

She sat. "It's true. My life is complicated and she's going to see that before long anyway. Better she got wind of it on our first date than twenty years into something. I spent ten years hiding the drama that follows me, I'm not willing to hide anymore. I am a woman with some issues. The universe likes to screw with me by sending squirrels into my life to destroy my car and black mold into my walls. It got me laid off and unable to get a single worthy interview. Now, it sends me a woman who is going to a Latin dance party with her gorgeous, flirty *friend*, and I'm jealous. I'm freaking jealous of a woman hanging out with her friend. A woman I've only had one disastrous date with, no less. She has it all together. Everyone does. Even Bristol has it all together now."

Three stunned faces stared back at her.

"Oh God. I'm awful." Faith popped up. "I'm an awful person. I'm jealous of my own daughter for being happy. I'm so screwed up."

"None of us have it all together," Danielle said.

"Speak for yourself." Martina raised her voice. "I'm not going down that pity party. Neither are you."

Danielle sat Faith back down on the stool. "So life roughed you up a little lately? If it didn't from time to time, you'd be bored with the good stuff."

"She's right." Martina's red-painted glossy lips irritated Faith. "It's a choice. You go out there," she raised her voice again. "Find the good and stop looking for the bad. You hate squirrels. You hate them all because one or two made a nest in your car. They're not all bad creatures. They're looking for a home. You provided that. That's the good."

"You're too cheery for me."

"Faith," Danielle urged her.

166

"No, it's all right. She has every right to her opinion." Martina's jaw flinched up and down. A fiery passion lit up her dark eyes. "Remember this." She pointed her finger at Faith. "If you keep looking for bad, you're going to bring bad into your life. We've had enough bad here." She shook. "Stop bringing the bad." On that, she marched out of the kitchen leaving Faith speechless.

"She's superstitious," Lucia said, as if none of them had figured that out.

"Look," Danielle rolled an orange between her hands. "Candace is obviously fine with you. She took Bristol to Providence on a bus."

Faith resurrected a small smile. "That's true."

"Yeah. It is. So you hit a bump. You'll strike many, and you'll get past them."

"This one shouldn't even matter. At the end of the summer I go to Boston and she goes on her next adventure."

"Why do you have to go back to Boston?" Lucia cradled her coffee mug.

"Because everything is there. Stuart. The house, which should be fixed by then. Work. There's got to be work for me there. I need to be there and get serious about the job search."

"You're making your life way too difficult." Lucia poured her a cup of coffee.

Faith pushed it away. "I can't have coffee right now."

"You obviously still need to wake up and smell the coffee, dear. Drink up." Lucia turned back to the coffee pot burner. "You need to let loose. Have some fun. It's summertime. You've been hurt. She's single, so she's likely been, too. Go lick each other's wounds."

Danielle and Faith busted out laughing.

Lucia began scrubbing the coffee stains from the counter. "Life isn't a torture chamber. Not everything needs to be plotted and dissected. If you want to plan out your breathing patterns and sleep cycles, fine. But trying to control summertime fun with a nice person who takes care of people's dogs? Come on now." She shook her hips. "Put a little zing into this, will ya? For all of our sakes."

"What is that supposed to mean?" Danielle asked.

Lucia pointed her finger at Danielle. "Don't pretend a wool blanket hasn't been tossed over this house for long enough. It's been ten years and I'm peeking out at life through the damned suffocating wool. It's nice to have some life back in this place, finally, even if it's temporary."

Martina inched back into the kitchen. "It has been nice."

Danielle folded her arms across her chest. "Have I not provided a nice place for you, Lucia?"

Lucia slapped the countertop with her rag. "You think *you've* been the one providing *me* with a nice place? What do you think I've been trying to do since Lucas died? If I hadn't moved in, you and the kids would've shriveled up and died too. So, don't pretend you're doing me any favors here. This has all been for you and the kids."

Danielle rose. A blanket of hurt crept across her face. She wrestled to get words out. Her eyes darted around Lucia's head as if trying to catch a hummingbird.

"What is happening here?" Martina yelled. "Stop this nonsense." She turned to Faith. "Tell them to stop."

Faith flung her hands up in surrender. "I don't know what to do."

Lucia and Danielle dueled stares, fueling them with angry puffs of air that ransacked the usual peaceful air.

Faith had to hand a winning card to Lucia. Danielle did die a little along with Lucas. She poured herself into the kids and forgot about herself. She let her hair turn an unflattering faded shade of gray mixed with saltwater. No wonder her clientele dwindled. She never wore mascara anymore. She wore clothes that hung off her skinny body like a tablecloth. When did *she* last enjoy herself?

My God, Faith rose and turned into her sister.

"Danielle," Faith began. "They might have a point about both of us. We're one and the same. Only you had a husband that died, and I had one that got caught wanting to put his hands down Gilly's pants."

"It's very different." Danielle squared off with her. "Don't compare what I've been through with your small entanglement. Lucas and I had a full life. We did everything in the right pattern. We got married in a church before God. Then, we got pregnant."

A battle raged inside of Faith. "How dare you go there?"

Danielle fumed like a bull ready to charge.

Faith stood tall. "Just because I got pregnant and miscarried before getting married, doesn't make what I went through any less traumatic."

"Don't compare the death of my husband to your situation," Danielle screamed.

Faith steadied herself against the counter. "Don't scream at me." They were preteens again duking it out through frustrated tears and yells.

"You're angry because you've spent your entire life hiding from yourself. It's time you stop acting so childish and admit the fact you're a lesbian and that's why your marriage failed. Not because you failed."

The room blurred around them.

Danielle continued. "It's frustrating to watch you go down this spiral. You point the finger at everything else. This caused me to lose my job. This caused me to have a squirrel nest in my engine. The sangria caused me to say stupid things. Listen, until you stop blaming and start rebuilding, you're going to continue to get drunk and make a fool of yourself."

Faith's eyes twitched. She wanted to punch her sister. She wished she was ten years old again so they could wrestle on the carpet and have it be slightly less strange than it would be as adults. She would win the match that time, and not because of strength. Because she had to prove to herself she wasn't pathetic. That everything her sister said didn't ring true. That she could rise and rebuild a better life. That she wouldn't spend the next ten years wallowing in self-pity blaming Stuart for her failed life.

Danielle softened. "It hurts to see you do this to yourself."

Silence permeated the space.

Faith clenched her jaw.

"You lost your job not because Stuart cheated on you and no one wants to work with you now," Danielle continued. "You lost it because you didn't like it in the first place. A squirrel built a nest in your engine not because he wanted to piss you off. They build nests anywhere it's warm. You take precautions so it doesn't happen again. Husbands go for a jog and end up dead on the sidewalk from a heart attack at the age of forty. These things happen! That's life! It's illogical!" She tossed her hands in the air and began to sob.

A strange guttural sound escaped from Martina.

Lucia stopped blinking.

The silence around those sobs echoed against the pitched ceiling, then rained back down on them.

Faith trembled in the cold wake of her sister's outburst.

Each of Danielle's sobs wobbled like a wounded animal.

Faith couldn't bear another second watching Danielle suffer. She ran up to her side and placed her arm around her, stepping into the nurturing role for a change. "I'm so sorry." She rubbed Danielle's back.

Danielle grabbed a tissue. "I didn't mean to say it all like that."

They sobbed together under the golden lights of Danielle's sunny kitchen with the ticking of the grandfather clock's second hand playing a somber soundtrack to their dramatic sniffles.

Several agonizing minutes passed before any of them spoke. Then, Martina whispered, "You two are forgetting something important."

"Let them be," Lucia whispered back.

Silence hung.

Danielle's truthful words poked Faith's mind.

She and Stuart did get married because she was pregnant. They did it backwards from Danielle. Faith didn't want to be a single woman raising a child on her own. Then, fast forward and three miscarriages later, she finally carried to term with Bristol. She didn't marry him for the same reasons Danielle married Lucas. Danielle loved Lucas. Faith embarked on a crusade to have a baby.

"I hate when you're right," Faith mumbled.

Danielle leaned into her and chuckled.

"Ah, see, I knew you'd come around!" Martina cried in joy.

Lucia whacked Martina's skinny arm.

Danielle hugged Faith and stayed quiet. The need to fight and lash back soon melted, and was replaced with a quiet acceptance by Faith that she had a lot to learn in life.

"Can I speak now?" Martina asked.

Her earnestness comforted Faith in an odd way. "Go ahead."

"Instead of crying over the past, how about we plan for the future?"

Danielle sniffled. "That sounds like a good idea."

Martina puffed her chest out and gripped her waist, taking on her superwoman pose. "Faith, do you see yourself working behind a desk again?"

She'd rather have a house full of pet squirrels than go back to what she did. "It's what I do."

"You're getting good at cutting hair. Four people called this week to ask for you."

Faith laughed. "Four people are hardly going to put a roof over my head."

"No, but four people will turn into four hundred people. You beam the whole time you're with a client."

"Building a clientele takes time. And, I'm running out of that." The negative self-talk pinged around in her head. She sighed deeply, fighting against the whiney inner voice. "Though, the truth is that I do like it." She liked it more than anything she'd done. She liked the consultation, the artistic approach, the happiness on the person's face, the selling of retail products, and best of all, when the person left with a bounce in her step.

"What if you gained access to a full clientele right away?"

Faith wiped the tears from her cheeks. "Are you quitting?"

Martina pulled in her lips and darted her glance around everyone. "I want to." Her voice stretched out like a red carpet ready to introduce the world to her idea. "Gabe is popular. For a scientist anyway. He plays golf. Now his golf buddies want videos for their businesses. There's a need. I can fill that need." Her eyes grew larger. "I've already started work on creating my own video production business. I'm a natural at it. Well sort of. I have been staying up late every night learning." She traced a finger underneath her eyes. "Am I getting dark circles?"

Faith laughed.

She dropped her finger from her face. "I slip out. You slip in."

Danielle caught her breath. "I thought you enjoyed cutting hair."

"I hate cutting hair." Martina's face stretched into pain. "I don't like it. I never did. My hands get all cracked and my feet throb. It hurts to wear heels now. And, I love heels."

"If you hated it so much, then why did you spend so much time doing it?" Danielle's eyebrows arched too high.

"Because we're family, and you needed my help. That meant everything to me."

Tears began their descent down Danielle's cheeks again. "You should do what you love to do. Life is too short not to."

Faith glanced at the opportunity in front of her and examined it with scrutiny. She asked the logical questions because that's what a logical, responsible person might do in such a circumstance, right? Ask questions like, *am I taking a step backward or forward? What about all that time spent on my graduate degree? Had I wasted that time? I still have to mail a monthly check to pay off my student loan debt. Should I continue to travel the more prudent path and stay the course of my chosen public relations field? Though, the hairdressing world had proven great for Danielle. Could it prove just as great for me, too? Then again, would Martina's clients even want me as their stylist? I'm not Martina. I don't walk around in a constant state of animation. I have so much to learn. I need better equipment. What about health insurance? More importantly, how will I ever convince Stuart of such a move's practicality if I can't even convince myself?*

Prudence won. "I'd love nothing more, but..."

Martina stopped her with the hand. "No buts. Please no buts."

"My life is in Boston. Bristol goes to school in Boston. Stuart lives in

173

Boston. He would never agree to such a long-distance arrangement."

"He travels seventy five percent of his time. He's hardly committed to Boston," Danielle said.

"That's his job, though," Faith defended him.

"This could be yours," Martina said. "Why does he get to set his sail toward the great horizon? Why can't you knock him off and then set an open course?"

"Money."

Martina flipped her hands. "His money? Like that should matter."

"It helps with the child support," Faith said.

Martina rolled right past Faith's argument. "He's an hour and a half away if he drives fast."

Faith stood, brushing lint from her pants. "That's a lot to ask of him. That drive to Boston is terrifying. Drivers are crazy. I don't want to put Bristol in that kind of danger." The sensible mother in her found the logical argument and clung to it. "Besides I can't afford to live around here. Not even with Martina's clientele."

"You could live here," Lucia waved her hands around.

"I've already told her that." Danielle leaned in. "You have to admit that it's nice having the home full of family."

"I'm not going to move into your house. I'm enough of a failure as it is. Now you want me to siphon your resources too?"

"That's the problem with this generation," Lucia said. "You're all so worried about being independent. You want your big houses filled with furniture instead of family and friends. You want cars the size of small RVs so you can drive alone on the highway and be miserable instead of driving together and helping to keep our planet healthy. You want to eat in front of the television so you don't have to talk to each other. You want to work in silos so you can prove you're brilliant all on your own without anyone's help. If you ask me, independence is a crock of bullshit that hurts families and societies. Why is it so wrong to live together and share resources? Why does anyone need a four-thousand-square-foot home for two people? How much space does a person require to be happy? That's why everyone is so damned miserable. We have too much space to roam around and get lost in our minds. No wonder squirrels are confused and nesting in cars. They have no more trees to build their family a home because we've cut them all down to put up these crowded neighborhoods where we stuff oversized houses into what used to be nature's home."

Lucia tossed the dirty dishrag into the sink. "That's all I have to say. Now if you'll excuse me, I'll go do the independent thing and stare at my bedroom television all by my lonesome while you all get out of your own way."

She left on a huff.

"She has a good point," Danielle said, staring at the empty space she left behind.

Faith couldn't argue. "I suppose."

"I'm sorry, again." Danielle smoothed her hand over Faith's wrist. "I didn't mean to lash out earlier."

"I get it. It needed to be said. I needed to hear it."

"Meltdowns are good for the soul." Martina lifted her chin at them. "I feel better."

Faith and Danielle chuckled.

"Well," Danielle said, "Now that we've all had a chance to get our meltdowns over and done with, I guess I should put a load of laundry in the washer." She heaved a great sigh. "I do feel lighter."

# #

Not until later that afternoon, when the girls returned from their bus trip to the dance studio, did Faith remember to call Stuart back to tell him he could pick up Bristol for Block Island the next day.

Some kind of long-distance parenting team they'd be.

Chapter Eleven

Faith walked out to the mailbox and spotted Bristol walking her bike as the other kids sped by on theirs. Faith chuckled at the sight of Emmy obeying traffic rules by using her arm as a blinker prior to turning. She couldn't help but wonder how much more fun Bristol would have if she learned to stop being so afraid.

Once they came in for drinks and snacks, Faith asked Bristol to join her on the deck.

"Sweetheart, why don't you ask Emmy to teach you how to ride the bike?"

"No, Mommy. She'll think I'm dumb."

Faith began to braid Bristol's hair. "Don't be silly."

"I want to walk it."

Faith kissed the top of her head and hugged her, letting her silky curls fall out of the braid. "I want you to be happy when you're out there with them."

"I am happy, Mommy."

"I mean happy riding a bike down the street like all the other kids. You should ask Emmy. I bet she'd love to teach you."

"I don't want to. Don't tell her. Okay?"

Faith squeezed her tighter. "Of course I won't, unless you ask me to."

Bristol tilted her head up. "Promise me?"

"I promise. But, will you promise me you'll ask her when you're ready?"

"I pinky swear." She offered her tiny pinky, and Faith latched onto it with hers.

"Good." Faith kept her pinky wrapped in Bristol's for a moment longer. "Because you know what, sweetheart?"

Bristol looked back up at her with her innocent doe-like eyes.

"You deserve to be happy. Always."

"You do too, Mommy."

# #

That night, Faith played Monopoly with Emmy and Bristol to keep her mind off Candace dancing with the blonde goddess. That proved impossible because the girls talked about Candace for the entire game. They spoke about how she spoiled them with candies and smoothies. How she taught them dance moves. And, how they asked her to come to Bristol's and Danielle's shared birthday party at the end of summer.

Apparently, Lucia and Martina would be throwing a big bash.

Later on, as Faith lay in her bed trying to sleep, she thought of Martina's offer and imagined what life would be like if she went for it. It seemed too good to be true. Her luck, she'd accept the offer, package up her life in Boston, and on day one, her nightmare would come true. She'd forget to turn off a curling iron and burn the salon down.

She fell asleep a while later and dreamed of Candace.

She fed Faith grapes, and kissed her in between. The kisses led to a steamy interlude where they danced on puffy clouds. In her arms, Faith blossomed, opening herself up to a profound moment where Candace lay her down, straddled her, and explored her curves with awe. Her tongue took her to places she'd never traveled before. Faith woke on a startled breath, panting and buzzing from the realness.

The next morning, Faith lied to everyone during their dream analysis. "I

178

didn't dream about anything last night. Nothing to reveal."

"Well, I had a crazy one." Lucia reached for her notepad. "We were all naked. Everyone. The entire Orchard Pond community."

Faith stood up. "Okay, as much as I'd like to analyze that one, I need to get Bristol's stuff together for her trip with her dad."

"He'd be sad to know your breasts were perky," Lucia yelled out as Faith slipped into the safety of the kitchen. "Oh, and hey, mine were too!"

# #

A short time later, Stuart arrived wearing a colorful Hawaiian shirt, khaki shorts, and a fedora hat.

"I see Gilly has given you a makeover."

He took off the hat. "The hat keeps the sun off my face."

Had she poked a vulnerable, self-conscious spot? After all, he did now date someone much younger than himself.

He tossed the hat back and forth between his well-manicured hands. Always so meticulous about his nails, he never missed his weekly manicure appointment at the nail salon around the corner from the university. They even stocked his Blue Moon beer in their mini fridge. He always joked how that helped him maintain his masculinity as the manicurist filed and buffed his nails to a pretty shine.

Faith looked over her shoulder at the front door, waiting on Bristol. What was taking her so long to get outside? "So you'll be back in three days?"

"You bet."

"Is Gilly meeting you there?"

"She's not feeling well. Morning sickness, I think."

"Oh, what a shame," she said with too much sarcasm.

179

Bristol finally came running out the door and into her dad's arms. He lifted and spun her. "Ready for a three-day adventure?"

"Are we going to walk bikes again?"

"You bet we are."

"Oh, goody. Oh, and Daddy I can't wait to show you some new moves I learned at dance class."

"Dance class?"

"Yup! I'm taking Salsa lessons from Candace."

"Candace?"

"Yeah, Mom's new girlfriend. They went on a date. Mom got sick from eating seafood."

Faith froze.

He opened the back door for her, and then closed it. "Seafood poisoning, huh?"

Faith shifted her feet. "Yeah."

Stuart went over to the driver's door. "Candace?"

Faith dug her fingernails into her sides, clenching her jaw. Even divorced, she couldn't tell him her truth. All her words piled up on top of each other, cementing themselves into a doomful demise where they disintegrated before their release. "We're just friends."

Stuart studied her. "Huh. Okay." He opened his door. "Well then, I'll see you later."

"Yeah," Faith crossed her arms over her chest. "See you soon."

# #

After saying goodbye, Faith went to the salon to work with Martina on techniques. Martina's clientele ranged from teenagers wanting to have hair as

180

thick and trendy as Martina's to older women who favored curling irons and perms to their natural straight, wiry hair.

On the flip side of that, Danielle's chair always sat empty. Few clients called and asked for an appointment with her. The ones who did come in left looking older and less polished than when they arrived.

Martina caught Faith eyeing Danielle's client at the register. Her fresh bobbed haircut looked unfinished with a few strands falling past the sharp line of the squared cut. "She's growing tired of the haircutting aspect. She loves working the front desk, talking with the clients, selling them retail. If you ask me, now that Christian is on board and booked, and if you come on board, we'll see her ease into what she loves to do. She'll shine as a manager and hostess."

Faith watched Danielle laugh with her client, touching her wrist on a thoughtful word and offering her empathetic nods from time to time. She warmed up the reception area and smiled more when pouring someone a cup of coffee or packing up bottles of shampoo and conditioner into pretty gift bags.

As the day progressed, Martina taught Faith easier ways to fringe the bangs, highlight and lowlight, and add volume to even the thinnest of hair.

In between clients, they hung up new artwork that arrived that morning. Catering to local artists, Danielle agreed to showcase a new artist's work each month. Artists expanded their platform and the salon gained a new look every few weeks. That particular month, the artist was a woman who used photos to create a mosaic effect. Faith admired one picture in particular of two young girls smiling at a butterfly. "I'd like to hang this one near my station, if that's all right?" she asked Danielle.

Danielle gripped the frame in both her hands, extending her arms. "Your station. I like it. Has a nice ring to it."

# #

Later on, Faith and Martina went down to the lakeshore to sunbathe. They sat on beach chairs while Christian hung out with his little sister and her friend in the water.

Martina scooped up a handful of sand and let it filter through her fingers. "Stuart didn't like me before. Can you imagine how much he's going to hate me now if you decide to stay here?"

Faith studied the fine grains of sand falling from Martina's fingers. "It would be because he fears losing his daughter."

"So he *didn't* like me?"

"I didn't say that."

"You didn't tell me he did. Same thing. Even more powerful. But I don't care." She flipped her hair over her shoulder. "Like you beforehand, he didn't take time to get to know me. If he did, maybe he'd come around too."

Faith shrank in guilt. "I never had anything against you."

"It's okay." She cocked her head. "I like you now, too."

Faith's jaw dropped.

Martina put on her sunhat. "I'm going for a stroll. If Emmy wants a snack while I'm gone, can you tell her not to kick up sand all over my chair? I hate the way it scrapes my ass."

"Of course."

Faith leaned back against the chair and closed her eyes. She loved the way the sun warmed her face and how the soft sand tickled her toes. She wore a new tankini, and felt surprisingly sexy in it. She tapped her fingers against the chair arms, anxious to hang onto that peaceful feeling. But, it vanished before it had a chance to take any root. The nightmare from two nights before returned and pinched at her temples, causing her brain to hurt.

A few minutes later, Faith scanned the beach.

There before her, she spotted Candace strolling along the pathway wearing a colorful one-piece bathing suit. Pretzel trotted alongside her. They headed her way. With each of her steps forward, Faith's mind scrambled to devise some kind of excuse for her drunken state the other night.

"How's your head feeling?" Candace asked as she approached.

"Better now. Yours?"

Candace plopped down on Martina's chair and sand kicked up into the fabric. "Mine's been fine. I only had half of my sangria."

"Only half?"

"I should've warned you better about how potent it could be."

Faith stared at the soft lines around Candace's eyes. "I'm sorry you had to see me that way."

On a smirk, Candace looked down at the sand. "It's all right. But, you did seem pretty upset when Pat came up to us."

"Pat?"

"Yes. My friend, Pat." She drawled out the words as if trying to spoon feed them into Faith's stubborn mind.

"For a friend, she's quite flirtatious. Does she always toss herself at you like that?" The jealousy flamed on the edge of her words.

Candace repressed a chuckle. "Flirtatious, maybe. But, toss herself at me?" She shook her head. "The sangria may have played a critical part in that impression. Do you think?"

"Well, it tasted like punch, so in my defense, it snuck up on me. I don't get drunk like that."

"Don't worry. I've been there, too. It happens." Candace looked back down at her sandals, rubbing her legs with her long fingers. "One thing I noticed though, you didn't say much to me after Pat left."

"The liquor played a critical role in that, too."

She gazed up at her. "I was hoping it might've been a little more than that."

Faith looked into her beautiful dark eyes. "Really?"

Candace laughed. "You seemed jealous, and I found that to be kind of adorable."

A tingle swept up the back of Faith's neck. "Well, I mean who does that? Who goes up to a romantic looking table and throws herself at one of the guests? We could've been on a date."

"Weren't we?"

"You said we were friends. Friends don't date, do they?"

She sat up and pinched Faith's wrist. "You *were* jealous."

The tips of Faith's ears burned. She needed instant liftoff out of the wreckage. She dove into defense mode and prepared to evacuate the embarrassing disaster. "Hey listen, what you do and who you date and take to Latin dance parties is none of my business."

Candace cupped her hand around Faith's hand, and whispered, "As I had told you that night, she owns the dance studio. And, I don't want to date her. We really are just friends."

Faith nodded nonchalantly, then pulled her shades back over her eyes. "By the way, Martina's going to raise hell when she gets back here. You got sand all over her chair. She hates the abrasive feeling of sand on her ass, apparently."

"Then, I guess Pretzel and I will wait here to face her fury."

Faith scanned the lakeshore again. She noticed Emmy and her friend, along with Christian, splashing in the water a few hundred yards away.

Martina stood far away from them and yelled something, which intensified the rate of those splashes.

We really are just friends. Funny how a few words could erase the residue of a few ugly days of buildup.

Maybe Candace really didn't have any desire to date the blonde superwoman who could dance.

She let that marinate.

Slowly, the wad of jealousy in her gut dissipated. A hopeful flicker of light replaced it.

The sun beamed brighter than usual. It glistened on the waves and caused Faith's heart to bounce. The water had turned a prettier shade of blue. If she narrowed her eyes enough, the water resembled the teal blue of the tropics. In fact, the lake, which only a few minutes ago reflected the dullness of the overhead clouds, now sparkled.

Life waited on her to open her hands and accept the granted gifts. She needed to let go of blaming Candace for something she hadn't even done wrong.

Hell, a shiny new path glistened before her, one where Bristol giggled and spoke, her family gathered around the dinner table to eat *arepas* and, yup, even flaxseed muffins, and a creative career existed within feasible reach.

Things actually looked up.

Her hangover from two days ago had cleared, too, and thankfully didn't leave any permanent damage. At least physically. Finally, she could open her eyes without summoning a headache.

She took in the view. "This place is so peaceful." She breathed deeply and felt her soul shift into balance on the exhale.

"You have such a charming smile," Candace whispered. "Your whole being glows. It's incredibly sexy and beautiful."

Faith floated. Somehow, despite the detour from the other night, she ended up on the sunny side of the curve. She leaned back and hooked her arm over the back of the chair, gazing at Candace through relaxed eyes. "You know how to make a woman feel special."

Candace offered a satisfied sigh before half-closing her eyes and gazing out at the blue sky and colorful ripples on the lake.

Martina's overly-dramatic yelps from the water created just enough chaos to fill in the silent moments and remind Faith of the fun times she might uncover in the remaining weeks of her summer vacation.

"Should we go help Martina?" Candace asked.

"Nah." Faith lifted off the chair. She reached for Candace's hand. "I say we help Emmy and Christian."

Candace grabbed hold of Pretzel's leash. The three of them dashed toward the water, kicking up sand and giggling.

They played like kids.

Pretzel did, too. She jumped and chased a Frisbee that Emmy and her friend kept flinging toward the shore. When she got it in her mouth, she leaped and ran it back into the water.

Faith and Candace floated peacefully, watching the scene unfold.

At one point, Candace saved her from banging into the wooden pier. She hugged her from behind, cradling her arms around Faith's tummy in a tantalizing moment. Time suspended. The rest of the scene blurred around them. The sand at her feet softened even more, and the breeze delighted even the small hairs on her arm. And then, as if Faith's spirit hadn't ballooned enough, Candace whispered, "My heart races when I'm around you. What are you doing to me?"

Before Faith could respond, Candace dipped her shoulders into the water. She drew in closer, gathering her tightly in her strong arms.

Faith nuzzled against the softness of Candace's body. They treaded water as they watched Emmy and Christian antagonize Martina. She could've floated with her like that for eternity. Just stick a hose in the lake for access to clean drinking water and she'd happily live life as a mermaid falling for a yoga goddess.

Christian, Emmy and her friend dragged Martina into the water and got her hair all wet. She screamed like a little girl being chased by a mountain lion. Soon, Faith and Candace moved in closer to the group and together they all began splashing each other and swallowing water in between their laughter.

Faith basked in the delight of the lazy day.

By the late afternoon, Emmy and her friend asked if they could walk Pretzel around the lake. Candace handed off her leash to Emmy. "She will love it."

The three galloped off toward the pathway.

Faith and Candace gathered their belongings and headed back up to their respective houses.

"I haven't had that much fun in forever." Faith swung her arms and strode forward carrying her good mood like a prize. She might've even started to skip had she not turned around to find Candace a few paces behind, pulling in her bottom lip.

"What's wrong?"

Candace stopped walking altogether. "Faith, I'm wondering about something."

Her high shrank. "About what?"

"I'm curious where your heart is right now, and whether it's close to where mine is."

Faith dug her toes in the sand to stop the twitching of her upper lip. "Hopefully in the same place as yours."

"Do you want to just keep this to friendship?"

Friendship? What happened to the beauty in the water, hugging her and whispering sweet things into her ear? Had she inadvertently said or done something to upset her?

"Is that what you want?" Disillusionment congealed in her chest, blocking oxygen.

Candace stepped forward with a softness that sang a different tune than her words. She moved in and traced Faith's cheek with her finger. "I asked you first."

"Why would you ask me that?"

Candace studied her for a moment. "The summer is short, and I want to be sure we both know what we're getting ourselves into if we decide to take it a step further while we're here."

A long pause ensued where Faith stared at Candace and watched her eyes turn from serious to playful. The sun peeked through the trees lining the houses, and hinted of the warmth hiding somewhere in between their evolving circumstance. "I'm not exactly sure about much these days, but I don't want to let that get in my way."

Candace's face relaxed even more. The soft lines around her full lips turned upwards along with their mood. "I'm so happy you said that." Candace clasped Faith's hands and looked into her eyes. Her gaze went deeper than merely glancing in the window of her soul, but of actually opening up that window and stepping inside of it.

Faith wanted to kiss her. She wanted to taste her breath and indulge in her softness. She dropped her belongings, leaned in, and brushed her lips against Candace's cheek.

Then, flirting with the moment, Candace dropped her belongings, too. She led her into an intimate dance, carrying the weight of uncertainty for Faith and allowing her the opportunity to feel as sexy and beautiful as Candace believed her to be.

"What are you doing?" Faith laughed and looked around to make sure no one saw them.

Candace's energy uncovered a teasing and longing, and connected them as if by an invisible band. "This dance is called Rumba." Candace lifted her arm, leading Faith into a turn. Then, she pulled her back in close to meet face-to-face. "It's known as the dance of love."

Faith's heart beat in fast pulses. The air swaddled around them, cushioning them against the outside world. A small giggle found its way to the surface and floated in the space between them. Faith latched on for the ride, the kind of ride she'd experience right before going over the edge of a water slide, where her hair whipped behind her as she raised her arms in the air and screamed with delight.

"I thought you were serious about the *keep to just friendship* thing," Faith whispered, finally able to string together a few words.

Candace drew her closer. Her eyes relaxed and a look of desire pooled in them – the kind that hinted of a passionate kiss. "I wanted to be sure."

Faith melted as Candace's vulnerability bathed her in sensual joy.

"Come for dinner at my place." Candace lingered her gaze on Faith.

Their noses brushed, and then Candace's lips landed on hers as a feather might float against the sand, sensual and light, playful and brief. The soft kiss hinted of what could come had they not been standing on a public lakeshore under the blazing summer sun.

Chapter Twelve

The first time Faith had experienced an orgasm, she was twenty-eight and a new mom. She read an email from her bestie, Sally, and had an orgasm. Not about Sally, of course. About the woman on the centerfold of a magazine Stuart hid between a *National Geographic* book on polar bears and a book on how to build a deck.

Sally had confessed she fell in love with a woman named Natalie. They met through a mutual friend and connected instantly. They had been dating for three months and Natalie moved to Boston from New Hampshire to live with her.

Something opened up in Faith in the moments following that email. Her body lifted. Life rushed at her and she spun. Alone in her basement office, Faith came to life. Sexually charged by the news that her best friend was a lesbian lifted her from the chair and brought her to that magazine. She opened up to it and traced her finger down the woman's neck, collar bone, curve of her breast, roundness of her nipple. Faith's entire body buzzed.

Overcome by something wild and intoxicating, Faith continued to trace her finger down the woman's curvy waist and past her dark mound. When Faith's fingers landed between her thighs, she imagined the softness of her folds.

Faith trembled and lowered herself to the carpet. In the privacy of that basement, Faith explored her own body, imagining she was that model. When her fingers landed on her wetness, a warmth traveled through her. It started as a dream in her brain, the kind where she closed off the harsh outside world

191

and snuggled up under a pile of softness. Then, that warmth flowed into her heart and in between her legs. The heat heightened as Faith instinctively flicked her swollen folds. Each new flick created a fire between her legs. Soon, she floated high into the corner of the room. Her entire body trembled in a state of bliss Faith had never before experienced.

On that day, Faith discovered her true self. Like flipping on a light switch, Faith woke to a new reality. That reality was one where no man would ever satisfy her. Not even someone as nice as Stuart.

After that, she bathed in her oversized Jacuzzi tub most every night, reading romance novels about women in love, and not with men. She sprang to life in those moments when the pulse between her thighs quickened and responded in spontaneous spasms. It's where she sipped her expensive bottled wine from Argentina and ate seasoned crackers topped with port wine cheese. She stepped out of her mundane life void of romance and into a world overflowing with exciting rendezvouses with exotic, flirty women. They lifted her out of the dankness of insecurity and into the limelight of sexy and desirable.

Behind those bathroom walls, although fictitious in nature, Faith lived as her most authentic self.

Before long, Stuart accepted more travel with his job as an athletic recruiter for Harvard, and Faith encouraged him. That's when things fell apart.

He would return from his long road trips with eyes ablaze and a discernable swagger to his walk, and Faith didn't question it. To rock the boat would disrupt everything. Her home, her daughter, her friendships, her work life and balance. If she asked him about that mischievous smile, and he disclosed the truth, she'd have to do something about it.

Faith suspected there was someone else. A person could tell such things. He became extra friendly. Began working out more. Only wanted healthy foods in the house. Brushed his teeth a lot more. And even smiled differently, with a flirt. Though, Faith doubted Stuart meant that flirt for her. It had been something he'd picked up from the road, like a phrase or inflection heard often enough.

Now, many years later, Faith still didn't trust she had what it took to maintain the landscape of another person's heart. She had a lot of weeding to do in her life before she should consider any new relationship. But a fling? No reason to wait on something like that. A fling allowed her to be whomever she wanted to present. She always wanted to be confident and bold. You know, walk into a room and own it. Put on a pair of heels and dig into the floor like it owed her something. Stretch her neck a little more and appear stronger and wiser, like the superstars of movies did whenever they sat across from the media and showed off their quirky and lovable dispositions.

She stood before the mirror and examined herself. What she saw worked. The summer sun had tanned up the puckers around her butt and thighs. She glanced at her side profile and sucked in her gut. If she walked around without breathing, she might even look like someone who worked out.

Faith cradled her hands around her mid-section. All her life she avoided her tummy. She stuffed herself into slimming bodysuits and suffered gas pains to look a few inches thinner. Those suits eventually had to come off and reveal all they hid. What did they hide? Her?

Faith rubbed her palms over her tummy. She had spent her life disassociating from it. She covered herself up and pretended a part of her didn't exist. But, there she stood in the flesh, every last ounce of her. That tummy had been through everything with her. Yet, despite all the annoying

193

issues along the way, it still hung in there. Still wanted to experience the journey of being part of her.

She traced her finger around her belly button. "We're healthy, but more than that, we're sexy."

If she said it enough times, eventually it might sink in.

#

Faith knocked on Candace's door, and Pretzel barked. "Come in. It's unlocked," Candace yelled.

She opened the door and Pretzel twirled in circles, wagging her tail and whining. Thankful for the distraction, Faith knelt down and petted her.

She peeked into the kitchen and noticed Candace's cute yellow, polka-dotted sundress and black wedged sandals. She had primped for her, yet again.

Faith's tummy rolled. "I brought sparkling cider."

Candace appeared in the doorway to the foyer. Flour smothered her hands. "No sangria?"

Faith rose and hobbled over a sandal. She tossed it into the pile under the coatrack and continued toward the kitchen. "Likely never again."

Candace chuckled and headed back into the kitchen. "I'm running a little late. I wanted to have this pizza already prepped when you arrived. I bought salad fixings, too."

"You don't have to go to any trouble for me. We can have toast with peanut butter." Her voice shook. Her energy vanished. Her knees weakened.

"Make yourself at home," Candace turned back to her pizza.

Faith paced the kitchen, looking for something to do. She noticed the laptop on the counter opened up to a webpage with cartoon dancers and a list of songs.

"You look nervous. Are you?"

Faith shook her head no.

"How about some of that cider?" Candace motioned to the cupboard by her side. "There are glasses in there."

Faith rounded the kitchen island and reached into the cupboard. A minute later, she handed Candace a glass full of cider.

Faith raised hers. "To a great pizza night."

Candace clinked Faith's glass. "To pizza night." Her voice dripped with sex appeal.

What to do with the lure, Faith hadn't a clue.

Candace took a bowl out from under the kitchen island. "You're in charge of chopping the veggies." She took a knife down from the magnetic strip on the backsplash. "I'll finish the pizza."

Candace spread the sauce in long, nurturing swoops. Faith imagined the spatula as Candace's tongue against her skin. Faith turned away from the sight, but the flutters continued their travels through her.

"Oh, can you get the olive oil from the pantry? My hands are all pasty from the dough." Candace swiped some hair away from her face with the back of her hand. Lucky for the dough, it found its way to her face.

Faith wandered into the pantry. She could've fit her entire kitchen in it.

"Do you see it?"

She scanned the shelves. Canned beans. Gluten free pasta. Rice crackers. Organic tortilla chips and salsa. Olives. Pickles. Basmati rice. Bottles of wine. "Not yet."

Candace came up behind her. "Oh, here it is. She reached from behind and pressed up against Faith's back. She remained, and wrapped her arms around Faith. She folded her floured hands and rested them near Faith's navel.

195

The pantry blurred and all Faith wanted to do was turn and kiss Candace the way she wanted to kiss her on the lakeshore, with unbridled passion.

Candace rested her chin in the crook of Faith's neck, now circling her fingers around Faith's tummy and teasing her bare neck with warm, breathy tickles.

They began to sway in the tight space, and Faith let herself fall into her embrace. Candace placed her lips along Faith's neck, in the space right below her ear, and Faith trembled. She lost her sense of place as she had that first time she orgasmed at the sight of a naked woman in a magazine.

Faith's heart pounded and her throat began to itch. Candace caressed her with more intensity, showering her in affectionate kisses across the side of her sensitive neck. Then, Candace's fingers traveled down her neck and past her breasts in a slow, sensual move.

Faith's knees turned weak, and she lost her balance. She grasped onto the shelf and stared at a box of pasta noodles. An undeniable surge of endorphins coursed through her and before she could blink, the room blurred and her head swam in that sweet nirvana where everything turned hazy and tingly.

She was having an orgasm.

An orgasm in a pantry!

No! No! No!

Everything happened too quickly.

She didn't want their first time to be in a pantry. She wanted soft sheets and romantic music, and a candle or two.

She stilled herself, trying her best not to pant, to tremble, to hint she lost control before they even got started. Faith had no clue how to handle sex with a woman, especially one as sexually charming and adept as Candace.

Fear seeped in and soiled the moments that followed the rush.

"I can't," Faith said. "This is all too much."

Faith pushed past Candace, through the kitchen with their unmade pizza, past the picture of the beach at Camp Cronin, and straight out the front door. Pretzel chased after her, and ran all the way back to her sister's with her.

She heard laughter coming from the back deck. The house sat quiet, otherwise.

Faith dodged the steps three at a time, and Pretzel didn't miss a beat. She landed on an excited hop in Faith's room.

"What have I done?" Faith dropped her head in her hands and tugged at her freshly-styled hair. "What am I doing? I can't be shacking up with her." She looked at Pretzel whose ears flopped over and waited on her to toss her a sock or something. "My life looked promising, and now I'm twisting it up into a mess again." Faith tossed her head back in her hands.

Pretzel licked her face.

"I'm already attached and I only technically kissed her cheek." She stared into Pretzel's understanding eyes. "Well, all right, I lost control of myself in a pantry, too." Faith bent over and groaned.

She stood up and paced the room, and then called Sally.

"I'm an idiot."

"Yes you are. I called you three times since yesterday. Now it's too late."

"Too late for what?"

"I called you about a job, but you missed the deadline. It would've been perfect. We could've worked together at the Miller Center with the Success Program."

The Miller Center hosted international students from ten different countries, and ran programs to help them succeed by providing tutoring, counselors, and communication partners. "I don't want to work at the Miller

Center."

"Well beggars can't be choosers."

"I'm in deeper trouble."

"What did you do?"

"I ran away from Candace. Just now. She cradled me in her arms, and I ran away from her. All the way back to my sister's. Her dog followed me." Pretzel's ears perked.

"Why did you run away?"

"Because I acted like a nympho while staring at a box of pasta noodles. Gluten free no less. I don't want to be known as the pantry woman she once dabbled with one hot summer night in July."

"So now you're the woman known as the runaway?"

A heap of dread sat on Faith's shoulders.

"I had an orgasm while staring at pasta noodles, Sally. Who does that?"

Sally laughed. "You're my hero."

"Get serious, will you," Faith cried.

She laughed some more. She started coughing and hooting. "I am dying over here."

"Stop." Faith paced the room.

"You need to stop being so serious and let loose."

"There's no coming back from this. I left her hanging."

"Go back there."

"I can't."

"You're having a summertime fling. Why do you care so much? You're the lucky one who gets to experience one. You'll be out of there in a month anyway. So, enjoy yourself. Before long, you'll be back here hunting for a job. Big deal if you made a fool of yourself. You'll never see her again after this."

Faith stared out the window at Candace's sloped roof. "You do have a point." Pretzel grew tired of the drama and dropped to the ground on a thud. She rolled her eyes up at Faith. "I do have to get her dog back to her."

"There you go. Call me later to fill me in."

Faith hung up and sat down. She petted Pretzel's head. "I'll wait on you."

Pretzel jumped to her feet and twirled a few times.

"Why?" Faith flung her hands in the air. "Why are you so damned active?"

Pretzel yipped and leaped toward the door.

"Fine. You get your way." Faith stomped after, following her all the way down the stairs into the oddly quiet living space, through the front door, and back to Candace's house.

# #

Candace opened the door wearing a concerned frown. Pretzel strolled in behind her, strutting her little butt toward her water bowl.

They both watched her.

"So," Faith began, "I'm sorry I ran."

"I'm sorry I freaked you out."

"No, you didn't. I tend to do that all on my own." Faith shrugged, but that didn't massage the wrinkle of concern off Candace's face. "I shouldn't have run."

"You don't have to be afraid of me." Candace waved her into the foyer. "I'm sorry if I came on too strong."

Faith stepped into nurturing mode. "You did nothing wrong. I got nervous."

199

"Nervous." She avoided Faith's eyes, and turned her attention to Pretzel. She folded her arms over her chest, which didn't help the situation because now her cleavage expanded. "I make you nervous?"

Faith avoided her cleavage and took up refuge in the unfinished pizza. "I'm terrified."

Candace gazed at her with concerned eyes. "I terrify you?"

"I'm terrified because I'm out of my element. I have no idea what I'm doing. I don't know how to flirt. I don't know how to be sexy." She flung the words out. "And, I've never had sex with a woman."

Candace wandered her gaze around Faith's face, then reached for her hands. "It's okay."

"I'm basically a virgin, and I'm terrified to mess things up with you."

Her hands softened in Faith's. "I don't want you to be terrified."

Faith pulled her hands back. "I'm not wired for this whole fling thing."

"Fling thing?"

"We're not in positions to go beyond that. And, on top of everything, I'm embarrassed."

Candace opened her eyes wide. "Embarrassed?"

"I don't habitually orgasm in pantries. How did that happen? Beats me! That's the problem, right there. I'm out of control when I'm around you. I don't like when I can't stay grounded. What do I do with all the air under my feet?"

Her face relaxed. "You orgasmed?"

Faith looked for a quick getaway. The bathroom would offer a brief rest, enough time to collect her ego and put it back together again. "You didn't know?"

"You ran. When did I have the chance?" Laughter seeped into her eyes.

"It's not funny."

"No, it's not funny." A grin danced across her face. "It's adorable. It's honest. And, I understand." She walked over to the couch and sat down. "Come here."

Faith walked over to her and sat down.

"So, you've never been with a woman?"

The intimacy of the question caused Faith's insides to quiver all over again. "No." Faith lowered her head. "Well, not exactly. In my imagination I've been with them, a lot of them, if that counts?"

Candace stroked Faith's forearm. "A lot? So are you saying you're sort of a fantasy slut?"

Faith didn't know whether to laugh, cry, or flee again. She settled on pure honesty for a change. "I'm a fantasy slut, in the flesh."

A small grin crept across Candace's face again. "Imagination is everything."

She closed her eyes for a moment, trying to figure herself out and decide how much to reveal. Then, Candace reassured her with another soft stroke up her forearm.

Faith leveled a gaze on her. "I've never orgasmed with anyone present right up until an hour ago with you."

Candace drew in closer, spreading her warmth to Faith's freshly-opened core.

"It's crazy, right?" Faith giggled in spite of herself.

"So, you've never orgasmed with your husband?"

Faith swallowed dread. "Ex-husband, and no."

Candace lay back against the couch pillows, taking it all in.

The air conditioner turned on and eased the silence. Faith rested in its calming hum, praying it stayed on until she could somehow find a way to escape with her dignity still intact.

"Faith." Candace reached out for her hand. "Why did you run from me? Why do I scare you?"

Faith let her question sink in. "I've been working hard to get my life in order. Every time I turn around I mess things up. And, I like you. I'm not so much scared of you as I'm scared of messing this up because I enjoy being around you."

They both stared ahead at the enormous bookcase filled with classics like Huckleberry Finn and The Secret Garden. A statue of a naked woman holding a basket of bread stared back at them.

"So what do we do?' Candace asked.

Faith bit her lip. "We've already established that neither one of us are in a position to commit to anything here. I don't know about you, but I don't want to complicate things. We should keep things simple. Maybe we take it down a notch?"

"Just a notch?" Candace kissed her hand.

Her lips excited her command center all over again, causing all her faithful soldiers to rush in and isolate the flutters. No amount of defense would be able to stop the flurry. "Or two."

Candace caressed her hand. "I like being around you, too. My heart beats faster and I laugh more. When I spring out the door to come and see you, I'm like a kid on the first day of summer vacation. I'd like to continue spending the remainder of this summer with you, and if that means as just friends, then friends it'll be."

They remained reclined against the big pillows, staring at the swirls of the plastered ceiling. The silence formed a vacuum and sucked out the comfort and playfulness, leaving it a lonely, dried-up wasteland of unrealized potential.

Faith had no idea how to proceed from there. Do they eat the pizza? Do they drink the sparkling cider? Maybe add in some wine? But, could she drink wine and control her attraction? What was the alternative? Be kissed and orgasm in her embrace? Did she have any self-control at all? Would actual sex tease her with a similar rush of adrenaline as it did when Candace brushed her fingers across her skin or looked at her with those warm, gentle eyes?

Candace sat up and rubbed her hands together, plucking Faith up and out of her rapid-fire internal questions. "The pizza turned out like a brick. How about popcorn and a movie?"

That's what friends did, right? They ate buttered popcorn and watched a movie on Netflix when they tossed sex aside. "You get the kernels, I'll do the butter."

They leaped off the couch and headed toward the kitchen.

After a few minutes of making small talk about the beautiful summers in Rhode Island and Pretzel's crazy antics, they settled onto the couch and decided to watch *Grey's Anatomy* on Netflix, starting from season one.

By the third episode, Faith basked in the glow of comfort. Her eyes grew heavy. Candace had fallen asleep already, breathing in gentle rolls. Faith studied her beautiful features. Her nose sloped at a smooth angle, accentuating the plumpness of her cheeks. Tiny, diamond studded earrings adorned her delicate ears. And her almond-shaped birthmark, that sweet marking, snuggled against the hollow of her neck.

Candace looked so comfortable, like a spot of refuge along a winding, challenging path. Like any reasonable hiker would do, Faith decided to seize the opportunity to rest in the warmth of that comforting oasis. She lifted herself up and snuggled against her.

Candace's hand fell to Faith's lap.

Faith caught it with her own and cradled it, fondling her fingers one long stroke at a time. She started with her thumb, and then worked her way down to her pinky. Even her fingers were soft and smooth. She imagined what those fingers could do to her if Candace were awake.

Her body tingled, as Candace's pouty lips stretched upwards gently.

She was like a soulful song, light and expressive. She took other people's daughters on a bus trip to teach them dance steps. She pet sat and accepted the help of a stranger to replace a broken screen so the dog wouldn't escape. She laughed at Lucia's and Marina's jokes and would rather spend time on their deck than lounging alone in that big, gorgeous, art deco home with wine bottles from all over the world. She agreed to be platonic because she enjoyed her company and respected her enough to keep her comfortable.

Faith's admiration for her ballooned. It took over the entire room, filling it with a sense of awe. Nice people existed who liked spending time with her doing things like watching marathons of the drama-infused derelicts on *Grey's Anatomy*. Could the world be a nice place after all? Maybe somewhere down the road the curves she encountered might lead her somewhere other than heartbreak and frustration.

Maybe squirrels would stop nesting in her car now and black mold might stop feasting on her plaster walls. Maybe she'd end up building a successful clientele, and then live happily-ever-after in a lake house full of family. Or maybe somewhere down the line the universe would open up room in her life and allow her to indulge in the fantasy, even if for one night, that someone like Candace wanted to take a risk with her.

One night.

What if that's all they had? Did she want to waste it? The opportunity might not be there the next day. In that moment, under the soft caress of the overhead track lighting and the scent of popcorn still lingering in the air, the opportunity waited on her to act. It dangled in front of her in that living room, on that couch, in that pocket of air that swaddled them.

That moment could be her chance to toss caution to the wind and embrace one of the most romantic opportunities of her lifetime.

In good conscience, how could she ignore it?

Powered by something stronger than her fears of the unknown, she leaned over and kissed Candace's lips.

Candace stretched. "What are you doing?"

"What if tonight was the last night of our lives?"

"Are we expecting an asteroid to hit?"

Faith feathered her lips against hers. "If so, would you want to watch television?"

Candace's lips swayed against hers, "We don't have to, Faith. We can talk instead." She placed her finger in between their lips. "I can be a good friend."

"I have enough friends, and they can't give me what I want right now."

Candace kissed her back with a hunger. "We can watch something different."

Faith drank from her smiling lips. "Are you not enjoying this kiss as much as I am?"

"Are you crazy?" Candace covered her in tiny kisses, followed by sweeps of her tongue around the ticklish part of her neck and down to her collarbone.

Faith traveled down her arms. Candace's muscles contracted and trembled. The heat from her silky skin warmed Faith's hands. She found her way under Candace's sundress and traveled across her taut belly, circling her navel, and then finally up farther to explore the beauty that awaited. Faith caressed her full breasts, and then massaged her erect nipples.

Candace moaned, and then she sat up and gathered Faith in her arms to pull her up and off the couch.

She guided Faith through the living room and up the landing to the second floor, to the master bedroom. To that gorgeous luxurious room with the creamy carpets and comforter.

Candace eased her down and straddled her, staring deep into her eyes. Earnestness took over, tossing aside all fears and what-if questions as Faith answered Candace's calling with a passion all her own.

Candace explored Faith's body with slow, mesmerizing caresses, smoothing her hands over her curves and taking her in with a beautiful, lazy smile.

Her finger slid under the edge of Faith's string bikini undies and in one intoxicating and liberating move, she eased them down her thighs and off her legs. They flew high across the room and landed before the doorway. Far away from being a distraction any longer.

Faith giggled and Candace drank it up with her lips, pressing into her and sealing them into a steamy interlude where no one and nothing else in the world mattered but the two of them sharing that incredible moment.

"You're a beautiful woman, Faith," Candace whispered.

Faith melted under Candace's sultry and irresistible regard.

For the first time in Faith's life, she forgot about her insecurities and let herself fall into the sweet embrace of vulnerability.

In the comfort of Candace's arms, Faith found her true self.

They engaged in a soulful dance, moving to the beat of an intimate song meant for them. Candace led Faith into a most enticing and intriguing sway, where the hard lines of reality faded into the soft edges of a dream. In that dream, Candace created a virtual cozy spot where they could dance without distraction under the warm glow of their passion and fed by their hunger to be closer. Cocooned in that surreal comfort, their souls swooned to the music. With each new inch explored, they moved in gentle rhythm.

Candace kissed her elegantly, her lips in tune with the slow and steady cadence of their bodies. Then, a fiery urgency drove her moves, like someone wanting to up the tempo and lose herself in the erratic instruments that livened it.

Candace filled her with a series of intoxicating sensations, intensifying the heat of their mingled breaths.

Candace was soft, and not at all subtle. She took charge of their journey, inviting Faith along the unknown path to somewhere delicious and exciting. Candace explored Faith's skin with great respect, stopping along the way to admire a freckle, a contour, inviting Faith to enjoy every move, every sweep of her hot tongue as she traveled down toward Faith's most personal space. Her tongue embraced every imperfection with ease and safety, calling Faith into the euphoric place she longed to experience her entire life, the place no one had yet to take her.

Every caress invited her to indulge in the pleasure of their entangled bodies. Faith floated like a woman wearing a gorgeous red dress of her own, being swept across the dance floor by someone skilled in how to move, how to pause, and how to bring her to pleasure with her loving and gentle touch.

"Candace," Faith whispered, "You're so good at this."

Candace caressed Faith's belly and continued leading her in that soulful dance that curled her toes and arched her back and caused her to moan from deep within, from a place so raw and real, that she could taste the joy on her tender, sensitive tongue.

With that, Faith allowed herself to let go and be swept up into the romance. Her heart lifted as she handed it over to Candace's loving care. She savored the euphoria, taking the time to indulge as she let her take her anywhere she pleased.

Chapter Thirteen

Faith returned to her sister's, floating on a cloud she never wanted to leave. She plopped down on her bed and marveled at how the sun teased the edges of the plastered ridges on the ceiling. The room looked sunnier than she remembered, too. Even the wicker furniture took on a new shine, not looking as dull and faded as it looked one day before. She rolled over on her tummy and placed her chin on top of her folded hands. She delighted at how far those fingers had journeyed and what pleasure they gifted to Candace.

All that worrying about not having the experience. For what?

She stared into the picture hanging above her dresser of a cottage with an archway porch and a wide path full of blooming lilacs. She always hated that picture when it hung in their parent's living room. It came from someone's junk pile. Like Stuart, her father loved picking other people's junk and making it his treasure.

If she looked closely enough at the right hand corner, she could see the sun poking through the large trees that shaded the blooms in the hottest part of the day. The sun always hung out, a constant companion shining its light on the cottage. For some reason, she never noticed it until then.

She swam in a pool of surreal joy. So much had just happened. She needed to tell someone. So, she picked up the phone and called Sally.

"I did it! I had sex with Candace!"

"You slept with Candace?"

"I did!"

They squealed like little kids on the Christmas Eve.

"I have good news, too."

"Tell me!"

"We bought a house. We close next month!"

They squealed again.

"I'm sleeping over her place again tonight. She's making me lasagna! Bristol is with Stuart at Block Island."

"With the bimbo, too?"

"She's technically not a bimbo."

"Wow, you're in deep with Candace."

"Bristol likes Gilly. She speaks to her, so that's something."

"She speaks to Candace. So that's something even more. Life is really coming together for you!"

"It kind of is, isn't it?"

"Don't let anything steal the mojo."

"Deal."

# #

Faith entered Danielle's kitchen carrying her joy. The brewed coffee took on a new scent, a richer, bolder, livelier one. It even tasted better. No more bitterness on the tail end of a sip. Hell, she didn't even need creamer.

Cheers to sex and orgasms!

She rested her chin on her hand, tiptoeing through the pleasures of the night before. Her posture straightened. Her hair fell in softer waves on her shoulders. Her lips plumped up. Her eyes focused better.

Love.

She felt loved, admired, and at ease with herself.

She wanted more. She wanted to experience the highs of more orgasms.

She wanted to have more sex, for the first time ever.

Did sex do that to everyone? She'd avoided it all those years. What an oddball! She spent decades hiding from it, rolling her eyes whenever Stuart hinted. Sex turned into a chore, like washing the kitchen floor or scrubbing the toilets and shower of mildew and soap scum. She had learned to dread it.

Not with Candace. She could spend the rest of eternity curled up in that woman's arms, writhing under her in ecstasy. Why did people do drugs when sex offered a shiny alternative with the enhanced features of euphoria? Sex with Candace lifted her out of her dull reality and into the dreamy upper atmosphere where stars blazed.

Lucia entered the kitchen wearing a purple, polka-dotted head wrap and humming a song. Emmy and Christian tossed pillows at each other and one knocked over the ugly statue of the giraffe. It broke in half on the floor, and its short neck sat in the middle of a pile of plaster crumbles. Lucia cried, "No, not Charlie!"

Charlie?

She ran over to it and crouched. She cradled it in the palm of her hands, like it was a bird knocked down by the blades of the ceiling fan. She cried into it, and Emmy, Christian, and Faith stood silent.

Her cries grew higher. Faith looked to Emmy and Christian to do something. Lucia was their grandmother after all. They looked scared, backing away as if they themselves took the neck of that giraffe and broke it with their bare hands on purpose.

Faith lowered herself to Lucia and placed a hand on her shoulder. "It's going to be okay." She picked up a piece of the mangled giraffe and Lucia slapped her hand down.

"No. Please leave me alone."

211

Faith looked to Emmy and Christian again, and they bit their lips.

"I can help you put it back together again. We'll just need some glue."

She whimpered. Giant tears rolled down her cheeks. "This was all I had left of him."

Faith scratched her head, uncomfortable with nurturing a woman over a broken piece of plaster. "All isn't lost." She patted her shoulder, eyeing the chards and willing them to put themselves back together again so she could get Lucia to stop whimpering and Emmy and Christian could stop biting their lips.

"How can I help?"

"You can't." Lucia cradled her hand around the giraffe's broken eye.

Faith's knees began to ache.

The front door slammed open and then shut. In came Martina carrying a grocery bag from the organic market. "I'm here and I'm ready to make Tamales." Her voice came out as a song. "I found the juiciest tomatoes. Of course, don't tell the neighbor." She laughed.

She placed the bag down and gasped at Emmy's scared face and Christian's dropped jaw. "What's wrong? What happened? Did someone die?"

She turned to face Faith and Lucia, and then screamed. "Oh my God!" She ran over to the carnage and kneeled.

Impatient, Faith stood up. "Okay somebody tell me what the hell is happening here."

Everyone cupped their hands over their mouths in sync the way one would if told someone had died in a car wreck.

Martina turned to Emmy and Christian. "Who did this?"

They pointed at each other.

212

"They were playing," Faith said, afraid for them. "Like they always do."

Martina pointed to her. "This does not concern you."

Faith backed away.

Lucia lowered Martina's pointed finger. "She's right. They were playing. They didn't mean it."

Martina stared at the wreckage with sorrowful eyes. "This was Lucas's favorite."

Poor Lucas, to be remembered by a statue; a piece of inanimate plaster with no beating heart, no laughter, no words. It was chalky, heavy, and ugly.

"My God," Martina sat back on her knees. "My psychic told me to watch out for signs. What if Lucas is trying to tell me something?"

Always about Martina. Why couldn't Lucas be talking to one of his children or his mother? Why would the first sign of his spirit be to his sister?

"Like what?" Lucia asked concerned.

Their drama suffocated Faith at times.

"Well, I'm dating Gabe. Maybe he doesn't like Gabe? Does he see my future as a homemaker wearing an ugly nightgown with stupid flowers all over it and wool stockings? What if I'm sleeping next to him in those pink spongy curlers? Or worse! What if Gabe eventually blows up in a lab? It could be anything."

"Wow, yeah, it could." Lucia's straight face worried Faith.

"Oh, come on." Faith couldn't take it. "Statues break. Accidents happen. They were tossing pillows."

Martina's eyes flew open. "He loved pillow fights." She turned to Christian. "He loved them, didn't he? Remember you used to drive your mom crazy because you screamed and he screamed and she feared one of you would roll over and bump your head and crack it. Don't tell me that's not true. I remember. I remember everything."

He lobbed his head up and down in agreement.

Faith remained the only sane person in the house.

"Or," Martina yelled out as if solving the great mysteries of the universe. "What if Lucas is trying to tell me this video business is a bad idea." Her hand flew to her chest as if things finally dawned on her. As if Lucas had whispered the secrets of the afterlife.

Faith couldn't take another second of the ridiculousness. She went over to the statue and carefully placed its broken pieces in a plastic bag. "Pillows were tossed. Gabe is a nice person and treats you well." Faith placed the neck of the giraffe next. "As far as this video business, it's brilliant. So, if you want to sit on the sidelines and decipher messages from your psychic, and miss out on life, then you're crazy."

Suddenly, life with all its twists and turns dawned on her. She was no different than the giraffe. The best thing for it was to break. Like she did. She couldn't put herself back together if she had never broken. "It's time to pick up the pieces and move on."

"You're mean." Martina snarled.

"I'm realistic."

Martina eyed her, sniffing her out like a dog on the hunt. "You're different." Martina folded her arms over her chest. "What happened? What's different? Why are you carrying around this smirk?" She waved at Faith's face in disgust.

"It's called a glow." Lucia climbed to her feet on a groan. "Something she earned the right to wear."

Self-conscious, Faith stopped collecting piles of debris. "It's the sun. I got too much yesterday."

"You had sex, didn't you?" Martina asked on a lighter note. She punched her arm with a little too much force. "You did. You had sex with her. You're glowing."

Faith shot Martina a glare. "We're not discussing that right now."

"Gross" Emmy said, twisting her face again. "I'm out of here."

Christian followed.

"Get back here," Lucia said.

They stopped short before the sliding door.

"Get the broom and the dustpan. Faith is right. We need to move forward from this. So together, as a family, we clean this up."

They did as instructed. Faith backed away and allowed them the dignity to clean up the dust as a family.

"Why are you just standing there?" Lucia asked her.

"I don't want to get in the way. I'll put on some water for tea."

Martina pointed at her. "You're as much a part of this as we are. Finish what you started."

Despite the rudeness in her tone, Faith took Martina's words as a compliment. It had been a long time since she belonged to a family. For so long she tried to liven her house up into a home. But, the light never shined right. The furniture dampened the cozy vibe. The air never flowed. The negative energy overpowered her. But here, amongst all the oddball differing personalities, Faith was home. She knelt down with the family and picked up the pieces to part of their brokenness.

It wasn't long though, before a flush of heat raced across her face, brought on by not only the peace in her heart, but the memory of Candace's scent and the promise of what would come that very night on their second date.

#

As Faith prepped for the day ahead, Stuart called. "I tried to withdraw money from Bristol's bank account. She has no money left in it."

Faith dropped her mascara wand on the sink. It left a black smear. She wiped it away with the back of her hand, and then she put him on speaker phone. "It's not empty. I put her allowance in it on Friday. She has a balance of four thousand dollars. And why on Earth are you making a withdrawal?"

"It's empty. Trust me. And because she wants to buy a gift."

"Stuart, that money isn't for gifts. We've talked about this. She needs to learn how to save, and, once in a while, make a donation. That money will help her buy a car one day. We can't hand over the keys to a shiny new red sports car and think she's going to learn the value of what it means to be responsible. Kids who are handed stuff like that turn out to be reckless. I don't want her to be reckless." Faith wiped a spot of mascara from underneath her lower lashes. She always managed to get some right where her finger couldn't fit.

"The gift is for you."

Faith stepped back from the mirror and bowed her head. "Still, Stuart. We can't let her do that."

"The teller confirmed someone withdrew the remainder of the funds last week."

"Withdrew? By whom?"

"I hoped you'd tell me."

"Someone stole her money?"

He sighed. "Yeah. It appears so."

"Well, can we get it back? Doesn't the bank have some protections with something like this?"

"They said we withdrew the money from the ATM several times over the

216

past two weeks. The ATM is in Rhode Island."

"From the ATM?" Faith ran over to her desk and opened up her briefcase. She shuffled through papers and books to the place she usually kept the checkbook and debit card for Bristol's account. "The debit card isn't here." Panic coursed its way up her spine. "Stuart, we brought her debit card here. Where did it go?" Faith panicked.

Just one more thing to fuck with her. Always one more thing around the corner.

Shuffling and clanking filled the background. Then, finally Stuart's soft voice returned. "Bristol, sweetheart, did you take the debit card from Mommy's briefcase and use it?"

What a ridiculous question.

"Yeah it's in my room."

"Here, you mean?" he asked.

"No. At home."

"No," Faith said. "Tell her we brought her checkbook and debit card here to the lake house. We didn't leave them at home. We had the checkbook two weeks ago when she donated five dollars to the animal shelter here."

He relayed the message.

"No Daddy, it's at home. My new home."

"You mean Aunt Danielle's?"

"Yes. In my sock drawer like you always tell me to do."

"I'll check." Faith darted across the hallway to Bristol's room and opened up her sock drawer. She rummaged through her ankle socks and there it sat at the bottom. "Oh, it's here." Relief spilled through her.

"I don't understand then. How did someone get her debit card and withdraw multiple times?" Stuart asked.

That little pin prick of a hole in her happy bubble grew too quickly, causing her to lose balance. Had their daughter turned into a little thief over the summer? "Can I speak with Bristol?"

Stuart's voice grew more distant. "Now tell her the truth, Bristol. No one's going to get mad."

"Hi, Mommy."

"Hi, Sweetheart. Listen to me, okay? You're not in trouble. We won't get upset if you tell us the truth."

"Okay."

"Can you tell us if you went to the bank and got some money out from the machine?" She rolled her eyes at the absurdity of a seven-year withdrawing funds from an ATM. Had she stolen a car, too? Maybe went for a joyride along Narragansett Beach with the four thousand small bills she collected. Maybe stopped at the liquor store, too, and bought herself a jug of Merlot and a pack of cigarettes?

"It was Emmy's idea."

The blood drained from her face and pooled at her toes. She sat down, attempting to balance herself with wobbly hands. "Now tell the truth, sweetheart."

"I am," she yelled. "I'm telling the truth."

Faith steadied herself, sitting taller and rolling her shoulders a few times to work out the kinks. She could imagine Stuart pacing the floor, steam rising out of the top of his head, flames shooting out of his eyes.

One more spark to the kindling. Fantastic.

"Okay, calm down," Faith said. "No one needs to yell. Tell me why you and Emmy withdrew the money."

"She said it would help."

Faith began to hyperventilate. "Would help what honey?"

"Keep the girl quiet."

"The girl?"

"Yes the girl."

"Can you put your daddy on the phone again?"

Stuart greeted her with an exaggerated sigh. "I don't want Bristol to spend any more time down there. It obviously hasn't been a good influence."

Flashes of light appeared in Faith's peripheral. The beginnings of a hell-banging migraine. Her warning sign. Her visual aura or whatever the stupid doctor said. She ran to the bathroom and dug her migraine pills out of her makeup bag. She swallowed two without water, and then cupped her hands under the faucet to wash them down better. "I'm sure there's an explanation."

"Your niece stole money from our daughter. How much more evidence do you need that there's a problem? She's not safe there now. Martina probably put her up to this."

A heaviness sat on her chest constricting her airway. "Martina is a nice person and a good influence, so don't you dare go there."

Stuart sighed.

Faith panicked about their future.

I don't want to go back to Boston. I'm turning into a skilled stylist. Martina wants to hand me a clientele. I will finally be able to sleep at night because I can provide for myself and my daughter and be happy at the same time. I'm supposed to move to Rhode Island and have real live orgasms with a woman named Candace, who by the way, I'm pretty sure I'm falling in love with. Her arguments jumbled up like a traffic jam, one piling on top of the other in a mad frenzy to escape the wickedness of a brewing storm.

She cupped more water in her hands and drank to clear the blockage. "I want to hear the rest of the story."

"Fine. She's on speaker with us now."

"Bristol, sweetheart," Faith said, using her calmest voice.

"Mommy. It's not my fault."

"We know it's not," Stuart said.

"It's not Emmy's either."

"You don't have to defend her," Stuart said.

"She helped me," Bristol whined. "She's my friend."

"Of course she is, sweetheart," Faith said, straining not to cry.

"A friend doesn't steal your money," Stuart said.

"She didn't steal it. I took it."

Stuart cleared his throat again the way he always did when losing grounding on a debate.

"Why did you take it?" Faith asked softly.

"To pay the girl."

"What girl?"

"The girl from school."

Long pause. "From dance school?" Faith managed to ask. Please not another roadblock.

"No, Mommy. The girl who hits me at school."

They both gasped. Someone could've pulled the heart right out of her chest and it wouldn't have hurt as much. "A girl hits you at school?"

"Yeah." Her voice came out as a puff of air.

"Sweetheart, it's okay." Stuart said softly. "Everything is going to be okay."

Was it? How could he be so sure? Life according to the man who had everything aligned. A job, a girlfriend, a baby on the way, an understanding ex-wife who didn't sue him for alimony, a nice apartment, a car with no nest-infatuated squirrels.

"Why did she hit you?" Faith asked.

"Because I answered questions at story time." She spoke so low, Faith had to take her off speaker and press the phone to her ear to hear her.

"Story time?" Faith asked. "Did you say story time? Like in kindergarten?"

"Two years ago?" Stuart fired the question before the poor kid could answer the two before it.

"And now, too. She doesn't want me to ever talk she said."

Faith fumbled against the bed. She studied the plaster swirls in the ceiling. So many bumps, hills, and valleys. Couldn't things just be smooth? "So she keeps hitting you?"

"Yeah."

"Why do you want to pay her?" Stuart's voice rose to incredulous levels.

"Emmy thinks she'll stop hitting me."

"Well, paying her off isn't the answer," he said.

Faith hoisted herself up to a sitting position, relieved Emmy didn't turn out to be a bully and stealer. "Emmy's a good friend. But, sweetheart, Daddy's right, you can't pay the girl."

"Where's the money now?" Stuart asked with a gentler tone.

"Emmy told me to hide it under the porch in her safety box. She says the rain won't get to it that way, and if the house catches fire, it won't burn too badly."

Faith stretched her neck, working out her new kinks. "We'll talk to your teachers. This girl will never bother you again."

"Do I have to go back to school there?"

221

"It's your school, sweetheart. And, you have to go to school," Stuart said. "But, don't worry. She won't bother you again. We promise."

"Daddy and I will talk. Everything's going to be okay."

"Why can't I go to school in Rhode Island? Emmy goes there. Then I can dance with her and Candace still."

Faith squeezed the bridge of her nose wanting so badly to make everything okay for her daughter.

"You can dance all you want, sweetheart," Stuart said. "We'll all discuss it when we're together."

Faith dropped her head into her free hand and eased into a deep, long restorative breath. "I trust I'll see you tomorrow, then?"

"See you then," Stuart said, then a second later added, "You're off speaker now."

"Was there something else you wanted to discuss?"

"I just wanted to say that I'm sorry," he whispered. "I went a little overboard. I didn't like the fact that Bristol would be spending so much time with Danielle's family. Martina is so brash and Emmy is a little diva. Then this happened. I just want Bristol safe."

"She's safe here. Everyone is good to her."

"I can't stand to think anyone is messing with her, that's all."

Faith softened. "I understand. We want what's best for her."

"That's it, yes." He paused. "We'll talk tomorrow about next steps." Then he added, "If that's okay."

Faith sealed her eyes closed. "Yes, that would be fine."

Chapter Fourteen

"Wear this tonight," Martina said, wiggling the colorful dress in the doorway.

Faith laughed. "I'm about three sizes too large for your dainty little dresses."

Martina emerged in the doorway wearing an apology on her face. "I acted rude earlier."

"Seems to be the theme of the day."

She cocked her head.

"Forget about it." Faith waved off the apology. "You know what I need right now?"

Martina dropped to her bed and sprawled out. "Please say a huge scoop of vanilla bean yogurt with candy on top. You won't have to twist my arm to tag along."

"I was going to say a drink. A tall drink."

"I knew you were going to say that. I heard everything with Stuart and Bristol."

"You shouldn't be eavesdropping."

"It's a small house. We're a tight family. That's what happens here." She propped herself up and cupped Faith's face in her hands. "You're a good mother. And even Stuart knows it."

Emotion overcame Faith. Tears spilled from the corners of her eyes, leaving her less heavy. "Well, you're a good person. I hope you realize it as well."

"I know I am." She lowered her hands. She sighed and walked toward the door. "I'm not in the mood for a tall drink, though. Now, I want to take a walk." She turned to face Faith and a sadness overcame her usual happy face. "Is that okay?"

"Of course." She paused. "Are you okay?"

Her chin quivered, and then the tears rolled. "I pretend I don't care, but I do. It hurts that people don't like me."

"People are stupid. They decide on things without knowing all the details. You've got a good heart, Martina. The people that matter know that."

Her eyes brightened. "That means a lot. Thank you."

"That's what family does. We tell the truth."

Martina sprang back to life. She raised her chin. "This is a good family."

"The best."

"I'm going for that walk now." She pranced through the door and looked back. "You're welcome to join me if you want."

If Martina was anything like Faith, she needed some alone time to sort through her feelings. "I want to chill out in my room for a while. Maybe read a book or something."

"All right then." Martina waved to her. "If I don't see you, have fun with Candace tonight. Everything's going to be all right with Bristol. Everyone's looking out for her. Trust in that."

She believed her. "I will."

# #

An hour later, while sitting on the deck with Danielle, Faith filled her in on Emmy, Bristol, and the money.

"I'll have a frank talk with Emmy about how she should've come to one of us."

224

"She was being a good friend to Bristol," Faith said. "You've raised a beautiful daughter, Sis."

Danielle's forehead smoothed. "Thank you. Her heart's always in the right place."

Faith cradled her sister's wrist. "And we all know that."

"Poor Bristol. I can't imagine how scary being bullied must be." Danielle gripped a book in her hands.

"Well, at least now we know the root cause of her not talking. We're going to make sure she's never put in that position again."

Danielle nodded. "She's lucky to have you and Stuart as parents." And on that, she looked down at her book and began to read.

Faith pulled the rim of her sunhat down and closed her eyes, easing into the peace of the moment.

A few minutes passed and then Candace called Faith. "I'm so sorry, but I have to cancel our date tonight."

Disappointment pooled. "Is everything okay?"

"Oh, yeah, everything's fine. It's just that Pat needs my help with a dance event tonight. She's in a desperate position."

The wad of jealousy returned. "Okay, no problem." She tried her best to sound nonchalant.

"You're welcome to come and participate in the event, if you'd like."

Candace's sincere tone softened the wad, instantly. A smile spread across Faith's cheeks. "I don't want to get in your way. I'll take a raincheck instead."

"Well, I'm dying to see you again. Can I take the raincheck for tomorrow?" Candace asked. "I don't think I could last more than that."

"Yeah. That should work."

"I miss you," she whispered. "Really, really miss you."

"Me too."

"I might be sounding sort of desperate here, but, I should be home by eleven tonight. Can I call you and see if you're up to swinging by?"

Her heart fluttered. "That would be amazing."

"I can't wait to see you again," Candace whispered. "Until then, I'll just be replaying last night in my mind over and over again. I'll call you later." She hung up on a sexy tone.

Faith fell back against the lounger on an exaggerated exhale.

"What was that all about?" Danielle asked, putting down her book.

A smile grew on Faith's face. "She had to cancel dinner because she needs to help a friend."

Danielle tilted her head to the side. "You seem oddly happy about that?"

"I may see her later on." Faith stroked the chair's arm, lingering on the memory of Candace's sweet breath and softness.

"Why don't you come with me to my book club to make the time move faster? I'm picking up some pastries. We can get those cake things you like with the powdered sugar on them."

"No thanks."

They sat in silence for a few minutes, and then Danielle slammed her book shut. "I've been trying to read this trashy romance for the past month and I'm tired of reading about how well-endowed a certain character is and how faint another one is every time she lays eyes on him."

"Oh."

"Fuck the book club. Let's you and I go out tonight. A sister date! We'll make the best out of it. Embrace the curveball!"

"You just said fuck."

"I did."

A surprising deep giddiness rushed through Faith. The last time they went out on the town was her bachelorette party when Danielle treated her to a Garth Brooks concert. They filled up on beer and nachos at a pub, danced and sang at the top of their lungs to Garth's brilliant lyrics, and then ended the night with huge slices of Pecan pie at Greg's Restaurant on the East Side of Providence. Five pounds heavier and filled with giggles, Faith had slipped into her bed that night wearing a peaceful smile. That was probably the last time she had felt in harmony with herself.

"I'd love to." Faith perked up in her chair.

"We'll embrace the night at a charming seaside restaurant that serves salads with shrimp in a giant tortilla bowl. Then we're going to have a drink and tell stories. We'll laugh so hard we may even pee our pants. Deal?"

Faith could make lemonade out of lemons like Lucia, too. "That sounds incredible."

"Cheers to a canceled dinner date!" Danielle fist bumped her.

"And to a trashy romance book," Faith said.

Several hours later, when she should've been dancing in a candle-lit living room with Candace, she found herself walking down the same quaint street where she and Candace had their first date.

Not long after, they ate a delicious meal in that crunchy tortilla shell and sipped mojitos at the curbside bar while they people watched. By the time they paid their bill and walked the cobblestone street, Faith found herself longing for later on when she'd see Candace.

"This has been a lot of fun tonight." Faith grinned at her sister as they trekked up the small incline.

"Much better than sitting around in a circle with a bunch of women who don't know the first thing about hot sex."

They giggled.

"Do you miss it?" Faith asked. "The hot sex?"

"It was loving sex. And yeah, I miss that. A lot."

Faith's heart pinched. Candace had treated her with such love. When she stared into her eyes while exploring her with a gentle touch, she did so with a sense of love Faith hadn't ever experienced while having sex with Stuart.

They ventured farther up the inclined cobblestone sidewalk, and then Faith noticed a group forming in the street ahead. Lights strung from lampposts and a fresh Latin beat filled the air. Couples danced romantically in the middle of the closed off roadway.

"I always wished Lucas and I would've taken dance lessons. It's such a romantic way to be together. Look at all these couples. They look so in love."

Faith and Danielle approached the circle and nudged forward to get a closer look. That's when she spotted Candace dancing with Pat. They danced without taking their eyes from each other. The crowd watched, mesmerized. They glided as if on ice, across the street and back, passion firing in their eyes, whipping their dresses in snappy flashes.

Danielle grabbed Faith's arm and pulled her away. Faith fought her. "I want to see the show," Faith hissed.

Just friends? Like hell! They probably had a bottle of champagne chilling for their arrival at the quaint restaurant with the potent sangria. They probably reserved the same table, too.

Danielle tugged her. "Let's go."

Faith flung another glance toward the two of them. They breezed around the cobblestone street flashing flirty glances at each other. They had to be sleeping with each other. No one gazed that long if they hadn't rolled around under the sheets together.

What happened to monogamy?

"Yeah, let's go."

Faith clung to her sister's wrist and pulled her into a sprint. They ran so fast Faith's ankle twisted on the cobblestone as they rounded the corner to where her sister had parked the car.

Then the tears sprang, and Faith swiped at them. She wouldn't cry over Candace. No way. Let her have her blonde bimbo with the makeup instead. Let them spend the rest of their lives dancing around cobblestone streets without breaking their ankles.

The whole Candace distraction wasn't helping her to put her life back together anyway. Faith had to do a better job of focusing on what mattered. Like call her daughter and tell her she loved her. She would pour her love and attention on her daughter and no one else. She would become a success story on her own and prove to anyone who doubted her that she, Faith Miller, was a strong, capable woman with more going on than chasing after women who had eyes for others.

"Faith, I'm sorry," Danielle said as she helped her off the ground.

Faith stopped the nonsense by putting up her hand. "It's okay. They have a lot of chemistry, and that can't be denied. Honestly, I'm glad I saw the way they looked at each other. Now I can finally get my mind off her and onto figuring out my life."

"I'm sure it's not what it looked like."

Faith shook her head with defiance. "I've been down that road already. I'm done second-guessing the moves of other people." She laughed from deep in her stomach. "I don't even know her enough to be upset."

"No?" Danielle folded her arms over her chest. "Why are you trembling, then?"

229

"I landed on the ground because of the way they installed this cobblestone all crooked. I'm lucky I didn't break my ankle. I better get home to get ice on it."

"Do you think we're jumping to conclusions about her?"

Faith stammered to find the right words to describe her humiliation. "I doubt it."

"She likes you. I can tell. I see the way she looks at you when you don't notice."

"It doesn't matter. I'm not cut out for this new dating landscape. Especially with women who aren't satisfied with monogamy."

"You only have to communicate with her."

"Oh really? Ms. I-date-all-the-time."

"Look, I'm saying if you want an exclusive relationship with someone, then don't settle for anything less."

She walked forward, limping slightly, holding her head high. "It was only a summer fling anyway."

Later that night, as she waited on sleep with one arm behind her head and the other petting the cat, daring the allergies to fuck with her, she impressed herself. She didn't wallow in self-pity. She planted a big ol' smile on her face and forced it to remain for a full five minutes.

She could be happy.

Yup.

She saved herself from suffering a lot of heartbreak. Her future lay before her a shiny prism. She could do what she wanted with it. The choice remained hers. With that much focus, imagine what she could accomplish? She would no longer have to worry about anyone cheating on her. That was something.

Her life could be anything she wanted it to be.

She didn't need to be wined and romanced by anyone. She could self-service. That's how she got along all her life anyway. She didn't need anyone to jumpstart her libido. She learned how to do that a long time ago without anyone's help.

That's what enterprising women did. They could talk a good talk, run a business and household, and fuck themselves at the end of the day in a bathtub of soapy water if they so desired.

She would be okay.

After about an hour into her positive self-talk mumbo jumbo, reality poked in. She began to imagine Candace's hair flying around behind her toned back muscles and her eyes steamy with lust over the blonde-haired woman in her arms.

Faith shoved her face in a pillow and groaned.

Friends. Yeah right!

Ugh. Why did she have to lie to her?

An inferno began to blaze in her mind, flickering and shooting flames all around. All the positive talk ended up charred on the floor, unable to escape the burning notion that Candace did hurt her.

Were they now sitting across from each other feeding one another bread and cheese while toasting their romantic evening? Was Antoine staring at them from his server counter with a pleased smirk on his face that he got to keep secrets from unsuspecting people like Faith?

The stories that man could tell.

Now Faith was one of them. Again.

Anger steamed.

What would be the point of romancing her as she did the other night only to flip the switch and try again with someone else? Who had the energy for such nonsense? How could she be so loving one night and again the next with someone else? Had they had revenge sex? Maybe she and the blonde-haired woman had gotten into a fight and Faith walked through the door and offered Candace resolve? A brief escape from the horrors of having the blondie yelling at her?

Nah. That was a ridiculous thought.

Something else must've happened.

Had Faith forced her into an unreasonable and uncomfortable position?

But her kiss. The way she looked into her eyes. Her soft touch. Had she read the signs all wrong?

She buried her head again.

When Candace texted her at eleven fifteen that night, she ignored it.

And, by the time she rolled over and fell asleep, she settled on a reality. Candace wanted to be friends, not lovers.

The morning came too fast and Faith met the harsh reality that she would be better off without the distraction. The insecurities that came with a new relationship overwhelmed her. At least now she could settle into her new life with a clear conscience and a lighter heart. The future had lots waiting for her, and as she climbed out of bed, she refused to let the weight of the restless night bog her down any longer. That morning she would make blueberry pancakes with the maple syrup Lucia had bought for Bristol and Emmy. And dammit, she would enjoy them without fear of adding an extra pound.

# #

Faith ate four pancakes, despite Lucia's concern. "I have diabetes. Believe me, you don't want it, too." She stared in horror at Faith.

She was a single woman who could eat what she wanted. She was okay

232

with how she looked, and the rest of the world could suck it if they weren't.

She stuffed the last forkful of heavenly blueberry fluff into her mouth and savored it.

When she finished, she brought her plate to the sink and washed it herself, having to nudge Lucia out of her way three times. She placed the washed plate in the dishrack, swiped her wet hands together, and sighed.

She would be fine.

Next task, writing to Bristol's school principal. If she did decide to go back to Boston, Bristol needed to be safe.

She typed out that email with extra gusto, not stopping once to worry about if she sounded too harsh or not.

Nope. She would write that email in whatever tone she desired. When she finished, she took a quick glance at it and then sent it to Stuart for his review.

That week, she would take Emmy and Bristol with her to the bank and have them redeposit the savings.

Watch out world. Faith Miller was on a roll.

Since her time in Rhode Island she found a new side of herself, one that didn't rely on another person to set things straight. She could do anything. Well, except for skydive. She could never skydive. But get over a lover. Easy peasy.

Chapter Fifteen

A little while later, Stuart pulled up in front of the house. Faith ran out the front door and toward her daughter, gathering her in her arms. "I missed you." She smelled sweet like apples on a crisp fall day. She clung, wanting to savor the beautiful treat of Bristol's heartbeat against her chest.

After the reunion on the front walk, Bristol ran inside to say hello to Lucia and her auntie. Then, Faith faced a suntanned Stuart.

"Hey," he said, squinting at her.

"Hey."

He wrestled with a loose strand hanging from his button hole. "So about what happened with Bristol…"

"I drafted an email to the principal and sent it to you for your review. And I plan to take her and Emmy to redeposit the funds this coming week."

"That's great about the redeposit, but we need to do more than send an email." His voice dripped with an authority that Faith despised.

"Don't do that," she pointed at him, still powered by her can-do attitude from earlier.

"Do what?"

"Toss me that condescending tone like you're the boss and I'm some idiot who has no clue. I'm perfectly capable of handling this."

"Condescending tone?" His jaw flinched. "I'm her father. I get a say in what goes on in her life. You took her away for the entire summer without asking me. You pretty much told me you were taking her away. So, if anyone is being the boss here, it's you. Not me. What you did was unfair."

A jolt of anger sprang in her. "You want to talk to me about fairness? Seriously? You?"

He covered his mouth with his hand, then swung it down. "I've said I'm sorry a thousand times. And, I meant it. How I acted was wrong. I never wanted to be the man who cheated on his wife. But, I did, and I can't take it back now. So Faith, what can I say or do at this point to help us move forward for Bristol's sake?"

What more could he say? He fell in love with someone else. That hurt her, even though she had zero desire to have an intimate relationship with him.

He was happier in life without Faith. He changed into a softer and more affable Stuart with Gilly on his arm. That woman changed Stuart's life into one that he appeared to love living. Faith couldn't do that for him.

That's what hurt the most.

They stared at each other for a few intense moments, both breathing hard and uncomfortably.

Then finally, he stepped toward her with sorrow in his eyes. "I'm really sorry I hurt you. I'm sorry I hurt Bristol. I wish I could've been the person you deserved me to be, and also the person who could've made you happy in every way."

His words carried truth. They both knew that he never could've been who she needed him to be any more than she could've been what he needed her to be.

Faith nodded her acceptance of his apology. "For now maybe we should just agree that we want what's best for our daughter."

His face softened some more. "That's a good idea. She's been through a lot, and I want her to be happy and stable. I know you want to send an email,

236

but I'd really feel better if one of us could have a face-to-face with the school administration. They need to see how deeply this has affected her so no other child will suffer like this."

Faith folded her hands in front of her. "Yeah. You're absolutely right. Let's plan on us both being there for that meeting."

"I was also thinking that I don't want her going back to that school. So, I'd like to pay for her to go to a different school. Like maybe St. Mary's."

Faith let her gaze wander around Danielle's plush grass, and then the morning air finally settled around her in quiet surrender. "A different school would be great. Let's think more on which one and talk later."

"Okay. That sounds like a good plan." He pulled in his upper lip. "Are we okay?"

Faith nodded. "We're okay."

"I just want what's best for her."

Faith twisted away and headed up the walkway, leaving gentle taps behind. She glanced over her shoulder. "Me too."

# #

Once inside, Lucia and Bristol waved heartily to her from the back deck. Faith had wanted to avoid the deck that day. She didn't want to run into Candace doing her yoga and risk her looking up to see her gawking down on her sun salutations.

But Bristol's happiness. How could she resist?

As she walked through the sliding doors, she scanned the grassy field and lake for signs of her. No one but a few joggers set the scene against the backdrop of trees and shimmering water.

"Why don't you grab yourself a cup of fresh coffee?" Lucia asked. "Then come back out and relax." She lifted her oversized mug to her lips.

Faith returned to the kitchen to get her coffee. Next thing, a shuffle and giggles from the deck piqued her interest. Then, Bristol called out Pretzel's name and up the steps came Candace, glowing and laughing as she chased Pretzel around the deck furniture. "Come here you little stinker." More laughter curled up in the air, seeping into the screen of the sliding door and looping around Faith.

Finally, Candace grasped Pretzel's collar and attached the purple braided leash. Candace looked through the slider's screen and spotted her.

Faith froze. All her resolve from the night before and that morning melted and left her naked and vulnerable standing behind the kitchen counter.

Candace handed Bristol the leash. "She apparently wanted to come see you, so here you go. I'm going to say hello to your mom."

Faith's heart bucked. She grabbed onto her steaming mug of coffee for lack of anything better to do with her hands.

Candace came inside. "It's a gorgeous day. What are you doing cooped up in here?"

"I like it in here."

Candace scanned her apprehensive eyes. A slow recognition came to play, one that said things like, *Faith is upset. Faith looks like she wants to toss that hot coffee in my face. I should run.* Instead of running, she waltzed right up close to her.

Could she not read a clue?

Candace stepped around her backside. She placed her hands around Faith's waist and whispered, "So I texted you last night. When you didn't answer back, I imagined you tucked under the blankets with a peaceful smile on your face as you dreamed."

Faith pressed her lips together.

"So," she continued to whisper, "where do you want to have dinner tonight?"

With the first unhitching snap of her restraint buckle, Faith stiffened. She would not walk into her trap. She could dine with the blonde bimbo instead. Faith had better things to do. Redeposit Bristol's money. Balance her checkbook. Make a list of hair color she needed for Danielle's trip to the supply shop. So many things to do. She backed out of her embrace. "I can't make it tonight."

Faith went over to the paper towel rack and tore off too many. She needed to stay focused on something. So, she knelt down under the sink and dug out the disinfectant spray. A moment later, she doused the counters with it.

"Faith," Candace said with an authority she had not heard before.

Faith pretended not to hear. She swiped the counter with more force, trying to beat the shine into it.

"Are you upset with me?" Candace asked.

"Upset?" Faith laughed. "Of course not."

"Why aren't you looking at me?"

"I have things I need to focus on right now."

Candace looked at the pile of wet paper towels dripping with cleaner. "Yeah, I suppose you do."

Faith wiped the counter feverishly, pushing crumbs into the sink. Candace's eyes followed her.

The woman didn't take a hint.

Candace liked being with multiple women, and Faith wouldn't beg her not to be. Faith accepted her true nature, a womanizer. Some people did that. She wouldn't judge. She was a modern day woman with strength and confidence now. She didn't need another person to complete her. Candace could go on her merry little way, back to her wandering lifestyle and Faith would eventually be fine.

"Faith, talk to me."

She bit the inside of her cheek to stop her chin from quivering. She hated how she fell apart so easily. Faith had spent her whole life forfeiting arguments for the sake of keeping peace. She was tired of trapping her true feelings. "Well, okay, the truth is I wish you could've been honest with me. I'm a grown woman. If you wanted casual sex, I could've handled that."

"What?" Candace's face contorted with disdain and bewilderment. "Who said I only wanted casual sex?"

Faith had handed her a golden ticket, a free hall pass to be honest and state her truth. Why lie to her still? Time for Candace to stop with the charade. "You could've told me."

"Told you what?"

"The truth. The gathered crowd could've gotten high off your flirty buzz."

Recognition spilled across her face. "You saw me?"

"I did. Dancing the night away with your blonde *friend.*"

"Dancing? That's why you're upset?"

"A lot more than dancing transpired between the two of you."

"She's a friend. A dancer. It's what dance instructors do. We dance."

"Dance instructor? Friend?" Faith's voice flew up to the high ceiling and paraded around the two of them like a detective drawing out the criminal's secrets. "Come on now, be honest with me."

"You thought I'd rather be with her than you, even though I invited you to join us?"

"You're free to be with her. We're not exclusive."

240

"Well, you've made that clear." She wrapped her arms around her chest. "She needed my help to fill in a gap. The show needed to go on, and I couldn't leave her without a dance partner."

Irrationality surfaced. It stomped on all reason, squashing and trampling over all good intention. It landed on top of them, suffocating the magic out of whatever could've evolved. "I saw the look."

"The look?"

"The passion. The longing gaze. The sensual prowess. I saw it all." The anger licked at her ankles, burning her at the stake of a hunt she found herself on again.

"We performed at the annual summer dance-a-thon. That's what dancers do."

Faith's argument began to buckle. It snapped one band at a time until it ripped apart and fell at her feet.

Could've she been wrong?

No. That blonde woman had passion dripping off her and wrapped Candace right up into her gooey, sticky lusty arms. Jealousy grew in Faith. It built up into a thick, hard residue and clung to her, unwilling to loosen its grip. "I assumed you canceled because maybe you would've rather spent time with her doing what you love most."

"Why would I cancel on you to be with another woman? Is that what you think of me? That I spend a night making love to you and the next I hook up with someone else?"

Faith shrank in the wake of Candace's frustration. "Well, you have the right to live how you want to live."

"That's not how I want to live."

"Well, now I know that," Faith shouted.

241

"Why are you shouting?"

"I don't know. I'm still mad, I guess. I've been mad since last night. I can't shut that emotion off like I'm turning off a faucet. It's ridiculous, I know. But, this is me and how I react when I think I'm being screwed." She still yelled despite her best effort to take it down a notch.

Candace bowed her head. "I have to go, Faith. I've nothing else to say."

She walked away carrying Faith's shredded dignity in tow. It trailed behind her, blowing in the wind, flying away for good. Soon, it would take flight up into the wind patterns and then fall back to the lake and get pummeled by the late evening breeze. Back and forth, it would slowly drown in the ebb and flow.

She screwed up, and she couldn't do anything to put the pieces back together again.

#

Danielle snuck out from around the foyer, wagging her finger. "You wanted to fight. You wanted to catch her. You wanted to because you're afraid."

"Afraid of what?" Faith snapped.

"You're afraid you're going to lose yourself all over again."

"Well, can you blame me?" Faith slammed her palm against the counter. Tears followed.

"Why do you always think the world is out to get you? Because Stuart cheated?"

"I trusted him," she said through gritted teeth.

"You both had issues. It happens."

"Says the woman with the perfect marriage."

Danielle's eyes twitched. "I never should've said those things to you and Lucia that day. Sometimes my emotions get the best of me. I hope you know I'm sorry for that."

Faith had crossed a threshold not to be crossed. "I do. Of course." She exhaled and pulled in her lower lip. "I screwed up bad."

"Everything is fixable. First you have to admit you sometimes place blame where it's not deserved."

Her trusty flotation device. "When did I turn into the person who finds comfort in bad things?"

"You always have. Like when we were kids and you used to rummage through dad's sock drawer to uncover his hidden cigarettes, only to find a picture of him and another woman. If you hadn't been seeking the bad, you wouldn't have found worse."

"He cheated on Mom."

"Mom didn't care. She wanted it to stay hidden. Her life worked with dad. Without him, she'd have to struggle with a lot more than his girlfriend."

"So you blame me for their divorce?"

"I'm not saying that. I'm illustrating a point. One Martina already made. If you seek bad, then you get bad."

"Mom deserved to know."

Danielle sighed. "Not everyone is strong like you, Faith."

That sentence nearly knocked her to the ground.

Her sister met her on the other side of the counter and hugged her. "I love you and admire your strength. I want to see you rise, not fall. Stop looking for problems and start looking for solutions. Set things right before you can't. This is a great opportunity."

"A great opportunity? How?"

Danielle looked around the kitchen as if an answer would pop up out of the toaster. "She loves my flaxseed muffins. I've got a few left from the other day. You could bring some to her as a starting point."

Faith giggled into her shirt.

"Why are you laughing?"

"No one loves those muffins, Danielle."

Danielle backed out of her arms. "She said she did."

Lucia came into the kitchen at that moment. "How about we make *arepas* instead?"

"This place is too open. There's no privacy," Faith stated.

"Not an ounce." Lucia smirked. "Now get the bowl, I'll get the mix. And we're making these by hand. We're not using the Ziploc bag today."

A few minutes later, as they formed the *arepas*, they fell flimsy in Faith's hands.

"You've got to add more mix," Lucia said, pouring more. "Now work it in like you mean it."

Faith kneaded the dough so it would withstand the heat and the flipping.

Faith then began to form the bread. Eventually, she molded it into a perfect circle.

"There you go." Lucia glanced at the beautiful *arepa*. "Sometimes you need things to fall apart to understand their fragile nature. Only then can you start to put things back together again in a stronger way."

"So poetic, Lucia," Faith said.

"Cheers to flimsy *arepas*," Danielle said, eyeing Faith's concentrated effort with pride.

Like the *arepa*, maybe she only needed to add more substance to her own life to prevent it from falling apart into a flimsy mess.

# #

Faith stood in front of Candace's front door, trembling as she brought her finger up to the doorbell. She snuck a peek into the window slit and wondered if her heart would hold up as she waited. It pounded much too hard, stealing the oxygen from her lungs and causing her blood to run cold.

As Candace opened the door, Faith drew herself up tall.

Candace leaned against the doorframe wearing a tired frown.

"Hi," Faith said meekly, shrinking back in her sneakers as the grooves on Candace's forehead deepened.

"Hey."

Hey?

"Can we talk?"

She took a step back, and narrowed her eyes. "I'm still mad."

Faith stood before her embarrassed. A car sped down the road. A strong gust swirled around her. Birds sang. Dogs barked. The world continued to spin despite Faith's immature disregard for all that was still good in it.

She dug for her voice, finding it packaged up like an old parcel with gummy duct tape in the back of her throat. "I'm sorry." She handed her the plate of *arepas* wrapped in foil. "There's Colombian cheese under the foil."

Candace glared at the plate without grabbing it, then back up at her. "You were way off, and I didn't deserve the way you treated me."

Faith unearthed her voice, yanking on the faded tape that imprisoned it and freeing the words. "You're right. You didn't deserve it."

"I'm not somebody who sleeps around with just anyone, and I don't appreciate that you accused me of doing that."

Faith bowed her head, still gripping the plate. "I worked myself up into a frenzy and got way out of control."

245

Candace finally accepted the *arepas*. "Faith, I know you've been through hurtful times with Stuart. So I get it." Candace backed into the foyer, softening her gaze. "But, at some point, you have to stop assuming everyone is out to hurt you."

"I know," she whispered back.

Candace headed toward the kitchen, and Faith followed her. She placed the plate down on the counter, and then spun to face Faith. "We have two separate lives, and at the end of the summer, we have to get back to them. So, I know this feels a lot like a summer fling, and I don't like that. I don't have summer flings. I'm not that kind of person. I've never engaged in a temporary relationship before. So, it's scary for me, too."

Faith swallowed hard. She preferred certainty over impulsivity.

"I don't want to hurt you. I don't intend on hurting you. But, I think we need to discuss what we want." She folded her hands on the counter. "What do you want out of this, Faith?"

I want you all to myself. I want to appear ready. I want to have it all figured out for a change. I don't want to screw this up. "To enjoy it for what it is."

Candace's dark brown eyes studied her intently. "And what is this, exactly?"

Instinctively, Faith placed her palm on Candace's soft cheek. "I suppose a break from life's curves."

She arched her eyebrow. "I like curves, though."

"They're beginning to grow on me, too." A relaxed smile grew on Faith. "Literally. Too many of these *arepas*, I guess."

Candace smiled softly. "Curves are one of life's greatest assets. I prefer embracing them."

Faith flushed. "I get a little erratic about them, I suppose."

She leaned in slightly on a chuckle. "A little?"

"Okay, a lot. It's only because I'm…" Faith stopped herself. No more excuses. No more placing blame on someone else. "I overreact. I tend to do that. Danielle tells me all the time I have a bad habit of overlooking the good because I'm always looking for the bad. My mind goes into overdrive. I cooked up a steaming pot of bad and plopped you in it. I'm sorry for that."

Candace looked at her with gentle eyes. "I promise you that I'm never going to lie to you and treat you badly."

Faith's heart warmed. Candace had an easy way of melting the rigid ice that built up walls. "And I promise you I will *try* to not overreact."

Candace opened up her arms and Faith fell into them. "I'll take a good try." She kissed the top of Faith's head. "I'm not Stuart. Please don't look for ways I will screw up. I'm trustworthy and not interested in defending that. I can't be happy like that. You have to trust me. Okay?"

Trust. What a loaded word. Faith didn't trust herself, let alone another person. Trust required she stand naked and allow life to take over. If she wanted to ever mend herself and find trust again, she needed to stop looking for ways people would screw her over. She needed to trust that whatever happened, she'd be okay. Because really, wasn't she?

Faith pulled out of the embrace and stared into her eyes. "I promise I will."

Candace hesitated on a wavering smile, as if weighing Faith's intent. "Okay." She squeezed her eyebrows together. "I want to enjoy the time we have left together and not get caught up in worry over things that aren't real. Let's enjoy this for what it is. A sweet gift of time to put anxieties over the future aside. What do you say?"

"I say that's a great idea."

"Thank God." She held Faith's hands and swung them, bringing her hand up to her lips. "Because I've missed you like crazy."

Faith's tummy broke out into a series of flips. She cocked her head to her shoulder. "You've missed me?"

"Especially that look." Candace laced her fingers through Faith's hair. "It's a look that buckles my knees every time."

Candace kissed her with renewed energy. She led her backwards toward the foyer, toward the staircase that led to her bedroom. Moments later, she placed Faith onto the bed and stared into her eyes while teasing her with her touch. Faith craved her touch more with every caress.

They kissed and tightened their embrace. Air didn't have a chance of passing between them.

They weren't just having fling sex.

No, they enjoyed much more than that. They expressed their love for one another. She read about such romance in fictional books. She heard about it in hushed whispers between best friends over cocktails. Danielle had shared it with Lucas.

Love.

They made love.

Sweet love.

Chapter Sixteen

Time floated by too quickly, as with any good vacation.

As the summer progressed, so too did Bristol's speaking. She ordered breakfast from perfect strangers and made friends with the dancers in the kids' Zumba class. She and Candace grew closer, and Faith stopped herself each time she worried about when the end would come. It would come on its own whether she worried or not. Until then, she indulged in their time together.

She also dove into her commitment to Danielle, as Martina dug into her video production venture and healing her ulnar nerve.

Still, to keep a steady finger on the pulse to her future, once a day she'd check her email and respond to any potential job interviews. A few sailed in, the usual sales-type jobs offering bonuses and high commissions to the right candidate. She didn't have the proper credentials. That fact didn't bother her nearly as much as it had a few months earlier.

She wouldn't force things. She didn't want to waste the little time left of the summer biting her nails over jobs that didn't exist. She'd land somewhere right eventually. In the meantime, Martina and Danielle kept her busy with clients. Between that money and the money she collected through unemployment, she did okay. She paid her half of the mortgage on time and even managed to buy Bristol some new outfits for dance class.

Faith thrived, better than ever.

Even when Bristol came back from a visit with her father one day and told her, "Daddy's getting married to Gilly in two months. I'm going to be a junior bridesmaid!"

They were having a baby. Marriage logically followed, as it did for them.

Faith waited for the usual anger and jealousy to bubble up inside; anger and jealousy over his wins, despite him being the one who disrupted their lives.

The heaviness never came. It no longer mattered to her what Stuart did in life. In fact, she got to a point where she wanted to thank him for his selfish act because had he not hooked up with a younger woman, Faith would not be sipping coffee and watching her girlfriend do yoga on the lakefront.

Cheers to Stuart's cheating.

# #

That night, Faith told Candace about the news of Stuart and Gilly's wedding.

"Why did you and Stuart split?"

"That's not obvious?"

Candace ran her fingers through Faith's hair. "You know what I mean. How did it come about? Did you one day have enough and tell him I prefer breasts and soft curves?"

Faith indulged in Candace's lips, inhaling her deliciousness. "I've never spoken with him about it," Faith whispered.

Candace lifted up on her elbow and stared at Faith. "Did he cheat on you?"

Faith hesitated. In the past, she allowed Stuart to take the blame in everyone's eyes. "He did, but I take part of the blame."

Candace squinted. "How so?'

"We had a great relationship with no obstacles right up until we decided to try and get pregnant again."

"Again?"

"I had miscarried before that. Anyway, something changed in me. My hormones kicked into full gear, cranking my biological clock and ordering me to act. Once I gave birth, I had what I needed. I didn't need Stuart in that way anymore. I had zero desire."

"That's normal with pregnancy hormones, isn't it?"

Faith twisted her mouth. "Things unraveled quickly. I wanted companionship, not sex. He wanted both. I turned my back on him, and he looked elsewhere."

Candace traced her finger along Faith's cheek. "He should've been honest."

"I should've been, too."

"Well, what's important is you're both okay now. You can both find the happiness you deserve." With that, Candace rolled Faith over and showered her in soft kisses, starting at her lips and slowly working her way down the length of her body.

In those precious moments, Candace bathed her in the possibility that maybe, just maybe, she was put together enough to be worth it.

# #

As the days progressed into weeks, they spent most nights curled up on the couch in Danielle's living room with the family. At one point, Candace whispered to her, "I love being here."

Faith squeezed her hand. "Me too."

One weekend, when Bristol stayed over her dad's, Candace wanted to treat Faith to dinner. On the drive to the restaurant, she stopped for gas. While she pumped it, Faith scanned the car. She noticed a yellow post-it note on the

251

floor of the car. She plucked it up. A smiley face started off the note. "Thank you for being so great the other day."

Flashbacks of snooping through Stuart's things came rushing at her. That's how it all began, her finding out about Gilly. She'd find little hints of her and Stuart, and then brush it off as nothing but coincidence. *Oh that hairpin? That's my mother's. She must've dropped it when I took her to the doctor the other day. Oh that's not your lipstick on the car floor? Uh. It must be from my sister. She always throws her pocketbook down on the floor. It must have rolled out.*

Faith examined the writing. The letters danced across the paper in flirtatious vibes with its curly letters and thick exclamation point.

When Candace fell back into the seat, Faith cut right to the chase. "What were you great at?"

Confusion took over her face. "What?"

Faith tightened her shoulders as she raised the post-it note. "You were great the other day."

Candace twisted her mouth "Where did that come from?"

"Right here on the floor."

Candace reached for it, confused. "Maybe Lucia? I helped her carry in some groceries the other day and she handed me a plate of food. Probably fell off it."

As usual Faith's alarms bells rang out false signals. She'd eventually work through them and begin to recognize them. She was a work in progress. Things like sneaky suspicions didn't disappear overnight. "Sounds like something Lucia might do."

"So, how about Mexican food?" Candace asked, oblivious to Faith's internal battles.

"Sounds yummy."

A few minutes later, they sat in a cozy booth in a quaint Mexican restaurant where they enjoyed delicious overflowing plates of chicken nachos. Then, later on, they went to a jazz bar and sat at a small table overlooking the room. Their knees brushed together under the linen tablecloth.

With one touch, Candace could soften Faith's calloused heart. She stirred the air with a healthy dose of confidence, and it flowed into Faith, turning her into someone worthy and desirable.

She wanted this leg of the trip in her life to last forever. How she wished she could manipulate time, slowing it down for moments with Candace and speeding past chaos and the unavoidable twists.

They sipped drinks and talked about trivial things like the time Faith locked her keys in the car in the middle of Providence with the engine still running. "I had to leave it there and get a ride back to my place in Pawtucket. I left it running all alone in Providence at midnight!"

"Well that's nothing. Once I hit a car with my bike. I ran right into it, flipped over its entire length, and broke my leg. Oh, and my mother grounded me for an entire month. My mother ordered me to scrub the toilet every day once my leg healed."

"You broke your leg?" Faith asked.

"And, I broke our neighbor's car. Do you think I cried? Oh no. I wouldn't dare. My mother would've sentenced me to a year of double house duties. She ran a tight ship."

"Sounds like jail," Faith said, brushing her knee firmer against Candace's.

"I thank my mom. Without her being that way, I would've been married and selling avocados out of a truck parked in South Providence."

Faith leaned back and extended her leg out so now her calves flirted with

Candace's leg. "You're so disciplined."

Candace's eyes flickered.

They gazed out at the dance floor, watching straight couples sway to the soft jazz. Meanwhile, they enjoyed their own dance under the privacy of their white linen tablecloth.

"You're driving me crazy right now." Candace's eyes shimmered, massaging Faith's heart and changing her into someone less cynical, and more graceful.

"Shall we go someplace more private?" Faith's voice came out husky.

A sheen of ecstasy eased across Candace's face. "I'm having a great moment right here and now."

Faith caught sight of Candace's sway in her chair. "Are you... you know," Faith leaned in, "being naughty."

"I am." She clasped Faith's hands, staring deep into her eyes. Her cheeks flushed as she squirmed side to side in the chair.

Faith shifted her gaze across the room to see if anyone noticed the two of them grinding against the soft seat cushions. Candace's hand fell upon Faith's knee, calling her back to their special moment when everyone else blurred and only the two of them danced in their chairs to a song all their own. One undulation at a time, their gazes grew more intense as did their breathing. Caught up in a whirl of sensual ecstasy, Faith let herself go to that sweet place where gravity let go and sent her flying.

# #

The next morning, the wind whipped sand against the window in Candace's bedroom. A thick fog hung in the air, one that normally would've had Faith depressed. She suffered from that seasonal thingamajig when the

254

sun didn't shine. But, that morning, a torrential rainstorm could've been pelting the windows, and it wouldn't have fazed Faith any.

Light emitted from her soul because she woke with sunshine on her heart.

When Candace woke, Faith tore the covers off her to peek at her beauty; perky nipples, round size-B boobs, muscled abs. What didn't she have?

Faith lay exposed, and Candace treated her like a gem, exploring every inch of her with awe and reverence. She treated Faith like she'd never before laid her hands on another woman or embraced someone with curves.

The woman erased all fears of inadequacy with her tender gaze. Faith opened herself to the thrilling ride of being in the arms of a woman who caressed her with loving sweeps, carrying her to a place where she mattered.

They spent the rest of the day wrapped up in each other's arms, exploring their gifts. When not exploring, they read magazines and ate popsicles. Or they watched *Doctor Who*. By early evening, Faith stood up. "I should go back to my place." She must have looked like a mess. Her hair tangled. Her makeup gone, likely smeared on Candace's pillowcases. Her feet were cold because she didn't have socks. The t-shirt Candace let her borrow acted like shrink-wrap, cutting off her circulation. She didn't want to be that person who overstayed her welcome, even though Bristol wouldn't be returning until the following day.

"Come back later. That's if you don't have plans." Candace twirled her hair seductively.

"You're not tired of me yet?

"Well, I'm tired, but not of you." She stood up and hugged her, kissing her earlobe. "Stay over again tonight. We can make eggs and rice and play a board game."

"Eggs and rice? Hmm. I've never had that combination. I'm open to anything these hands create." Faith cupped her hands over Candace's.

"My mom is going to love you as much as I do when she finds out you're open to eating anything." A bout of awkward silence followed her premature love admission. Then, Candace nuzzled her neck. "It'll be fun. I'll let you pick the game if you stay."

"I need to slip into something more comfy and warm. My toes are freezing."

"I have socks. They may not be fluffy, but they'll keep your toes warm."

Faith needed a shower and to brush her teeth. "I need fluffy socks. I'll be back in two hours."

"Perfect."

So, later on after she returned and ate a huge pile of Canilla white rice flavored with eggs and salt, Faith relaxed into the perfect evening. She loved being with Candace. But, as the night progressed and her Monopoly winnings dwindled, she grew sad. Soon, it would be time for her and Bristol to pack up and head back to Boston. Life would go back to working in a stuffy office under bright fluorescent bulbs, worrying about Bristol taking a bus in the city, trekking the rocky coast of Stuart's new love life with Gilly, and of course, opening her car hood every day to check for squirrel nests.

The end to their summer fling sped toward them, full throttle with no brakes. The humid air served as added fuel to the friction and sparks flying out from underneath their passion.

Soon, that ride would end on a deafening screech and toss them out into the cold harsh world of reality.

Faith slept in Candace's arms and woke when the sun peeked in through the slits of the wooden blinds. She got up to use the bathroom and once inside, her eyes landed on a pair of pink, fluffy slippers with a note, "I ran out to get these while you took a shower. Hope you'll always think of me when you're wearing them."

Those slippers meant she cared enough to invite her into a special place in her heart, reserved for her. Despite the hundreds of miles that would eventually come between them, they would always have that special place.

#

"Do you think if I decided to stay in Rhode Island, Candace might, too?" Faith asked Sally.

"Ease up, wild one." Sally laughed.

"She surprised me with the slippers," Faith reminded her.

"They're pink and fluffy?" Sally asked.

"Yes, and squishy like marshmallows," Faith said, closing her laptop.

"Do your feet stink?"

"Stop! It was sweet."

"Still begs the question."

"In all seriousness, I'm thinking of relocating here. I'm going to tell Stuart next time I see him."

"Is that wise? Right now, Rhode Island feels like a good choice because you're living in a happy bubble. Happy bubbles are nice. But, they burst. I don't want you to get hurt."

"Why would you say such a negative thing? I thought you'd be happy for me."

"Basing your life decision on a pair of fluffy slippers seems dangerous, that's all."

"This has nothing to do with fluffy slippers." Faith bit her lip. "Danielle invited me to stay with her. Bristol loves it here. She's talking. Even Stuart could eventually come around and agree Rhode Island is good for her."

"Okay," Sally sighed. "Those are good motives. I just want to be the voice of reason to make sure you aren't changing your entire life for the wrong intentions."

"Love?"

"It's a fling."

"But she bought me slippers."

"Based on a fling."

"I don't like this pessimistic side."

"I'm being sensible. Don't move there and uproot everything for someone else. Do it for yourself because it's what you want to do and what's best for you as an independent woman."

Faith digested her friend's advice, but not for too long.

Shortly after hanging up with her, she decided to leave Stuart a message before she chickened out. "Can you call me back when you have time? I have something important I want to talk with you about."

# #

Later that day, Candace invited Faith to tag along with her to a friend's house in Providence.

Faith would meet her friends. That meant something grander than pink, fluffy slippers.

When they walked up the front steps and rang the bell, Faith swallowed her nervousness.

A friendly couple answered the door, arm in arm. Their exuberant hugs calmed her nerves instantly. They were regular women wearing cargo shorts and flip-flops, no makeup or false pretenses. Faith felt at home, instantly.

They took them out to the back yard where more people gathered. Families tossed balls to little kids and dogs played. The excited dogs dashed around people drinking Bud Lights and eating hamburgers and potato chips.

Faith loved seeing Candace in her element with her friends. She loved what she saw, a real woman with a real life outside the fantasy world of Orchard Pond.

She learned some fun things about Candace, like how she used to put on neighborhood dance shows and charge people a dollar to hear her and other neighborhood kids sing things like the National Anthem and John Denver songs. She was so bossy," Tina, a plump and happy woman laughed and pushed her eyeglasses up to rest on her nose. "You used to stop me mid-stanza because you didn't like the way I sang a note."

"I didn't do that to you." Candace laughed. "Did I?"

Tina punched her arm. "You did. Of course you did. You used to send your baby sister home by lying to her. Don't leave that out."

Baby sister?

"She used to stand around and cry," Candace said. "No one could hear the show."

"Poor thing probably waited hours for you to come home and make the promised crafts with her. Did you ever make crafts?"

Candace rolled her eyes. "Let's talk about better things."

"Yes, let's." A sporty woman wearing a bandana around her head said. "We need to talk about a friend in Wyoming in need of a house sitter. She's going to be hiking the Appalachian Trails for six months."

Six months. Faith's blood ran cold.

"When?" Candace asked, perking up to the great news.

"Early fall, I think. She's got someone lined up for most of it, and needs help with part of the time. Interested?"

"I might be. I'll let you know."

Faith followed the conversation, trying to pick up hints and put them together like a jigsaw puzzle. Housesit in Wyoming. Part of time. May be interested.

At one point, right before delivering more clues, one of Candace's friends, Karen, pulled her aside. "Want to help me put together the dessert tray?"

"Sure." Faith stood. As she pushed past her lawn chair, she caught the beginning probe of another question by the sporty woman. Something about dance camp in New Jersey, end of summer, one hundred kids, tent camping, needing one more instructor.

"Are you coming?" Karen asked.

Faith shook off the concern of Candace's nomadic life and followed the slender woman with a ponytail through the back door of the house. If Candace liked being a nomad, Faith couldn't stand in her way. She'd have to move aside and let Candace pass by, carrying her worldly possessions in a satchel over her shoulder and whistling a sad song full of dull cadences.

"I've never seen Candace so relaxed," Karen said. "She's usually tense. With you, she's different. Happy, I dare say."

"Candace is tense?"

"To protect herself. She's been hurt."

Karen continued to speak about Candace in a foreign way, as if two people lived inside of her, a dancer by day, super wound-up woman by night.

"Candace had a rough time when her ex bailed out on her." The woman slurred her words. "That was rough. Talk about a low point. I should stop talking so much. She wouldn't like it."

Faith should stop her from revealing all her secrets. But, she needed to hear more. "What happened?"

"Melanie is a super bitch." Karen tripped over the tile on her way to get the brownies.

"Melanie?"

"What a crazy ex she ended up being. None of us saw it coming."

"What did she do?"

"She didn't tell you?"

Faith stumbled over that sad fact. "Just that it didn't end well."

"Didn't end well." She laughed. "What an understatement. The bitch did her in."

"What did she do?"

"I shouldn't be talking about this. The drinks are going straight to my head." She tossed a casual glance over her shoulder toward Candace. "We all look out for her. But, she's aloof. By the way, how long have you been dating?"

"The summer."

She shook her head. "Oh, such a short period of time. Candace won't open up to you that soon. She's a hard one to crack since Melanie did her in," she said, her words slurring some more. "It's nice to see her happy again, though. Please promise me you're not going to hurt her."

Me hurt her?

"Here she comes. Don't say a word."

Faith had so many questions. For starters, why didn't Candace mention anything? Faith pushed the hurt down as Candace approached.

Candace handed her a plate of macaroni and cheese. "It's better than you've ever had. I promise."

Faith took the plate. The uncomfortable vibe mulling around her head must have been obvious because Candace looked at Karen and arched her eyebrow.

Karen scattered off like a frightened raccoon after being caught digging in the trashcan.

# #

Once they arrived back at Candace's, they sat on the couch together and Candace took her hand. "So did Karen talk your ear off?"

Faith blinked and avoided her stare. "Not too badly."

Candace glanced at her with a softness in her eyes. "Did she tell you about Melanie?"

Faith toyed with the remote control, examining it like it carried the power to fast forward through that moment, far enough away from it so the omission she was about to launch would blur and disappear. "She mentioned a few things."

Candace twisted the edge of her t-shirt. "I learned something about Melanie today that upset me. I was afraid Karen would say something before I got a chance to tell you."

Faith took her hand. "If you want to talk about it, I'm a good listener."

Candace lifted Faith's hand to her lips and kissed it tenderly. She studied Faith for a brief moment. "I found out from Karen that Melanie's adopted a dog. And, frankly, it bothers the hell out of me."

The room began to shrink. "Because you still have feelings for her?"

Candace laughed. "Oh, hell no. I'm upset because of her track record. My aunt needed a place to stay a while back, so I invited her to live with me and Melanie in Providence. Then, she moved out, abruptly. Melanie told me I had upset my aunt with something I said to her. I couldn't eat anything solid for days. She wouldn't return my calls or even let me know where she had moved. Then, I found out she died a few months later. Not long after that, I overheard Melanie talking to her sister. It turned out Melanie had told my aunt she needed to leave because she didn't like her dog."

Faith cradled her wrist.

"She didn't like her dog, so she kicked them both out. Now, she's adopting a dog." Candace bowed her head. "That makes me angry."

Faith moved closer to her, running her fingers through Candace's hair. "Justifiably so."

"How could I have loved someone so careless? How did I not see that ugly side of her?"

"Sometimes love puts blinders on us."

Candace bit her lip. "You know the whole kicker here? I wanted to adopt Pretzel. She was a cute little puppy who took to me right away. Melanie never wanted dogs. So, I had to say no. That's how Pretzel ended up here. That's why I spend my summers down here, to be with her. Now Melanie says yes to another woman and dog. I was irrelevant to her, just like my aunt."

Faith stroked Candace's cheek.

Candace obviously lived a nomadic life to outrun the pain Melanie had caused her and her family. "Love doesn't have to hurt." Faith moved in closer until their lips touched. Candace didn't fight the kiss. She let Faith take her in her arms and lay her against the couch. Faith eased on top of her.

One moment Faith suffocated under a vulnerability only to be the one erasing a different one from the beautiful woman who trusted her. Candace responded to her touch with gentle moans and an eager sway.

Faith took the lead that night, nurturing Candace with her love, proving to her that she did matter and was far from irrelevant.

Chapter Seventeen

When Stuart dropped off Bristol, he dashed away before Faith could talk with him about her thoughts on relocating. It wasn't until he called her after he returned from a recruiting trip to Texas later in the week that he asked her about it. "Sorry I didn't have a chance to ask you about what you wanted to discuss. Is this a good time?"

"Um." Faith tripped over her thoughts. "I was thinking, you know, I can't find work in Boston. I've been trying, but nothing. Yet, right here in Rhode Island, I've been handed a golden ticket at my sister's salon. Clients are starting to request me. I'm making some money. And, I'm happy. So is Bristol. She's adjusting so nicely, making friends, loving dance. I think it might be a good time for me to consider relocating here."

"Relocating? That's drastic, Faith. She's going to think I'm abandoning her. My father did that to me, remember? And it sucked."

He lived two hours away at most, with traffic. "We can make this work between the two of us."

"No, we can't, Faith." His voice grew bitter cold.

Just then Bristol came into the kitchen. "Is that Daddy?"

Faith covered the mic. "Not now."

"Is that Bristol?"

"Yes."

"I want to speak with her."

Faith handed her the phone. "Be quick."

"Daddy!" she screamed. "Guess what?"

A pause.

"Auntie Danielle and I are having a birthday party in two weeks. Can you come? Please?"

Another pause. Then she jumped up and down. "Yay! Wait until you see. I can dance the salsa!" She started wiggling and giggling. "I love you too, Daddy."

She handed the phone back to Faith.

He had hung up.

Just then, Martina busted into the kitchen wearing a blue striped mini skirt and tank top. "I'm going to Gabe's for a few days. We're sailing."

Danielle came into the kitchen wearing her gardening apron. "Sailing?"

"Yes," Martina said. "He's packing a romantic picnic lunch and taking me out on the sea."

Martina was so spoiled and so far removed from reality.

Lucky her.

"I'm heading out too. Faith, there are fresh tomatoes in the garden if you want to make yourself a tomato sandwich." Danielle snatched up her keys. "Bristol, ready?" She turned back to Faith. "I'm taking her strawberry picking."

Bristol hugged her goodbye and galloped down the foyer with her aunt.

Faith needed to clear her head. She couldn't stand alone in the kitchen and brood about her life. She hoped to find Candace at home. She'd say something inspiring that would melt Faith's reality into something fluid and manageable. But, maybe that wasn't such a good idea.

Candace didn't need to hear her problems. Besides, complaining would mess things up. Faith would end up clinging to the comfort of unleashing, and as she tucked into that softness, she'd lose her grip. She'd slide down the side of her messy chaos and land on a thud, covered in the slime of negativity.

She couldn't be that person anymore. She would call Candace and see if she wanted a tomato sandwich. She would enjoy her company to get her mind off Stuart. She sent her a text and received a response a second later.

"Hey you! I'm at a meeting. It's going to be a long one. How about I try and swing by afterwards, if I get done at a decent hour?"

Although a little disappointed, Faith responded with a joyful, "Great!"

Lucia opened the front door on a giant whoop. "Anyone home?"

The walls squeezed in on her, stealing the privacy she craved. "In here."

"What's wrong with you? You look like death came in and decided it didn't want you."

Her voice pitched too high for Faith's mood. "Gee thanks."

She plopped a few shopping bags on the counter. "Trouble in paradise?"

"No." Faith shook her head. "Everything's good. I mean as well as temporary can be, right?"

"What is that supposed to mean?"

"It's almost the end of summer. Time to start heading back and getting on with life."

"Wow, what crawled up inside of you?"

Faith tired of the slams. When would obstacles leave her alone? When would good things happen and remain? "I'm kind of in a pickle."

"I love pickles."

"Not this one. This one sucks. This one is going to cause some indigestion."

Lucia pulled out a stool and pointed to it. "Have a seat. I'm going to make you something that'll help you get rid of that taste."

She began pulling produce out of the bags, and then pans from the hooks above. "Tell me about these pickles."

So, Faith proceeded to summarize the morning.

Lucia stuffed Faith with delicious potatoes and scallions sautéed in chicken and rice. She would miss Lucia. Although eccentric, she put things into simple perspective. "Laugh at everything," she said finally.

#

Later that night, Candace stayed true to her word and swung by. She looked exhausted and tense, though.

Emmy and Bristol pinned her captive as they brushed her hair and practiced braiding techniques on her. She didn't laugh when they joked with her. Her eyelids creased and her cheeks faded into an unwelcomed sadness. Not even Lucia's plum pudding cheered her up. The girls didn't even notice. They babbled about their dance moves and what they would wear.

Once they braided her hair ten times, Faith asked the girls to let her have some peace. So, they took their combs and brushes and went to find Danielle, leaving Faith and Candace alone in the kitchen.

"Are you okay?" Faith asked.

"I'm exhausted, and I have so much on my mind."

Faith hugged her. "You've been a million miles away tonight. Anything I can help you with?"

Candace lowered her gaze to the floor. "There's something I've got to talk with you about."

Faith froze. Whatever words would catapult out of her mouth would change things. Faith had experienced enough change in her life to fear it. It always brought rapid descents and scary landscapes cluttered in grime that smeared the positive side of the status quo. Though she expected the impending shift to happen in a few weeks, nothing prepared her nerves for the sudden onslaught of unease that appeared in the deep furrows of Candace's eyebrows.

"What's going on?"

Candace licked her lips and sighed. "Well," she started with an uneasy quiver to her voice, "I have a new housesitting opportunity." She paused. "In Hawaii."

Hawaii?

"How soon?"

"By the last week in August."

Sadness trickled in and blurred Faith's vision. "That's a whole week before we planned to say goodbye."

"I know." The color drained from Candace's face. "They have to leave on a yearlong expedition to Brazil. It's a last-minute thing. They've got four dogs and a huge estate on the Big Island."

"Is this something you want to do?"

"It's a dream gig."

The room squeezed in on Faith. Her head pounded and Candace's face turned fuzzy.

"So you've accepted the offer?" Her voice came out squeaky and desperate.

"I'm thinking of it, but wanted to talk with you first. The only problem is that they need to know tonight." Candace squeezed the bridge of her nose.

Faith's system shut down. The relationship would end. All good things did. Why not this?

Faith began to back away, numb. "You need to go, of course."

In the next few moments, reluctance spilled across Candace's face. "I

269

want to talk about this."

Faith would have nothing to do with that reluctance. She would not carry that burden so in five years her friend Karen would reveal in hushed secrets to another girlfriend how Faith Miller screwed Candace's opportunities.

"We don't need to talk about it." Faith bumped into the chef's cart and basil, oregano, and parsley jars toppled down and rolled between them. "The opportunity is too great." Faith stooped to pick up the remnants of her clumsy, sloppy disregard for order. Did she expect Candace to surrender the offer for her? A woman who couldn't even secure a stable paycheck or roof over her head that she could afford on her own? A woman willing to pull an innocent seven-year-old away from her father because of a summer fling? "We've made this into something more than it ever should've been in the first place."

Candace cupped her hand over her mouth and shook her head. "Wow."

Faith rose and placed the spices back on the cart, lining them up in alphabetical order. She should run. Bolt and not look back. Pull off the Band-Aid and deal with the sting until it healed over. It always did. Her life had become one giant scab turned scar. She was still alive and kicking, as Lucia would put it. So, she'd get over Candace too.

Faith rearranged the spices to align against the backing of the cart.

A ball of sadness sat between them. Candace stepped forward and grabbed her hands. "We still have two weeks left."

Faith pulled her hands back. "I've got a lot to do." The basil container didn't match the oregano or parsley. It stood too tall and ruined the order Faith worked to create. She plucked it up and marched over to the pasta cupboard. The room squeezed in on her. "You know, packing, getting Bristol ready for the new school year. Tying up loose ends at the salon."

"So, that's it?"

Faith bit into her pain, willing it to remain locked up inside. She blinked back her tears. Hanging on to her would cause more harm in the long run. Someone as put together as Candace deserved someone who could match her eloquence, not destroy it. "You should go." Faith folded her arms across her chest and braced for the heartbreak.

"I'm sorry you feel that way." Candace backed away wearing her disbelief like an ill-fitted dress.

As she turned and walked away with little fight, Faith's heart clenched. Faith wished she could rewind life back to the time when she first saw her outside in the street chasing Pretzel. That way, she'd never have to find out how much deeper her heart could love, and therefore never have to experience the breadth of its consequential pain.

She braced against the counter, sobbing until the pain evaporated along with the wetness on her cheeks.

An hour later, she climbed into bed with her daughter and hugged her. Bristol snored gently, despite Faith's rapid onset of more flooding tears.

Martina and Lucia would likely look at Faith's bonding moment with her daughter and whisper something stupid like *cheers to breakups*. Faith squeezed Bristol, praying no one would ever extinguish her baby girl's happy vibe.

# #

In the days following, Faith dodged phone calls from Stuart. He left messages asking about Bristol's birthday party and whether it would be all right if Gilly came, too. Then, he'd leave another one not more than an hour later asking about whether Faith had purchased her school supplies from the list St. Mary's mailed to them. A few more hours later, he left another message asking what he should get Bristol for her birthday gift.

He had motives that stood out. He wanted to get her on the phone to ask the real question of when he could expect them back in Boston. Well, his incessant messages did the opposite. Faith ignored them and went for many long walks along the lakefront to think about her life. She even dared to go by Candace's house and see if she could talk to her. She hated how they left things. She wanted closure. She wanted to see Candace one last time before she left on her new adventure. She peeked inside. The empty counter where her laptop usually sat and the missing pile of her shoes near the coatrack, spoke volumes. Candace had left, and without saying goodbye. She lowered to her knees in defeat.

She'd lost her chance.

Pretzel didn't lunge or bark at her from around the corner, either. Which meant, she had left and likely had taken Pretzel to the kennel for the remaining days until Bob and Mary returned from the Sahara Desert.

At least the heartbreak shined light on her hard decision of whether to stay or go.

Moving back to Boston made sense in all practical ways. She could move right back into the house. She had two years left before they would sell it. She and Bristol could have fun selecting new colors for the walls. They could sew new curtains at night before bed. When they wanted to do something more exciting, they could play board games or read books. They had plenty to keep themselves busy.

Sally even mentioned another position would become available in her new job at a research lab. They could work together. They could even take their coffee breaks together. Sure, the position was temporary. That was a plus. Faith didn't want to answer phone calls for a company executive for too long, after all. The good news according to Sally was that in six months they would be hiring for a new public relations representative to launch their newest nanotechnology.

Things could work out.

#

One morning Bristol hugged her after returning from Zumba class. "I don't want to dance anymore."

"Why not?" Faith pushed her hair away from her small cheeks.

"It's not fun without Candace."

Faith understood all too well. "When we get back to Boston, we'll look for a new place. I hear they've got a fun afterschool class for kids your age."

She narrowed her eyes. "Is Candace coming back, Mommy?"

"I don't think so, sweetheart."

"Why didn't you tell her to stay?"

Faith let that question marinate. She never did ask her to stay. She let her walk away. She hid her truth, and again hurt others as a result. "Well, sweetheart, I suppose because sometimes Mommy has a hard time finding her voice."

Bristol emptied all the air from her little lungs. "Like me?"

"You're doing a fine job of using it." She hugged Bristol. "The finest job."

"I can do better." Her voice came out as a tiny puff in the large echo of Faith's sadness.

They remained in a tight embrace both dealing with their own form of loneliness.

Then, Bristol said, "I like it here."

Faith scanned the warm room with its oversized pillows and shiny wooden floors. Her heart pulled. "This was just a vacation, sweetheart."

"Why can't we live here?"

"This isn't our home."

"Yes it is. Aunt Danielle said it is. I want to stay, Mommy."

Me too. Faith hugged her tighter, wishing she could protect her from all the hurt life continuously tossed her way.

Later on, as Faith walked by herself around the lake, she kicked and poked at her predicament.

They could stay in Rhode Island. She could take Danielle up on her offer to live with them and work for the salon. With Martina chomping at the bit to get her video business thriving, Faith could slide right in and build an incredible opportunity doing something she enjoyed, something creative, something that tickled her from deep inside and brought her back to life. Faith loved the salon. With that kind of taste on her tongue, going back to the blandness of press releases and chunky office desks without a window view caused her to wilt.

In the short term, the choice might not pay great, but in the long term, with a little care, she could earn a lot more money than by promoting nanotechnology.

Did she want to spend her days creating press releases that talked about nanotechnology? She could barely pronounce it let alone define it.

She wouldn't have to ride the T or hail a cab anymore. She wouldn't have to breathe in the fumes of busses and cars. She could say goodbye to the cement and brick buildings and hello to green grass and the lake.

She could take the time to teach Bristol how to ride a bicycle so they could enjoy long bike rides around the lake every weekend. They could picnic every night and talk about their adventures in school and the salon.

Danielle could use her help at the salon. Martina would be able to go after her venture without guilt for leaving Danielle empty-handed. Of course, Lucia would be thrilled to have her dreams to decipher still as they still pretended to enjoy Danielle's flaxseed muffins.

She could potentially even learn to like the muffins.

She sat down on a bench and took in the view. The sky radiated blue. The water flowed calmly. The trees brightened the landscape with their big leaves.

She noticed a squirrel eating acorns next to her. "Hey, little fella."

It ignored her.

"If your little friend hadn't eaten my car wires, I wouldn't be sitting here taking in this beautiful view. You little buggers fucked with me, and now I'm in control."

Especially in the salon. Each time someone sat in Faith's chair, she shared something. She educated on things like simple shampooing tricks and on things as deep as the client's beauty and worth. The client walked in one person and transformed into someone new, exuding joy and walking away with a bounce.

Behind the chair, Faith turned into a creative leader with purpose. She had so much to learn about cutting, coloring, and waving hair. Each detail relied on the complex ideas in science, math, and art, and that excited her.

Faith loved the support and encouragement that flowed between her, Danielle, Christian, and the rest of the staff. They embarked on building something beautiful together, something magical. Being a hairdresser granted her an opportunity to share special moments with people and help bring out the best in them. Working those shears and shaping hair formed the foundation for inspiration and fulfillment. Adding to that, Faith also transformed into a counselor, listener, and friend.

The squirrel darted off. A good cue to keep walking.

She walked past the rec center where Emmy and Bristol played basketball with a few other kids. Bristol shot the ball and missed, and one of the kids patted her back.

Lucia didn't miss a beat that first week when she said the place would have a good effect on them.

On her third lap around the lake, Faith spotted Bristol and Emmy now flinging a Frisbee on the lawn. It all made sense. They belonged right here.

She didn't have to think a moment longer on the matter.

She sat under a grand maple tree and called Stuart. No matter what he argued, she wouldn't let him have her peace and happiness too.

When he answered, she dove right in, finding her voice and giving him a piece of her honesty. "Bristol and I are going to stay here. We're going to live with Danielle until we can find something on our own. Bristol loves it. I love it. I have a job. She has a good school and great support system. She's making friends. She's talking again, to everyone. She's happy here, Stuart. So, we're staying."

He didn't speak. He sniffled, cleared his throat, and then sighed.

"Did you hear me, Stuart?"

"Yeah. Yeah, I heard you." Another heavy sigh. "Are you absolutely firm on this?"

Faith stood her ground. She lifted her chin like Martina always did. "Yes. I'll be cutting hair at Danielle's salon. It might not pay a tremendous amount yet, but there are lots of people who need haircuts in this place. So, the potential is great."

Another long pause. "You sound different, Faith."

She shook her head, stepping into her new attitude with confidence. "I am."

"You sound happy."

She looked up at the blue sky. "I am," she said again.

"I'm really happy that you're happy, Faith."

A strange muffled sob escaped. Years of bitterness drained out of her and landed in a puddle at her feet. The ground soaked it up and allowed her the freedom to stand on solid soil for the first time since she met him in college.

"And, I'm sorry about Candace. Bristol told me."

"Thank you."

"Why didn't you tell me what you were feeling, Faith?" Stuart asked softly.

His gentleness filled her with a sense of comfort. "How could I? We built a life together, Stuart. We had a daughter to consider. I couldn't toss something this big onto our life and expect it to withstand the impact. I didn't want to risk breaking the foundation we worked so hard to set in place."

"You deserve to be happy. Hiding who you are would never have served any of us."

"I couldn't live with myself if I acted on those feelings. I wanted to be who you needed me to be. Essentially, hiding protected me from hurting you and Bristol."

"And I did the hurting instead," he whispered. "I'm sorry I hurt you both, Faith. I never meant it to get to that point."

Faith swallowed the lump forming in her throat. "Everything worked out. Everything is as it should be. Things happened when they were supposed to happen."

"I suppose you're right. I'm assuming you knew long before Candace.

And if that's the case, had you left me when you discovered yourself, I would've likely met someone other than Gilly and our baby wouldn't exist. So on one selfish hand, I'm glad you didn't tell me right away."

His words soothed the soreness all that weight caused her shoulders. "I didn't know how to tell you back then. I wasn't ready." Tears rolled down her cheeks, ones born out of a gratitude for the freedom soaring in her heart.

"Things always have a way of working out, Faith. Your very name indicates that."

For the first time in days, Faith smiled.

Chapter Eighteen

Despite missing Candace, Faith went into full party-planning mode. Martina and Lucia jumped on the party wagon, too. Before long, sparkly decorations filled the dining room table. In one more day, the house would fill with laughter and hopefully erase some of Faith's hurt.

Christian took care of the music. He selected Bristol's favorite songs, according to Emmy. She loved Latin music, and so Christian downloaded song after song from Romeo Santos. "We like to dance Bachata to him," Emmy said, grabbing a chip and dashing off down the hallway.

Lucia remained hopeful she'd get Stan to dance a song or two. "If not, I'll pull Stuart on the floor and twirl him until momentum kicks in and we're both spinning."

"Good luck with that." Faith twirled yards of tulle around her wrist.

Martina swept in behind her mother and spun her. "I had a dream you were washing dishes and looking out the window, when a bluebird came up and flapped its wings. You know what that means, don't you?"

Lucia's eyes grew large as she swung to the left two steps and back to the right. "Someone is going to surprise me!"

Martina squealed and spun her again. "I know! Can you believe it?"

"They get excited about the strangest things," Faith whispered to Danielle as they walked out onto the deck and began looping the tulle around the window treatments.

"They do keep the laughter flowing here."

Faith stood on a step stool and stretched toward the top of the awning. "You know, I could certainly use–" She stopped. She didn't want to talk about her broken heart and how much it hurt that Candace left without saying goodbye. She still hadn't admitted to any of the women that Candace left. "– I could use more tulle around this awning."

Danielle snaked more through to her. "Plenty of it to go around."

Cheers to lots of tulle.

#

That afternoon, she returned from the salon and found Danielle in the garden, rearranging her pots. "I don't want anyone to kick them over."

Faith bent over and helped her move them under the deck stairs.

"So how was Mrs. Archer's appointment today?"

"She's thrilled I'm staying." Faith swiped her hands on her pants. "Apparently, Martina talks too fast and too much."

Danielle laughed, cocking her head. "How are you?"

Faith had spent too much time glancing at Candace's empty driveway before exiting her car. She wore her sadness like a scarlet letter. "I'm okay."

"Bristol told me Candace isn't teaching the dance class anymore. Where did she go?"

Embarrassed she screwed up another relationship, Faith resorted to shuffling her feet. "She moved to Hawaii, apparently."

"Weren't things going well?"

Despite going through more trauma than the average woman, Danielle could be so naïve. "I'm going to blame it on the curvy side of life."

"Ah, yes. Every choice taken or not taken has a consequence."

"This time, as is typical for me, it happened to be a bad one." Her sadness

280

caught back up with her.

"Are you crying?"

Faith began to sob.

Danielle hugged her. "Aw, come on. Don't cry."

She lowered her head onto her sister's shoulder, letting the warmth of the afternoon sun soak into her weary body. "I miss her."

"Have you told her how you feel?"

How could Candace not know? If she did, how could she so easily walk away? "It wouldn't matter."

Rubbing her back with small circles, Danielle handed her a tissue. "It might matter."

"She's in Hawaii. It's the gig of a lifetime. My telling her won't change things." Faith blew her nose and dropped her head again, taking up comfort in her sister's gentle ways.

"How do you know?"

Candace had chosen already. No amount of whining and pulling would've helped. "It's like she didn't even think twice about it."

"Well, why would she if you didn't tell her how you feel? You should've put up a little fight. Tell her how you wanted her to think twice about it."

"Part of me is hurt she didn't do the same."

"Sometimes you have to take the first step, Faith. You remained quiet with Stuart, never telling him what you wanted, what would make you happy. You allowed life to pass you by because you feared asking for what you wanted. The answer will never be yes if you don't ask for it."

Faith blew her nose again, letting Danielle's words sink in. Silence was a lot like black mold. It started off as a small spot and spread, eating up dreams and desires to fuel its survival. Before long, everything collapsed under it.

"I didn't want her to have a chance to say no."

"Or even yes, it would seem." Danielle arched her eyebrow, and then walked away.

#

The morning of Bristol and Danielle's party arrived. Faith woke and glanced out at Candace's roof and a lonely sense of dread rushed in. She wanted her there with them to celebrate.

Then, movement in the street caught her eye.

Bristol was riding her bike.

Riding.

Not walking.

Riding!

Bristol's earnest little feet peddled her forward toward a giggly Emmy.

Then, the bike wobbled. Faith braced against the window willing Bristol to save herself from falling. But, the bike proved too swift and dangerous under her small frame. It slammed to the ground, and Bristol fell on top of it.

Faith gasped, cupping her hands over her mouth.

A loud echo of rushing air forced its heaviness onto the room. All the progress Bristol made in the time leading up to her brave move, shattered. The shards stabbed Faith with gut-wrenching power, creating ripples of pain that restrained her to the front row seat of her daughter's letdown.

But then, Bristol raised her head, scanned her body, and climbed to her feet.

Faith grabbed the window sill and labored to breathe as she watched her daughter size up the situation.

Before Faith could knock on the glass to get her attention and offer her support, Bristol picked up her bike, mounted it, and with a smile on her face, began to pedal again.

Faith hugged herself as she watched her daughter blossom before her eyes. "Well, I'll be damned," Faith whispered. Tears rolled down her cheeks faster than she could swipe them away.

Bristol deserved to be happy, and she went for it. She stopped second-guessing herself. She tossed insecurities aside and listened to what life tried to tell her all along. It urged her to lighten up and have fun.

Bristol found her voice by saying yes to those things she wanted; to learn how to ride her bike, to make friends, to fling Frisbees, to bond with her aunt, and to ask Candace to teach her to dance. She would never one day have to face herself in the mirror and bite into the bitter taste of regret for not taking a chance on doing the things she wanted.

Her daughter devised a goal and achieved it. She took all the loose pieces of her fears, dug through the pain associated with them, and kicked them out of her way.

Bristol decided what she wanted. Then, she committed to it. She didn't look back on her time walking her bike. She mounted that bicycle and pedaled, leaving her fear behind.

She could learn a lot from her daughter.

She gazed down at her cellphone and into Candace's contact info. She didn't want to regret her inaction a month, a year, ten years from that point. She had to talk with her, to say goodbye at the very least.

Would the world crash down on her if she called Candace? Would she keel over and die? So what. She'd die one day anyway. She may as well die trying by tossing aside the certainty that came from not speaking her truth, and moving forward toward the opportunity of what might be.

She stopped staring at her cell and hit the call button. She braced for the unknown, squeezing her eyes and waiting for something to happen on the other side of that ring.

When her voicemail answered, Faith cringed. She could hang up and walk away. Or she could find her voice as Bristol did and speak her truth.

Pressing the phone to her ear, she took the risk. "I'm sorry for how everything ended." Faith paused and drew a deep breath. "I miss you already, and wish I hadn't wasted the opportunity to tell you in person before you left. I wish you could be here for Bristol and Danielle's party." Faith hesitated, then added, "And, thank you for the most amazing summer of my life. I'll always look back on it and smile. Don't be a stranger, okay." Faith strung the words out, not wanting to let go of whatever emotion it might stir in Candace. "I've decided to stay here for a while so, call me whenever you're settled in and want a recap on this crazy family of mine. And of course Pretzel."

# #

The sun shone, providing the perfect summer treat. The skies were bright blue with puffy white clouds. She stood on the deck and looked up at the expansive sky. The sun sprinkled golden hues all over the grass and trees. Inhaling the earthy scent of the great pines, her heart settled on the idea that eventually she'd be okay even if Candace didn't return her call after hearing her message.

The elegant tulle hung from the deck awnings. Pink balloons, tied to the wooden rails, danced in the breeze blowing in from the lake. Tablecloths decorated with a confetti print covered the long tables Danielle and her friend, Alan, brought over from the church hall. Everything looked festive and happy.

Later, as the afternoon sun lowered in the bright blue sky, the birthday extravaganza began. Guests from the salon and neighborhood began to arrive. Faith put on a smile and chose to enjoy her family and newfound friends.

When Danielle and Bristol came out onto the deck, everyone yelled 'surprise' from the patio below. Bristol played along, even gasping for effect. Faith's heart warmed at the sight of Bristol embracing the social scene.

Stuart and Gilly had showed up somewhere after Danielle and Bristol piled their plates with corn on the cob, barbequed chicken, and rice with lentils.

"She's amazing," Stuart said, coming up alongside of Faith.

They stood and admired their daughter. "She's the best thing that ever happened."

Stuart grinned. "She sure is."

"Of course she is," Martina said, tossing her arm around Faith. "She's got a fabulous set of parents who love her." She arched her eyebrow at Stuart. "Even if one of them doesn't like Auntie Martina."

An apology steamrolled across his face, causing his forehead to crease. "Whatever you may have heard, I'm sorry. I have no filter sometimes, especially when it comes to Bristol." He offered her a hesitant smile.

She reached across Faith and pinched his cheek. "Aw. That's okay. I'll take any brunt for that sweet girl." She released his cheek and it reddened up. "Now apologize for all those times you secretly rolled your eyes at me."

"I never–"

She went to pinch his cheek again, and he flinched. "Okay," he cried out. "Okay, I'm sorry."

"Why is this nice man apologizing to you?" Gabe came up behind Martina and placed his hands on her shoulders.

"This nice man apologized for not bringing his famous Boston baked beans."

"Ah, the man from Boston." Gabe extended his hand.

Faith swallowed her giggle. Stuart would never eat baked beans, not even if no other canned good remained.

As they all stood and admired the festivities, Faith scanned beyond the patio and out to the grassy field. That's when she noticed Pretzel sniffing Christian's plate as he grilled.

Henry barked and chased Pretzel away from the plate.

"Pretzel," Faith whispered.

"Pretzel?" Stuart asked.

"The dog, Stuart." Martina grabbed Faith's hand and smirked at Pretzel. "Should we grab her spare leash?"

"Nah. Let her be free." Faith scanned the lawn for Candace. No sight. Just Pretzel wanting to be lost for a few minutes. Maybe Bob and Mary had returned from their trip and would be joining them to retrieve Pretzel.

Faith settled on another sip of her iced tea, watching as Lucia and Stan opened up the dance floor to a Merengue song. Music pumped through the speakers, and Lucia marched to a beat all her own. Soon, a few more guests joined them and the party began to liven up. Even Bristol and Emmy found a spot and began twirling.

Martina nudged Faith, but kept her eyes peeled out to the far left of the yard. "Stuart, your fiancé looks lonely. You should ask her to dance."

"Oh, I don't–"

"Go! Now! Before she falls asleep." Martina pushed him away.

"Martina," Faith barked.

"Look." Martina nudged her again and pointed her eyes in the direction toward where Lucia and Stan danced.

The unmistakable silhouette of none other than her Yoga Goddess waltzed up to Lucia, grabbed her hand, and led her into a Merengue march. Lucia cackled and tilted her head back as Candace led her into a set of twirls and fancy hip flicks.

She wore the same red dress as the night Faith first fell in love with her. She snapped it left and right, before dipping Lucia. With Lucia hanging upside down from Candace's fingertips, Candace looked up at Faith and winked.

That wink traveled across the patio, past the drinks, past Stuart's clumsy legs, past Pretzel who had hung out by the food table, and into Faith's heart.

"Candace," Faith whispered under the tangle of her tongue.

Candace released Lucia from the dip, and twirled her back into the arms of Stan. Then, she locked eyes with Faith.

Those powerful eyes.

Candace walked up to her carrying a tease in her smile.

She would not get mushy. She would find her voice and talk like a civilized human being. She would send the woman off with a better sense of who Faith had turned into over the summer, that enterprising woman who embraced whatever life decided to toss at her with humor and grace.

Faith had so many things she wanted to say. All her words caused a bottleneck in the back of her throat. She would not let them marinate like she did every time something scared her. Not anymore. If she wanted something, she would not stand idle. "I never wanted you to leave," she blurted. "I wanted you to stay. I wanted you to say no to the Hawaii gig. I wanted you to choose us." Faith swung her hand at the crowd. "All of us. Every last crazy one of us." Faith squeezed her fingers together to keep them from trembling. She sounded like a crazed lunatic.

So much for staying civilized.

Candace chuckled.

"Why are you laughing?"

She moved in closer, casting her a sidelong glance. "You're adorable when you're flustered."

"No." Faith wagged her finger. "You don't get to do that."

Her eyes twinkled and teased. "Do what?"

"Look at me like that."

"Why not?" Candace asked.

"I'm still recovering."

"From?"

"You left. I didn't think you–"

"Shh." Candace placed a finger on her lips. "I decided to help my friend out with a dance camp. I spent a week with a bunch of wired and overly-dramatic teenagers. I just got your message, tossed on a dress, and am here now."

Candace smelled like a spring evening after the rain. Faith lowered Candace's finger from her lips and filled up on her beauty. "I thought I missed my chance to say goodbye."

"Dance with me."

Faith let go of Candace's hand and folded her arms across her chest. "No."

Candace peeled Faith's arms from her chest, and wrapped them around her neck as she took her in her arms. "Why not?"

"Because I know what this is."

Candace's eyes sparkled with a flirt. "What is *this*?"

"Our last hurrah. I'm not ready for that."

Candace studied her. "Why does it have to be our last hurrah?"

Suddenly, Lucia barged in between them and tore Candace away. "Sorry,

I need her for this song," Lucia bellowed.

The two women stared at each other as the space between them grew wider. Then, Christian grabbed Faith's hand and led her onto the dance floor, too.

The beat of the song intensified around everyone. Candace took charge and led Lucia into intricate moves, all while keeping a careful eye on Faith. The familiar longing captured Faith, pulling her into Candace's stare and creating an impossible escape from the love that had taken its place in her heart. She tried to push it aside, but it wouldn't budge. It turned into something untouchable, undefinable, yet every bit real.

As Christian led her into more twirls, Faith stepped confidently into her space on that floor. The music traveled through her and tossed all emotional ambiguity out of the way. A raw and powerful jolt passed between her and Candace, one that created a state of balance that allowed Faith to command control over her body. In their space, a palpable, delicate string secured them together. The music rose and fell. The pauses buffered the moments in between, creating an intimate pocket where their gazes melted into one another.

When the song ended, Faith retreated into her familiar existence of an outsider looking inward with longing on her heart.

Candace moved toward her carrying a look of love.

Faith bit the inside of her cheek. "I don't want this to be goodbye."

Candace took her hand and began to sway to a Rumba song with her. "Can I speak please?"

Faith swayed because if she didn't focus on something else, she'd cry. "Please don't. Not yet. At the very least, finish this dance before you say something that's going to break my heart."

Candace rocked her side to side to the sultry song. "Why are you carrying all this tension?"

Faith mumbled into her shoulder. "Because I promised I wouldn't let you break my heart."

Candace cradled her tighter. "Faith, why would I break your heart?"

"Because," Faith said, stammering over her indecisions to speak her truth. "You left."

"I didn't leave, though."

"But, you are."

Candace gazed at Faith. "Are you always this certain about everything?"

Faith swallowed hard. "I'm not certain about anything anymore."

"Well thank God for that." A mischievous grin took over Candace's face.

"What is that supposed to mean?"

Candace swept them across the patio, creating a gentle breeze that danced between them. "Just that life is fluid and always changing."

"That's a good thing?"

"It's a great thing. If every decision remained permanent, I wouldn't have canceled my flight to Hawaii tomorrow. I wouldn't have agreed to take my friend up on her offer to live in her home and manage her dance studio indefinitely."

Tears welled up. "You're staying?"

"My friend has offered me the chance to manage her business and live in her home."

"Wait, do you mean the blonde from the restaurant and cobblestone street?"

Candace tickled her side. "Seems, she can't leave us alone."

Faith nudged her. "So you're going to live with her?"

Candace smirked. "She and her *husband* are opening up a new studio in California, as I told you. And, she asked me to manage the studio here. That's why I've been in all these meetings. To figure out if I wanted to tackle it."

All the air surrounding the patio poured into Faith's lungs in that moment, causing her to lose balance. Candace pulled her back into her arms.

"Her husband?" Faith mumbled into her shoulder.

Candace nodded.

"Well now I feel foolish."

Candace rubbed her back and pressed her cheek against hers. "Don't, my love," she whispered. "I adore that you care." She gazed into her eyes. "And, I'm in love with the message you left me."

Faith lowered her head, then looked back up at her. "Is that why you decided to stay?"

Candace led her into a box step and into a turn. Then, dramatically, pulled her closer and kissed her. "I stayed because running from what I want in life has never worked. So, I decided to change my approach and stop running away from what scares me."

A question poked around Faith's mind. "I scare you?"

"Anything I fear losing scares me."

She kissed Faith with tender sweeps.

"You're losing Hawaii. That's a pretty big deal, no?"

Candace looked up at the early night sky. Her face beamed and peace rested in the fine lines along her eyes. "I'm done being a nomad. I spent this past week instructing one hundred girls at a dance camp in New Jersey, and something dawned on me. I miss having roots, having friends. Traveling the way I do swallows up any chance to grow that kind of comfort. I missed this." She scanned the clumsy dancing crowd, full of Faith's family and their friends.

"We missed you too."

They continued to dance and embrace each other tightly under the glow of the full moon and tiki torches.

At the end of the song, Candace took Faith's face in her hands. "Earlier in the summer, you may recall I asked you in the lake what you were doing to me."

Faith smiled from deep within. "I remember."

"Well," her eyes bore deep into Faith's, "I know now."

"What would that be?"

"You're causing me to fall–"

"Don't say it." Faith's lips brushed against Candace's.

Candace backed away and looked as though someone told her she'd never again be able to dance. "I don't understand."

Faith pulled her back and brushed her lips again. "I want to say it first."

Faith stopped blinking, and then whispered the words that had been brewing since the day she first watched Candace break out into a downward dog yoga pose on the lawn. "I love you."

Candace responded with a gentle cry and a delivery of love back to her.

They continued to dance to the romantic vibes of another love song. At one point, Candace whispered, "I fell for you the moment you entered my Zumba class. I thought, now there's a woman I'd love to dance a Rumba with."

Faith's heart twirled. "The dance of love."

Candace stopped dancing. She caressed Faith's face in between her warm hands. "The dance of love," she said on a whisper.

Faith melted. She sank into Candace's arms, not wanting Lucia's cackle or Martina's petting of her new boyfriend to clutter the moment. She wanted to relax into the softness of Candace's love and remain there forever.

# #

As the party guests began to leave, the family gathered around the fire pit that Alan had constructed for Danielle earlier that day. Stuart and Gilly walked up to Faith and Candace and said their goodbyes.

"Why don't you stay?" Faith asked. "There's plenty of room around the fire."

Stuart shook his head slowly. "Bristol looks like she's entertained enough. She wouldn't even notice if we stayed or left."

Faith looked back over her shoulder at Bristol. She and Emmy searched for the perfect sticks to roast marshmallows. Faith had a choice. Choose to agree with Stuart that his leaving would be inconsequential by not saying anything. Or decide on the better choice and insist they sit and enjoy the fire. Every choice she made or didn't had a consequence. She may as well be the one making the choice and directing that consequence to benefit them all instead of sitting on the sidelines waiting on everyone else to direct.

"Stay. Seriously, please." Faith placed her arm around Candace. "We'd like that."

Stuart and Gilly exchanged questioning glances. "Are you sure?"

"Never more." Faith waved them forward, and they followed her lead.

They joined the gang and soon fell into easy conversation and laughter.

After a while, Faith glanced around. Martina and Gabe told funny stories about blooper video outtakes. Christian, Alan, and Danielle shared laughs over some photos he had taken of a client who insisted on a mullet. Lucia and her *friend* Stan held hands as they watched the fire. Emmy and Bristol roasted marshmallows. And even Henry and Pretzel enjoyed the time chomping on marrow bones.

At one point, Lucia tossed Faith a wink. "I told you this place would have a nice effect on you."

That it did.

Faith stared into the fire and watched the flames dance. Her journey to get to that moment had taken her around some unnerving and exciting curves. If a squirrel hadn't eaten her engine or she hadn't lost her job at the university, or Stuart hadn't fallen in love with Gilly, none of that night would be real. It would all just be a grand dream of a life where good things did happen to good people.

Faith scanned the silhouette of all gathered. Everyone belonged right there and then, and if one of those things in life didn't happen, none of it would be real. Sometimes in life, people came across a curve that scared the crap out of them. Around every single curve in her life, there came a possibility to learn and grow from whatever met her on the other side of it. She had no clue what would come at her, and that no longer mattered. Whatever she met up with, she would view it with a humble and gracious heart, because good things did happen to good people still.

Faith raised her glass towards the women. "Cheers to the curvy side of life."

Lucia, then Danielle and Martina raised their glasses in salute. "To the curvy side of life."

She reached for Candace's hand and cradled it in her lap, free at last to finally be herself around the only people in the world who mattered to her. And, yes, that even included Stuart. They did, after all, share the most important gift.

Bristol's face glowed in the sheen of the firelight. She cracked a joke, and everyone giggled.

In finally finding her voice, everyone else learned to find theirs.

The very things Faith viewed as distractions were pieces to her puzzled life. The pieces never left her. She'd had them all along. She only needed to open her eyes and see them not as obstacles, but as stepping stones to a new phase in life.

Never in Faith's wildest dreams did she ever imagine she'd find herself embracing the unknowns of life. Yet, there she cradled the hand of the woman she loved, unaware of what would come next and excited about the opportunity in that uncertainty.

NOTE FROM SUZIE CARR

As with all of my books, I enjoy giving a portion of proceeds back to the community by donating to Hearts United for Animals www.hua.org. Thank you for being a part of this special contribution.

A SPECIAL REQUEST

If you enjoyed reading this story, I'd be so grateful for your honest review of it. Just a sentence or two will help others discover *The Curvy Side of Life* and help me to serve you better with future books! And, I'd be SUPER grateful, too, if you could share your thoughts of this story on social media (especially in reader groups on Facebook!).

(www.amazon.com/author/suziecarr)